THE SPACES BETWEEN THE THREADS

THE SPACES BETWEEN THE THREADS

A LEAH CONTARINI MYSTERY

LIBI SIPORIN

To Joe White z"l, one of the best of men.

Praise for the Leah Contarini Mysteries

Of *The Spaces Between the Threads:*

"*The Spaces Between the Threads* (a reference to lace-making) is the third entry in the Leah Contarini series, by Libi Siporin, and in my estimation, the best so far. In this installment, Leah is back in Scansansiano, the small Italian village she calls home for the part of the year when she's not back in Montana. She is also still a widow, her husband Nick having succumbed to cancer in an earlier book. This time around, three bodies are discovered and Leah, true to her uncontrollably inquisitive nature, quickly becomes involved in solving the murders. In the process, her sometime-romance with the otherwise nameless ('golden-skinned Sardinian') police Lieutenant, who finds Leah alternatively irresistible and meddlesome, continues to percolate just beneath the surface. This is a delightful read that moves along at a brisk pace. Fans of the series and new readers alike will enjoy it immensely."—Gregory Stout, award-winning author of *Lost Little Girl* and *The Gone Man*

Of *Bitter Maremma:*

"I am glad to report that I was quite stunned to learn the identity of the murderer. The descriptions of the landscape were mesmerizing to me. Murder is a fairly wild action (as in wild animal) so the murders taking place in the great outdoors were scary and reminiscent of mythology—almost with a dancing quality. Your array of local characters was great! My favorite was the cop."—Laura Fisher, M.D.

Of *If Two of Them Are Dead:*

"Wonderful! Can't get enough of this author."—Lesia, on Amazon

Chapter One

Crossing the field below the entrance to the trail, the man sweat heavily from the heat of the midday October sun. Salty drops beaded along the edges of his gray-flecked hair, fell from his nose and forehead, and wide, dark rings of moisture circled his underarms and spread toward his chest.

He tugged at his shirtfront in quick little jolts to stop it from sticking. His $235 aviator sunglasses, ordered from America, had slipped to the tip of his nose. He pushed at the bridge of the glasses, but within seconds, they slid down his nose again. Frustrated, he thrust them back into place.

At the far edge of the field, he stepped into the dark entrance to a *via cava*, one of the trails that threaded the forests around Scansansiano and much of the rest of the upper Maremma of Tuscany. Flanked on both sides by the trail's thirty-foot vertical walls of tufa stone, walls that created a murky dusk, he stopped, wiped the sweat from his face and glasses with a handkerchief, and replaced the glasses, carefully adjusting the bridge and temple tips. With a vain necessity to wear sunglasses, he waited for his eyes to adjust as well as they could behind the dark lenses.

Moving forward up the slick tufa trail, he slipped, caught himself against the wall, and, in a flash of irritation, cursed.

He could not understand why they had to meet in an isolated cave distant from town. It angered him, but with an uncharacteristic effort, he curbed his irritation and admonished himself, "It doesn't matter. It makes sense. Away from everyone. We've waited this long…"

The elation he felt at having received the phone call had given him strength to control his usually truculent character. The place was irrelevant as long as they could meet where the two of them could talk in peace with no one looking on, allowing them to cross the divide the years had made between them.

Neither of them wanted anyone else to know—or to guess—not yet. He could, he would, be patient. When the time came for others to know—he hoped soon—he would relish watching them hear the truth. How that truth would blossom like petals on the tongues of the community's gossips!

Imagining the surprised faces, he leaned with renewed energy into the gradual ascent of the trail, his heart racing with physical effort and excitement.

This was the day.

And those that depended on him, that had drained his life away for years?

Since the call, he could barely stand to look at them.

This—not them—was what he wanted. It was what he had wanted for decades. Now he had it. The others could go to hell. They could never fulfill his longing the way this revelation would.

He stopped and leaned against the wall of the narrow trail, breathing heavily. High above, a bushy canopy of holm oak blocked the sun.

The damp of the rock wall worked its way through his clothes. He shivered, and started once again on the descent.

He'd not taken more than a few steps when he felt a flicker of fear. He shook his head to dispel the sensation and continued upward through the gloom, careful to avoid any hole or rut in the rocky path.

"Can't fall now," he laughed nervously, envisioning himself standing in the middle of the cave: a leader, a man of power, of possibilities. This was the culminating moment for them both. From today, the new beginning, they would walk here often, and ultimately, it would be public.

All the losers would know.

They had agreed to meet at the Etruscan burial cave. A deep, high-ceilinged cavern, looted and left barren centuries earlier. Millennia past, a wide stone bench had been chipped into the rock wall at the back. There, they could sit together and talk unobserved. A perfect meeting place.

The trail opened from the walls, broadened, and leveled out. He was glad to step into sunshine, where the intermittent waft of wind through the trees created only a few trembling shadows.

An arc of rock at the entrance to the cave glistened in the sunlight. He was early, as he had planned. He stood in the entrance, hesitating a moment to let his eyes adjust again before stepping into the tenebrous air of the cavern.

Once inside, he shuffled to the back wall and took a seat on the cool stone bench, the same bench where, centuries earlier, Etruscan families sat for festive meals with their dead.

The wait was not long. He heard the gentle rattle of a pebble underfoot. He leaned into the dusky air, peering toward the cave's entrance, straining for the sound of footsteps.

Another light clatter of stones sounded, and then another.

His heart pounded in joyous anticipation. Still, he kept to his seat, waiting to make sure it was not a hiker passing by.

A shadowy apparition outlined in sunlight, legs spread, walking stick resting loosely in hand, appeared at the mouth of the cave.

A wide smile flashed across the man's face. He leapt to his feet, arms wide for an embrace, and stepped toward the dark wraith outlined with golden sunshine.

"You pathetic piece of shit!"

The shadow's laughter echoed against the walls.

"You expected some sort of revelation, a sweet greeting? My god! You're stupider than I thought you were. I know everything."

"But…" the man stepped back, cowering. "But, I thoug…"

Still in the form of shadow, the wraith rushed forward, raised the walking stick and struck, then again, and again, and again.

Twisted and cracked, the man's aviator glasses flew to the far side of the cave.

"Please!" The man wailed, "Please listen." Sweat and blood streamed down his face, "I can make it right…"

"Make it right! A lifetime of suffering, and you'll make it right? You want a revelation, a happy greeting? Take this revelation and rot in hell!"

At the next blow of the walking stick against the side of his head, the man's mouth formed an 0 of surprise, like a perfect tenor ready to sing in the choir of the dead. He toppled to the cave floor. Blood streamed down his face, flowed in rivulets along the dust, and spread a lopsided halo around his head. The air of the cave slowly absorbed the rusty, metallic smell of blood.

And the cudgel rose and fell, as if with enough blows, all the little minutes of a history of agony could be scattered to the wind, like a woman who beats a rug on the clothesline and fleck by fleck, the dust embedded in the rug rises and dissipates until all the dust is gone.

Outside, in a niche in the high stone wall near the cave's entrance, someone stood in shadow, listening, struggling to stifle a laugh of surprised delight.

Chapter Two

Black trench coat flapping in her wake, Leah Contarini walked through the sun-drenched piazza of Scansansiano toward the apartment of her friend, Angelica Piras, the master lacemaker Leah was interviewing for her next article. Tendrils of Leah's dark, curly hair twisted in the fall breeze wafting upward from the forested ravines and rivers that bounded both sides of the rock promontory on which the town was built. For a woman a clean five feet tall, Leah's long strides made her seem at least a foot taller. She wore a determined look that could have been read as somber, even angry, but in fact, Leah had an upbeat spirit, and her look reflected only a concentrated consideration of the best questions to ask Angelica.

Weaving in and out the stream of early shoppers, Leah's thoughts flowed into memories of all that had happened in the years since she had first come to Scansansiano with Nick, her husband, who had since been lost to cancer. She thought of their first walk on the *vie cave*, the ancient Etruscan trails that threaded through the forests around town. Leah smiled to herself. From that first day, she had loved the trails and had walked them in every weather. She had gone to them for their beauty, for solace, for joy with friends—and it was on these trails she had nearly been murdered twice.

The initial attempt on her life elicited in Leah a powerful desire to solve murders. So, in her own impetuous way, she slipped like an unruly child into the peripheries of local crime.

This invasion into his world infuriated the local police Lieutenant, a golden-skinned Sardinian who had been in love with Leah since she'd first come to town. Caught between love and duty, he watched as Leah blundered forward, driven by her vast, chaotic curiosity. More catalyst than sleuth, she jumped into crime with no plan, following what intrigued her, giving free rein to her deep reservoir of energy, her peculiar, undomesticated imagination, and her precipitate courage.

She drove the Lieutenant crazy. He wanted to kiss her.

Approaching Angelica's apartment, Leah stifled thoughts of the Lieutenant. "Italian lacemakers. The interview," she muttered, reminding herself that *Secrets Far-Flung,* the unfortunately named but well-paying American travel magazine specializing in the crafts and cultures of countries around the world, had made her their go-to writer in all reports from Italy.

The two women's friendship had long been more than business. A widow herself, Angelica had helped assuage Leah's grief when Nick died, and Leah, schooled in the skills of tending a dying cancer patient, now helped Angelica pass the hours of pain and boredom she was suffering in her own fight with the ruinous disease. As she raised her hand to knock on the apartment door, a smile broke across Leah's face. She would ask for Angelica's parents' story again and hoped this time Angelica might also tell her own story.

Chapter Three

Angelica laughed, shaking loose a strand of pure white hair from the scarf she wore. "My mother and father? Leah! I've told you that story a dozen times, and my parents' romance has nothing to do with lacemaking."

Leah blushed. She *had* heard the story many times.

Angelica relented, squinting her dark eyes and shaking a finger at Leah.

"You're thinking of Nick. Your own story—or perhaps the story you wished you'd had. You jump around like a chicken with its head cut off, as my mother used to say. It's no wonder it's taken you so long to finish this piece."

"One more time?"

"One *last* time! You're a hopeless romantic and troublemaker. As for my parents' story, paradise exists only in moments Leah and their love was one of those wonderful moments. And that's best. Eden wasn't sustainable, remember? You know that, and you should have had enough of murder to have cured you from listening to romantic stories. My god, you were shot!"

Leah was discombobulated by the change of topic to herself. "I know. It just seems that the story always leads to some new insight."

"*Mannaggia!* You and Arrammundu. I worry enough with him…"

Leah interrupted. "Why? He's a responsible young man. Attentive."

"He's both, but he's suffered." She turned to gaze out the window. "It's another story. I'll tell you later, or perhaps he will tell you; it's his story to tell." Abruptly, she turned back to Leah. "What am I doing? You're distracting me at every turn. I meant only to say that I don't want to be worrying about you, too. You have three skills, Leah, writing, being a good friend, especially to one so ill with cancer as I am, and getting into trouble. Now listen to the story of my parents—and finish your article." Angelica winked and made a funny face, which softened as she looked at Leah.

Seeing Leah's eyes tear, Angelica emitted a loud guffaw. "No histrionics! From either of us! Just listen."

"My mother came from Sansepolcro, in Arezzo Province. Her family had been there since the early Middle Ages according to my grandmother, and the women of Sansepolcro had been making bobbin lace at least that long, so it was normal my mother, my grandmother, and my grandmother's mother, all the women, all the way back, learned.

My grandmother was one of the best in town. I didn't tell you *that* before! Between her and my mother, I couldn't have escaped learning even if I had wanted to, which I didn't. I loved watching my mother, and I was anxious to learn.

Anyway, my father had come to Sansepolcro from the farm on some sort of business. For a peasant sharecropper in the early 1900s, that was an enormous distance, but he had to go, so he went.

He had finished and was hungry. He bought some bread and pecorino cheese and was wandering down a little alleyway to find a place to sit and eat when he came across three women—a grandmother, mother, and daughter, sitting in the sun outside their doorway. He said they were like peas in a pod, a progression in aging before his eyes. In front of each was a little table and on each table a sort of cushion with bobbins hanging from it.

He stopped to watch, and as he came closer, he realized that one of the women was not a woman at all, but a fine-boned, glossy-haired, delicate girl of sixteen who cast her sparkling eyes directly at him, studied him for an instant, then returned to her work with lean, strong hands moving quickly back and forth. The lace in front of her was the most beautiful of the three, my father said."

Angelica laughed aloud.

"He'd never seen lacework like that before and was hardly a judge! He'd never seen a girl like that before, either. He told me he fell in love with her like a bolt of lightning. Like big letters had suddenly appeared across the sky: 'MARRY HER!'"

Angelica spread her arms wide.

"Embarrassed by his attentions, my mother stood to go into the house. From the moment she rose from the chair my father could see she stood lopsided. He watched her dip and rise, dip and rise toward the steps of the house. His heart fell. He was thinking of the rigors of farm life. Still, he knew he couldn't leave her.

My grandmother watched him watching her granddaughter and grunted. 'Stop gawking. She's cripple, and she doesn't need any more rude stares than she already gets.'

'I want to marry her,' my father blurted.

'Didn't you hear what I said?' My grandmother barked, 'She's cripple! Can't you see for yourself!'

'Is she healthy otherwise? Does she cook and clean? Does she have the way of a woman?'

'She's strong as an ox, for how little she is,' my grandmother responded with great pride, 'but with the limp, no one wants her. Why would you? You're a peasant, and that means hard work."

'*I* want her!' My father yelled. 'And her work would be only housework, cooking, gardening, the chickens, and if she wants, the lacework. I'll buy the tools and material for her. My brother and I do the heavy work. Go! Go ask her if she'll have me.'

'You don't have to yell! I can hear just fine.'

She rose and shuffled toward the house.

My father was a tall, broad-shouldered man, dark skinned, with eyes blue as the sea and a beautiful, deep singing voice. He could be tough as any man and sometimes had to be, but he was also gentle and soft-spoken. He said the anticipation of waiting after he caught a glimpse of my mother peeking through the curtains of the house was almost too much to bear. She was looking. Did it mean she wanted him, or was she hoping he was gone?

My grandmother's slow shamble toward the house had made him edgy. He said he asked her to hurry in a voice harsher than he intended. She made a face, but went on into the house.

Muted voices came from inside, then scuffling, and then silence.

When my grandmother appeared at the doorway again, my mother was holding a little suitcase.

'She'll go with you,' my grandmother said, 'but first, the wedding.'

'I can't stay three Sundays for the banns! I have work. I promise she'll stay with my sister on the farm until we can marry. I won't touch her.'

'That's an old story, and we know how it ends. Those that are slow in making a promise are most faithful in the performance of it—and you made your promise pretty quick."

'Tell me her name!'

'Beatrice Sanna.'

They were married that afternoon. Sixteen and twenty years old. It was 1928. I was born less than a year later, and for a time, I had a happy childhood." Angelica sighed. "That's the story. Now, lace."

"Wait. The housework in those days must have been heavy work, no? How did your mother do?" Leah asked.

"More than well. She amazed everyone by how hard she worked, how pleasant she made our little house. And, the *fattore*, the farm manager, took her for the main house, so a few times a week she worked there as well, keeping his house. He was a brute of a farm manager, but he never hurt my mother."

"Fascist?"

"Later, yes. Some were mean, and some were meaner. He was the latter. I replaced my mother after I grew a little." Angelica's eyes darkened.

"And you married young in spite of all the troubles? You haven't told me about your marriage…"

Angelica's face flushed deep red and her voice cut the air. "I'm tired, Leah; we should stick to talk of the *merletti*." She tried to cover her abrupt dismissal. "You're on deadline, no?"

Bewildered at the sudden sharp tone of Angelica's voice, Leah reached for her notebook and the list of questions she'd prepared for her friend, but she wouldn't let her question go.

"Angelica, I've told you my story over and over. I've cried and moaned about my fate, and although you always tell me the story of your parents, you never tell me your own."

Angelica shook her head. "My story is of no interest, and I'm suddenly very, very tired. Cancer. You remember, yes?"

It was the trump card.

The older woman smiled, but her eyes flashed steel. "I'll call you."

Chapter Four

The following day, after a call from Angelica, Leah leaned into the brisk breeze that had risen overnight and walked toward the older woman's apartment. Stepping through the shadows of the tall buildings from one patch of sunlight to the next, she relished each thin slice of warmth and the occasional smell of bubbling sauce that wafted through the few kitchen windows that had been left ajar.

The broad expanse of the piazza was drenched in sunlight. Leah tilted her head upward and closed her eyes to take the warmth full on her face.

"Oooofff!"

She jolted to a stop.

"Are you crazy?" A rough-looking young woman growled. "Walking around with your head in the sky?"

"Sorry. The sun felt so good on…"

"Crazy bitch! Go sit by the fountain and wiggle your head around there."

Recovering from the initial shock of being called a 'crazy bitch," Leah regarded the young woman who'd spoken. Her dark blond hair, in need of a wash, hung in loose strings at her shoulders, and acne pockmarked both of her cheeks. The flesh around her strangely speckled eyes of brown and gold was marred by a sickly-purplish black-and-blue patch, as if she'd fallen hard, or perhaps had broken her nose and the bruise had spread.

"I apologize. It's my fault—and it looks like you don't need another jolt." Leah spoke with compassion.

"Damn right, it's your fault, ogling the sky like a crazy woman."

She rushed away.

"Wait!" Leah called after her.

Without turning, the young woman raised her hand in the air, her middle finger pointing to the sky. The last whiff of her cheap perfume dissipated, and Leah watched dirty jeans, ragged blouse, and disheveled hair disappear into the piazza bar.

"You look lost." Joel Stein had approached from behind her and put his hand on her shoulder.

"She's not lost; she's worried," Secondo said, moving to Leah's other side.

"You two!" Turning awkwardly, Leah kissed each one on both cheeks and squeezed Secondo's arm.

"I'm both lost and worried. I just ran into a young woman, literally ran into her. She broke her nose, I think."

"You broke her nose!" Joel blurted.

"Of course not! She already had a broken nose—or something."

"That's Lodoletta," Secondo said, rolling his eyes.

"Lodoletta?" Leah and Joel spoke in unison.

"Bini's daughter. She had a bad accident on her motorbike that wasn't an accident on a motorbike, and she's just getting over it. Broken arm, scrapes all over her body. Everybody knows that," Secondo admonished her, "You have to know these things; you live here—at least most of the time."

Leah changed the subject. "How long have you two been back?"

Joel glanced at Secondo, smiling. "Since yesterday. We've been in upstate New York meeting more family." He took Leah's hands. "It's wonderful to see you."

"You knew I'd be here! I'm always here, except when I visit Montana."

"I'm never quite sure you'll come back."

Joel Stein had shown up unannounced in Scansansiano some years previously and from the first had taken an interest in Secondo, the man most of the town considered the village idiot, but whom Leah knew as a courageous man who suffered from mental illness. Secondo had twice saved her life and had become a good friend. Her sense of responsibility toward him made

Leah suspicious—and jealous—of Stein from the moment she first had seen him.

Week by week, she had delved into Stein's background until Stein himself finally told her his story. Stein's father had worked as an art restorer in Florence during the war. Sent south to find and protect religious objects, he had narrowly escaped with his life from a *goumier*, one of the North African fighters who had joined the allies. The incident had happened in the Scansansiano countryside, and the elder Stein had stumbled, beaten, and half-starved into Scansansiano where, under the skeptical eyes of the community, he was rescued by Secondo's mother, the woman who became his lover.

When Leah learned that Stein and Secondo were half-brothers, Secondo, Stein, and Leah had become entwined in a confusing bond of Leah's protectiveness for Secondo, her admiration for Joel's commitment to him, and an unexpected physical attraction to Leah on Stein's part, which Leah chose to ignore, but by which she was at times embarrassingly overwhelmed.

Secondo, who had struggled with poverty and loneliness most of his life, felt an empowering warmth of love and belonging from them both, and he flourished. He convinced the City of Scansansiano, with strings pulled by the mayor, to give him a job as the street sweeper he'd always wanted to be, with a work arrangement that allowed him to travel with Joel on Joel's trips to and from the United States.

Leah watched Secondo flower in the relationships with Stein and with a new family. Secondo wrote letters and sent photos from the camera Joel had given him, and if Secondo made little of the fact that he had saved Leah's life twice, Leah never forgot. Learning from Joel of Secondo's courage, Secondo's new found American relatives treated the strange young man with respect and loving curiosity.

Leah let go her protective instincts, delighted in Secondo's newfound independence, and kept a distance because of her own confusion about the relationship with Stein.

She took Secondo's arm. "More family!! Feast or famine!"

"We ate a lot; there wasn't any famine." Secondo looked puzzled.

Leah laughed. "It's just a saying. Before, you had no family, and now you have a big family."

"A feast of a family!" He joined her laughter and clapped his hands.

Remembering Lodoletta, Leah's smile faded. "Lodoletta was acting strangely. I hope she'll be okay."

"She drinks." Secondo made a face.

Joel cut in. "How long have you been back, Leah?"

"I only stayed a month. Now I'm writing an article on lacework, interviewing. It seemed like you two were gone a long time." She glanced at her watch. "It's late! I wish I could stay to catch up, but I was just on my way to meet Angelica."

"Arrammundu's mother?"

"Um-hum. She's a master. Beautiful work"

"Always writing, as usual," Stein smiled.

An older lady: short, with smooth skin, a sturdy build, dancing dark eyes, and wearing a long fur coat, approached them.

"Of course, she's writing!" She barked. "She's a writer. Why wouldn't she be writing?"

Secondo turned and jumped forward to hug the woman, "Where's Idrissa?"

The Signora, as she was called, although everyone knew her name, attempted to hide her pleasure at being hugged by Secondo and gave a gruff response. "Idrissa is working at the store. And why aren't you working?"

Unable to keep up the austere façade, she broke into a smile and took Secondo's hand. "Don't tell me. I know why you're not working. You've been to New York again to see more family. You've got family coming out of the walls!"

"No, I don't. They live in houses and apartments, like everyone. You're just saying a saying."

"Yes," she laughed, "Well put. I'm just saying a saying. But now I've got shopping. Be good, all of you." She walked away, her rolling shopping cart rattling behind her.

Arrammundu answered Leah's knock. His pale face and the dark circles under his eyes startled her.

"Arrammundu, what's wrong?"

His neck looked impossibly thin, like a dying stalk that could no longer hold its fruit. He stood at average height, but seemed, in the few days since Leah had last seen him, to have shrunk and lost weight. What had been a handsome, square jawed and fine-featured face, was now gaunt; and a deep sadness clouded his eyes.

"Buongiorno, Signora Leah. Don't be startled. I'm not ill, just not sleeping well. Last night was particularly difficult so you're seeing the effects of that. I'm glad you're here. Mamma'll be happy to see you. Please." He gestured for Leah to enter.

Leah passed through the wide arch into the living room. "Buongiorno, Angelica." She leaned and kissed the woman on both cheeks before taking a seat beside her. "Not such a good day?"

"As you say in American, like a wet dishrag—but my spirit remains strong." She patted Leah's hand.

Leah glanced at Arrammundu, whose face was taut with worry.

Angelica's lace-work table sat in front of her, but she had leaned back to rest on a

pillow.

"Tea, Mamma? With honey and lemon, the way you like it? It would be good for you. Please." There was the child's desperation in his voice.

"No, no Arrammundu. I have water, and it's all I need. And why are you here? You baby me too much. Go on back to the store. Leah will get me what I need, and they are sure to fire you if you keep taking time for me."

"They told me I can stay whenever and for whatever time I need."

The plea in Arrammundu's voice carried the immediacy and desire of a child imploring his mother to buy him a gift. Each time she came, Leah witnessed Arrammundu's intense concern for his mother's health, his desire to be at her side, and his impossible urging to make her well.

Angelica answered her son gently. "'Need' is the operative word. Leah's here and you don't need to stay with me now. There's a limit to anyone's generosity, Arram. Later I may need you, so give more time to the store now, and they'll give more to you later. Go on. Shoo, shoo." She smiled and brushed the air with her hands. "It will do you good to get out of the house."

Leah nodded at him. "I'll be here."

Arrammundu bent to kiss his mother. "Try to eat something, Mamma. I made Pappa col Pomodoro." He glanced at Leah.

"And I'll have some, too," Leah assured him.

When Arrammundu had closed the door behind him, Angelica sighed heavily and shook her head.

"He's had a difficult path. Raised by a single mother, no other relatives. He joined the military when he was young. Did you know?"

"I didn't. He must have joined very young."

"Yes, and served with the UN Forces in southern Lebanon."

"But the UN mission…"

"I know. I know. I'll tell you the story sometime. His situation was exceptional and he's suffered for it. We'll talk about it another time. She fell silent for a few moments; Leah waited.

"He lives with what they call PTSD. So both of us have been through a war, each a war of a different kind, but both damaged. I'd take on all he suffers if I could, but I can't, and now he's got to deal with this cancer of mine."

Tears of grief rose in Angelica's eyes. Leah wanted to say that there were no words that had the power to assuage a mother's guilt, even when the guilt was unjustified, but she kept silent.

After they'd eaten, Leah asked Angelica to tell her about the war years.

"The war years? What about the lace?"

"We'll continue with that. I'd like more context, particularly what your mother's life was like. How lacework fit into life."

"It was as much a part of life as breathing. The war years wore my mother down, but she never stopped. The difficulties were the same for everyone, for all of us in town, in the country, but especially for the Jews. You should know."

"I don't, not really. My mother gave up any sort of Jewish practice she'd ever had when she married my father, and she didn't teach me anything—or even talk about that part of her life. I didn't even know she was Jewish and that that made me Jewish, until I was an adult. And then of course I studied, but my learning is late learning and sketchy."

"Then this story you should know, and I'll tell you the whole story sometime. But today, make us an espresso, take your photos, and when you've finished, I'll tell you just a little about the farm and the war."

Dishes cleared and washed, Leah moved around the room, doing a mental inventory of the lacework in the living room before she sat again across from Angelica. The furniture of the house was covered with delicate table runners with small circular patterns joined by a snake-like torso, an animal head on each end; dress collars of intricate flowers; elegant geometric borders on the window curtains; antimacassars of lace vines on the chairs and divan; stacks of handkerchiefs with diaphanous lace edges.

"So much beauty! I didn't know where to begin! How will I choose the last twenty photos?"

"You Americans seem to be practical people," Angelica pointed, "Choose the practical things: curtains, table runners, antimacassars. The handkerchiefs with fine lace are just for show. No one would imagine actually using them!"

"I know I wouldn't," Leah laughed.

"Um-hm. I need to rest my eyes a minute."

Signora Sanna closed her eyes and, with the rhythmic click of Leah's camera in the background, fell into a deep sleep.

Leah moved from one piece of lacework to the next, the soft click of the shutter punctuating the silence and Angelica's gentle breathing.

Finished with her work, she sat across from Angelica. Asleep, the signora's face had softened. Leah could see what she must have looked like as a young woman. Her high cheekbones, now riddled with wrinkles, would once have been smooth; her dark hair, now so light gray it seemed white, must have been long and flowing, a background for the chestnut eyes, which in conversation still glistened with life and excitement. But there was more to the eyes than excitement; there was a foggy undercurrent Leah detected in Angelica's warm look. Some sadness, or turmoil perhaps, that dogged her every emotion and prevented the two women from expanding and deepening their friendship. At times, in the middle of a conversation, a bolt of pain flashed across Angelica's face, and her eyes teared. It was as if in conversation they were walking through a minefield, and Leah felt she might suddenly trip a wire.

Angelica opened her eyes.

"I'm finished with the photos," Leah blurted, wondering if she had spoken aloud and Angelica had read her thoughts. "I've got over two hundred—that should be enough for the magazine to choose."

"I was dreaming about the *mezzadria*, about the farm."

Leah leaned forward.

"Don't get so excited. I can't tell you the whole story; I'm too tired, but I'll tell you a little.

"When the fascists and the Germans came. Everything got worse. By 1943, it was so bad the Jews had to hide or get out to whatever safety they could find. The father of Signor Bianchini, the Jewish man who taught us to read and write and who had been our family friend for decades, came one night and asked if he and his family could hide on our land.

My father didn't bat an eyelash before he answered yes. It was a dangerous offer. He could have been jailed or shot, my mom and me raped, the farm buildings burnt to the ground. That's what happened to a neighbor.

But God expects us to be human, my father said, and he knew what it meant to be human. He was afraid for all of us, but fear didn't stop him.

The Bianchinis came to us that night. We sheltered them in the mow of our little barn, and my father worried all the time about how to keep them safe because the Germans and their fascist stooges would come to the farms and search. Carabinieri came too, but our carabinieri overlooked many things.

I listened at the door one night and heard my father talking with my mother about his worries. The next day, I told him about a cave on a little creek far back in the hills of the Dry Forest near Lake Mezzano, near Valentano. Mezzano was formed by an ancient crater and there were caves, some of them well hidden. The forest is particularly thick. Above the lake and a ways above the river that runs into it, was a cave my brother and I had found. A perfect hiding and play place. We'd kept it a secret, even from our parents!

"But how did you feed the Bianchinis, get water for them? With the Germans everywhere?"

"I went at night. Every night."

"Alone?"

Angelica nodded and turned to gaze out the window as she often did.

"Those nighttime walks to the cave must have been terrifying."

"Not because of the Germans," she muttered.

"What?"

Angelica suddenly sat straight and cleared her throat. "It's enough for now."

Leah rushed to apologize without knowing for what, "I'm sorry. I didn't mean to push."

Angelica's eyes had gone blank. "I think you'll have to go now; I'm so tired. Can you come another day?"

"But Arrammundu…"

"Another day, Leah."

Her voice was firm, and she closed her eyes. Leah took up her coat and turned to see Angelica's forehead wrinkle in concentration, as if she were struggling with a thought.

Chapter Five

After quietly closing Angelica's door, Leah descended the front steps of the apartment building and walked toward the new town for her appointment with another laceworker, Baccia Mura, married to Cecco Bini. Leah had yet to meet Signora Mura, but she did remember Secondo's words about the young woman's bike accident that wasn't a bike accident. He had called the young woman Lodoletta and said she was one of the Bini family. She wondered what he meant by an accident that was not an accident.

The elevator of the building was out; Leah turned to the steps and soon stood at the Mura's door on the fourth floor. She knocked.

Inside the apartment, Baccia Mura reached with an awkward twist across her body to open the door with her right hand. The movement pained her left arm, swaddled in sling and swathe until the break healed.

"Signora Mura?" Leah tried to cover her surprise at seeing the Signora's arm in a cast and worse, her badly bruised face.

"Yes?" She followed Leah's gaze and glanced at her arm; her face flushed in embarrassment.

Leah rushed to divert attention.

"I'm Leah Contarini. I called you about an article I'm writing on merletti…" She hesitated. "We had an appointment today?"

"*Mio Dio*! I forgot… Please, come in, and please call me Baccia. I prefer it to the more formal. And I will call you Leah." She moved aside, gesturing to the right.

Leah stepped into the foyer and through a doorway on the right. The sparsely furnished room was elegantly unadorned and sparkling clean. A deep green, overstuffed divan sat across from two matching chairs, in front of which was a pristine glass table. On the table, Leah recognized what she knew to be a very expensive Kosta Boda handmade glass vase from Smaland, Sweden. The vase was filled with flowers and set on a small lace cloth, Angelica's work. Broad windows on the east allowed the morning sun to flood the room, emphasizing the austere neatness of the books on the shelves and two other shimmering ceramic vases filled with flowers so rigid and bright they seemed afraid to droop.

"Please," Signora Mura indicated one of the chairs. "I'm sorry I forgot our meeting. I broke my arm, and my mind is addled by the change it's made to my regular schedule."

"How did it happen?"

Signora Mura flushed. "Oh, the usual. I'm particularly clumsy." She changed the subject. "I certainly won't be doing any lacework for a while, so I'm not sure how much help I'll be. It wasn't clear to me what you wanted."

"I'm writing an article on Italian lacework for an American magazine. I've been interviewing a few of the local women, taking photos of their work, and trying to get some idea of their backgrounds in lacework. Whenever I mention lace, your name comes up. Do you feel up to chatting for a while? Perhaps I could take a few photos?"

Baccia flushed at the compliment.

"Of course. I'm perfectly comfortable sitting and talking; it's only moving in any way that affects the arm that bothers me."

Both turned when they heard the door opening.

"Oh, Pagolo, come," the Signora called to her son.

A short, trim, strong-looking young man of about nineteen stepped into the room.

"Mamma, I just came to take some papers."

"Pagolo, this is Leah Contarini. She's come to talk with me about merletti."

Pagolo stepped forward and offered Leah his hand. "It's a pleasure, Signora. I don't mean to interrupt."

Leah gave him a hesitant smile. "It's no interruption. I'm pleased to meet you."

He was a handsome young man, with thick, dark hair, a high forehead, strong jaw, and perfectly polite, but Leah saw a salacious glint in his eye when he looked at her.

He squeezed her hand slightly before turning to his mother and asking in a solicitous voice, "How do you feel, Mamma."

"I'm fine, Pagolo; I have to be careful how I move. I explained to Leah that I fell, how stupid it was of me."

Pagolo emitted a soft grunt, and Leah noticed the slight jerk of Pagolo's head, some unspoken communication between him and his mother.

"I'll go back to the library now, Mamma. Don't wear yourself out. I'll be back to make lunch by one."

"But I can…"

"No, Mamma, Lodoletta, and I will do it. You rest."

He nodded to Leah and left—with no papers in hand, Leah noticed.

"A handsome boy, Baccia," Leah remarked.

"And a good boy; he's protective of me."

"Protective?"

"Oh, you know, he likes to take care of me," she forced a laugh, "and now I've given him real reason. No matter, let's get back to lacework."

Her words left no room for any more discussion.

Leah nodded and reached for the notebook in her purse. "Shall we start with background? Where and how you learned?"

Signora Mura's face brightened.

"A good place to begin. My husband's family were farm managers, not far from here."

"What a coincidence; I interviewed Angelica Piras at length. Do you know her?"

"No!"

The answer came fast, emphatically, and Signora Mura's smile transformed to a frown.

"Sorry." Leah apologized without understanding why she was apologizing. "I thought since you both work in lace…"

"We don't know each other."

Leah glanced at the lace on the glass table. It was Angelica's work. "Well," she searched for the words, "let's continue with your background then."

Signora Mura smiled.

"My family's from Sardinia, but we moved to Calabria when I was little, and it happened that we moved to a village near Gioia Tauro, Maestra Melina's village…"

"You studied with the Maestra Melina!"

Baccia laughed. "Yes, my mother heard about her and decided it was a good idea for me to learn. She thought with lace I would always have a skill, always be able to earn at least part of a living, and earn it in the way a lady should earn. Maestra Melina had many other students, about forty, I think, but she took me anyway. We worked in embroidered lace, crochet, bobbin lace… but not just lace. The Maestra believed in education for girls, so rare in my family and in the village, and she taught us all to read and write. She had the combination of genius at her craft and infinite patience." Signora Mura laughed, "She used to say to us, 'Listen to me, girls. You get the chicken not by smashing the egg, but by hatching it.' So, I learned to read and write, and I learned lacemaking."

Leah glanced around the room. Sparkling curtains with lace borders hung at the windows, and on the top of a small bookcase was a delicate runner of white linen edged with an intricate geometric pattern.

"And excelled at all of them." Leah gestured toward the curtains and runner on the bookshelf. "How did you come to be here in Scansansiano?"

"I ran away from home." She said it with great sadness.

"And you're sorry?"

The signora, in the same gesture as Angelica's, glanced upward out the windows as if somewhere on the other side of the glass, she could see herself as a young girl. "Young people long for what is dazzling. I thought running away to the North was a dazzling prospect, and I was impatient for the future, for adventure."

"I can understand, but why Scansansiano? Such an isolated little town?"

Baccia laughed. Leah was pleased to see the laughter reach her eyes.

"I wasn't running away to Scansansiano! I was running to the Po Valley to work in the rice fields. One of my friends was going—lots of southerners went—and on a whim, I told my mother I was staying over at my friend's house—which I was—but the next morning early, we sneaked out of the house and ran to the edge of the piazza where there were lines of trucks and whole gaggles of young women. The owners of the rice fields in the north arranged these trucks as transport for their workers.

The driver of one of the trucks looked us over and asked for our papers. My friend had a contract, but I didn't, so initially, I thought I would have to stay behind and watch my friend go off on the adventure by herself. But the driver, a sort of manager, said I looked strong enough, and they usually had to hire extras, so he took me too, no questions asked. Since it was all girls except for the manager, and I was with my friend, I wasn't afraid."

"But your family?"

"It wasn't a real family. My own father was dead, and my stepfather kept mistaking me for my mother, so I left." Baccia stared straight into Leah's eyes to see her reaction.

Leah paled. "It's good you ran away, but horribly unjust."

"True. There was no justice. I wrote my mother and told her why I'd left, but she never answered. My sister, who also escaped, told me my mother didn't believe me. If she had, she would have come for me, or at least written. Anyway, given that I had run away, I had no alternative. I started a life on my own. We lived in big dormitories and broke our backs working in the fields twelve hours a day.

Then I met Cecco. His father, Diego, had been a fattore, but the mezzadria system was changing and Cecco had left the farm and come to the Po to manage women working rice. I got to know him; we married, and then we came here."

She stared out the windows. "I took up lace again once my hands were back in shape. I hadn't learned everything, but I'd learned enough to keep learning. And it was something I could do at home and could work at during my pregnancies.

"A young woman's odyssey! May I use some of your story in the article?"

"Some, perhaps. Let me know what parts. At any rate, feel free to take photos of the lace. I've got a dark brown cloth that would make a good background for the detail of the smaller pieces, if you'd like."

Leah was heartened to hear the excitement in her voice.

Baccia hesitated. "I'm excited to have you take photos, but I think maybe we should take them another day. I'm suddenly very tired.

"I'm so sorry; I've worn you out."

"Ciao, Mamma!" A voice sounded behind Leah.

"Be careful, Lodoletta," Baccia called.

Hearing the name, Leah turned to look and was startled to see it was the girl she'd bumped into while looking at the sky in the piazza, the girl with bruises and perhaps a broken nose.

Lodoletta made a warning shake of her head and rushed out the door.

Chapter Six

The following morning, Leah hurried toward the piazza, leaning into the wind, her thoughts tangled, her black coat whipping at her legs. She had spent a restless night full of the tears and the double-edged loneliness that strikes unannounced in the years following a loved one's death. Angelica had called, told her to come at 10, and abruptly hung up the phone. Her voice had sounded shaky, and the call frightened Leah. Why had Angelica been emphatic about meeting at 10 o'clock?

Leah's thoughts turned back to Nick. Memories could be lovely, but in certain moments, which came as suddenly as a slap in the face, the shock of loss seemed unbearable. Leah bore it; she would go on. She even had inklings of loving someone again, and when the weight of grief robbed her of rest, she reprimanded herself. Nick would be disgusted if she were wasting her time on grief.

"Is there anything dearer than being alive?" he used to ask her. And of course, there wasn't. But how did it happen without guilt, without confusion, without the past pulling you back and the future curling its finger to beckon you forward?

At the edge of the piazza, out of breath, she spotted Joel and Secondo talking to two men under the beautiful linden tree beside the bar. As Leah approached, Secondo's exuberant voice rang out on a gust of cool autumn air.

"Signora Leah!"

"Ciao, Secondo, Joel!"

The other two, Diego and Cecco, men she recognized from a New Year's

Eve celebration, turned to watch her approach. She now connected them with Baccia. Father and son, both were short of build, stocky, and looked as powerful as bulls. Both had close-cut hair, Diego's grayish, Cecco's black and smoothed back with what looked like a heavy oil. Both men, the grandfather and father of Pagolo and Lodoletta Bini, had snub noses set in round, tanned faces and deep brown eyes. Uncomfortable under Diego's and Cecco's gaze, Leah hesitated a step and then moved forward, hiding her repulsion behind the joy of seeing Joel and Secondo. She gave each of her friends a kiss on each cheek and turned to Diego and Cecco.

"Buon Giorno, Signori." Leah tilted her head. "We've actually met before, over a year ago, at the New Year's celebration in the piazza. I was sitting at the fountain with Signora Piras, and you stopped to talk. I remember you called her by Signorina. I was surprised by that. It seemed to be a slight."

Both men gave a slight jerk. Diego turned his palms upward and made a face. "I have no memory of that meeting. I certainly wouldn't have been purposefully rude."

Diego and Cecco glanced at each other, and Diego cast a false smile at Leah. "At any rate, I'm glad to meet you again. It's a fine day when one runs across such a beautiful woman."

"Me too," blurted Cecco. "Beautiful. We were just telling Joel about dad giving his land over to me." He glanced at Diego.

"Shut up, Cecco! She's not interested in our concerns." He nodded to Joel and Secondo, dipped his head at Leah, and grasping Cecco's arm, guided him away, hissing words Leah couldn't catch.

The two men had gone only a short distance when a young woman approached them, calling their names aloud.

Joel, Secondo, and Leah watched.

"Diego, Cecco," the young woman cried. "You've got to help me."

The men grabbed her, one by each arm. "Keep your voice down," Diego hissed.

"I won't keep my voice down, you bastards. You've ruined me! My parents have found out and they want to send me away to a place in Rome. You've got to help me; I don't want to go to Rome, and I can't stay here. You've got to find me a place somewhere nearby…"

"Shut your mouth!" They glanced back at the three watching, gave a weak wave, and rushed the woman away.

"Strange," Joel muttered as the three of them watched the two men pull the young woman into an alleyway.

"Those men make me very uneasy," Leah glanced at Joel.

"They're weird," Secondo blurted. "And they're mean. Their family has accidents that aren't accidents, and Pagolo's getting mean, too."

"What do you mean, Secondo?" Leah turned to him.

"I mean, they're nasty, and they hit people they don't like. And they're mean to women."

"Have they ever hit you?"

"No! I'm too quick."

"I'm surprised. They seem to have the respect of many of the people here. I see people nodding their heads to them as they walk by."

"It's their money that makes people nod their heads. Everybody nods their head at money. My mom used to say, 'There are people who have money, and there are people who are rich.' She said she and I were the ones who were rich."

"She was right, Secondo. You and your mom were the ones who were rich."

Joel broke in. "They do seem to cause trouble in every direction. There are several farmers around here who have been convinced to sell their vineyards after a few bad years. Diego and Cecco buy up the land and vines for a low price and appear to have the funds to wait until the weather cooperates. It's an old story. I think to many of the more moneyed in town, they merely seem like good businessmen, but to me, their dealings walk the edge of legal. One man killed himself after he'd sold. The land had been in his family for hundreds of years."

"No more talk about them!" Secondo interrupted. "The hike!"

"Yes, Sir!" Joel saluted Secondo and leaned toward Leah. "Secondo and I are off for a hike on the vie cave; why not come with us?"

"Can't. I'm on my way to Angelica's. She wants me to be there at ten, and it's almost that now."

"Couldn't you postpone for a day?"

"No. She virtually commanded me to come. But I'll take a rain check on the hike."

"How is she?" Secondo asked.

"Not well. She hardly eats, I don't think she's drinking enough water. And I feel like there's something bothering her. Lately she's had abrupt changes of mood when we're talking, and the other day she all but threw me out of the house. Arrammundu doesn't know what to do for her and neither do I."

"She's dying!" Secondo exclaimed, "Didn't you know that? She's got a lot to think about."

"Yes. Sadly. I guess there isn't anything to do but try to make her more comfortable. What I meant to say is that I wish she would talk about what's worrying her because there does seem to be something, and I'm sad to think she'll carry it alone until her death."

"Everybody dies with secrets."

Secondo's voice tinged with sadness. Leah knew he was thinking about his mother, who had left her life grasping a secret Secondo should have known.

Leah put her hand on his arm. "We never know anyone completely, even the ones closest to us, but I think I know enough about your mother to say she wanted to protect you. She loved you and hated having to leave."

He dropped his head and muttered. "I miss her. Everybody knew about me being an American soldier's son, everybody except me. I can't tell if I'm happy or sad. It makes me mad that Elia forgot to give me the letter explaining everything, but now that Joel's found me, and we have the same father, and we're almost brothers, and I've got lots of family, I'm sad for her because I don't understand why she wouldn't tell me that and because keeping a secret makes you feel bad, and she must have felt very bad. And I hate Elia for forgetting about the letter from my mother," Secondo stared up at a bird flying over, "but I liked Elia too."

"Keep the good parts in mind, Secondo. The rest will fade. Your mother would be so proud of you—and so happy that you've found family."

Secondo grasped Joel in a bear hug. "She knew you would find me!" he yelled with the eternal trust children place, against all odds and experience, in their parents and siblings.

Leah smiled at Joel.

Leah knocked on Angelica's door and waited. When there was no answer, she knocked harder, imagining Angelica in the kitchen preparing tea. The door swung open.

"Angelica?" Leah stepped into the foyer and through, to the living room.

Angelica was lying on the floor next to her chair, as if she had risen only to fall, crumpled as a piece of cloth. One of her hands extended toward the door. She had made a last attempt at saving herself.

Leah knelt beside her and put her fingers to Angelica's neck. She was still warm, but there was no pulse. Tendrils of her lovely white hair had slipped from the bun and had fallen over her forehead. Leah brushed the tendrils back with gentle sweeps of her hand and closed the eyes that, still open had been gazing into another world. Then, slowly lowering herself, Leah sat beside the dead woman, resting her hand on Angelica's head as one might assure a sleeping child.

Breathing deeply to calm herself, Leah thought of Nick's death and after, how she moved quickly, as if Death pushed at her back, forcing her to call for the nurses, the doctor, quick to cover the mirrors in the way of her family's practice, quick to wash his body, quick to do something, as if these awkward rituals might set things right, might assure Nick was being treated as he should be treated.

Do something! Do something! her mind had insisted. *Faster! Faster!* Death's urgent whisper in her ear, Death's hand at her back.

And then Nick was taken away, and she realized she had forfeited the time to live with his death, had not shared death with him. She had rushed through the business of death instead of being present in the moment, when there was no need for haste, no need for busyness. She could have moved gently, slowly enough to learn and to feel what it meant, to let Nick ease across the border instead of being rushed away from the world of the living.

After, when Anna died, she moved slowly, and when she found Elia murdered on the trail, surrounded by wild boars, she had moved slowly, carefully, and now, too, she would be quiet and give Angelica's body the slow respect the woman deserved. Leah quieted her spirit, dismissing haste. She closed her eyes and breathed deeply, and willed each breath to be a tribute to the woman, her artistry, to the painful secrets she carried on her shoulders into the dark.

Leah thought of Arrammundu, a son in anguish, how he had read a certain sadness in his mother. Leah guessed he must have felt like he was never doing enough to help her, to relieve her burdens of caring for him after his father died and then through her long illness. He would be left with this torment as well as the grief of loss.

And Leah herself wondered about the shadow weighing on Angelica as she walked the path to the other world.

"Mamma?"

Arrammundu's voice sounded from the doorway.

"Come, Arrammundu," Leah called. "I'm here with your mother."

The Signora came scurrying across the piazza toward Leah. "Leah, what's the matter? You look horrible! And," the Signora leaned closer to scrutinize her face, "you've been crying! What is it?"

Leah cast a sideways smile. "Angelica died this morning…"

The Signora drew a sharp breath.

"May her soul rest in peace. I'm not surprised; still, it's a sad thing. Were you with her when she died?"

"No. She called earlier to ask me to come at ten, but when I got there, she was already gone. Lying on the floor with her arm outstretched, as if she were trying to reach the door."

"Oh dear. Arrammundu?"

"I was sitting on the floor holding Angelica when he came. I was only a few minutes ahead of him. He seemed to take it fairly well, but by his eyes, I'd say he's devastated, as he would be. Still, he's usually so quiet, I'm not sure I understand his feelings."

"He's had a complicated life. You couldn't possibly know all the details."

"How so?"

"Let me buy you coffee, and I'll explain."

The Signora laid a gentle hand on Leah's elbow and guided her toward the bar. They took a seat by the window. With their coffees steaming in front of them, the Signora began.

Arrammundu joined the military when he was very young. He was by all accounts a very fine soldier in an illustrious regiment of the Granatieri di Sardegna, which was an old and prestigious group. From there, he was moved to a newly formed reconnaissance squadron, an elite group few people knew about. At the time, there was talk of Italy supplying troops for the UN mission in southern Lebanon. There'd been a UN peacekeeping mission since May of 1948 with a small number of UN military observers, but Italy wasn't involved until later. When they did make the final plans for the Italians to go to the area, Arrammundu was attached to that mission.

It was an honor; he was proud; Angelica was over the moon—and all of us were happy for him.

But it ended badly for Arrammundu. He and the others on the mission were just a little northwest of Qiryat Shemona, a town in Israel. There was an isolated area nearby taped off and posted with warning signs because of the danger of old mines that had not yet been cleared.

The soldiers knew about it, and the locals, including the children, knew about it, and had been regularly warned, but that particular day, there were three young, unfortunately impetuous, children guarding a flock of sheep not far away. Two of them had left the older one to guard the sheep while they played and wrestled. The two began chasing each other, and in the excitement of their play, they ducked under the tape that enclosed the mine area.

Arrammundu was the closet of his group. He saw the children roll under the tape, stand and start chasing each other again. He ran toward them, dashed under the tape, signaling and yelling at them to "come out" in the little Arabic he had picked up. One of them heard him, turned his head, and understood. But it was too late. Too late for anyone to save the two little boys, and too late for Arrammundu.

At the moment the one boy turned his head toward Arrammundu, the mine exploded. Arrammundu was hit with dozens of tiny fragments of metal, and the boys had both been blown to pieces before his eyes.

Arrammundu was in hospital for weeks. He was awarded a medal for his effort and then released from the military with an honorable discharge on medical reasons.

For a while, he was reclusive, but after some months, he seemed to come out of it, got a job, and spent his off time taking care of his mother, especially since the cancer."

Leah shook her head slowly back and forth. "I didn't know. How did you learn all this detail?"

"I had access to the final report, most of which had been taken in an interview with Arrammundu."

"How did you get access to that!"

"That's irrelevant. The important thing is that Arrammundu's hurt goes deep. I don't imagine he cried when he discovered his mother was dead, but he's in a great deal of pain, I'm sure of it."

"Thank you for telling me. What a painful story."

"What can be done about it?"

Leah shook her head. "Nothing. I think we just need to make sure to take food, offer to run errands, or whatever. He has a girlfriend, doesn't he?"

"Yes, but I think maybe she's left him for someone south of here. I forget the place. A farmstead I think."

"What made you break your rule against gossip by telling me all this."

"You already know. To help out with Arrammundu, you need to know. He's hurt in so many ways; he's vulnerable, and I imagine he'll withdraw again."

The two women sat in silence, their minds working on solutions that would never come.

Chapter Seven

Leah left her house and set out for the piazza through the early morning cold to have coffee. A shred of paper scuttled along the street toward her, and the chill fall wind curled under her collar and up the sleeves of her jacket.

At the edge of the piazza, Noah, a large, pure white Maremma Sheepdog, rose from a doorway and approached her. Leah waited. Noah stepped close, pressing against her leg as he always did. It was his way of hugging; he wanted her to pet him. Leah had never met Noah's owner, who seemed to live in town but was rarely seen on the streets. Cinzia in the bar, another close friend of the dog's, had told Leah that as a young dog, Noah worked in the traditional role of guard dog and herder for a local sheep farmer, but Noah's owner had moved to town.

Initially, Noah barked and snarled at people, as if to keep them away from an imaginary flock of sheep, but within weeks, he adjusted, became friendly, and enjoyed the run of the streets, forming friendships one by one with storeowners and housewives, who fed and cared for him and brought him in when the weather was too cold.

Now Noah's friend as well, Leah, was astounded that although he was old and moved slowly most of the time, he could run and jump over obstacles when he wanted. Once in the piazza, Leah had seen Cinzia's boyfriend yell and raise his hand against Cinzia. Lying nearby in the shade of the fountain, Noah heard the boyfriend yelling, bolted to his feet, bounded forward, and, in a flying leap, knocked the boyfriend to the ground, where he stood over the terrified young man snarling. Cinzia had delayed a long minute before calling off Noah.

Leah took Noah's face in both hands, ruffled his long, pure-white fur, and spoke gently to him. "It's a sad time, Noah. I wish you and I could have a discussion about the world, but we'll just have to be kind to each other. Our strength lies in our tenacity, right?" She petted his shoulders. "Okay. Gotta go. See you later."

Noah watched her walk away.

Arrammundu's reaction to his mother's death had been on Leah's mind. When he entered the room and saw Leah on the floor holding his mother, he stood staring at them and asked in a monotone, "Gone?"

Leah nodded.

He came near and sat beside them. With a voice gone ragged, he said, "She yearned for the fires of home. She was tired of living."

They both fell silent, aware they were witnesses to a moment neither of them understood.

In the aftermath, when the Lieutenant and the ambulance came, Arrammundu had watched it all, unmoving. Like a storm of insects, the examiner, the medical aides, the Lieutenant all gathered round motioning Leah and Arrammundu back while the Lieutenant checked the room for any signs of an intruder.

"A travesty," Arrammundu muttered to Leah, his eyes brimming with tears.

The medical team carried his mother away on a stretcher, briefly assuring Arrammundu they would call him the next day to release the body.

The Lieutenant had left last, holding back for a reason neither Leah nor Arrammundu understood. They waited, but the Lieutenant was silent.

A few awkward moments passed, and the Lieutenant turned and walked out. Once he was gone, Arrammundu stepped into the kitchen. Leah heard him rattle pans and mumble.

He returned carrying a flat box. "My mother wanted you to have this. She said to give it to you after she was gone."

Leah stifled a cry. "I know what it is." It's the beautiful set of curtains I admired and the beautiful blue spread that was woven on the farm. But she's given me so many other things; surely she didn't mean to give me such large, precious gifts?"

"She did. She told me specifically. And reminded me several times. It's just…I don't think either of us thought it would be so soon. I didn't." He wiped tears away. "She wanted the funeral soon, so I'll arrange for tomorrow."

"Tomorrow! But there's no…"

"It's the way Mamma wanted it."

Dazed, Leah walked home, saddened, perplexed about the haste of the funeral. At home, she set the box on her dresser, too emotional to open it.

The following day Leah, carrying the leftover food from the funeral meal, knocked on Arrammundu's door, but the black wreath swayed gently at her knock, and there was only silence from inside. She understood this to mean he needed to be alone.

Angelica's death recalled Nick's death, and as Leah left Arrammundu's apartment and walked toward the piazza, she moved along the narrow streets through shadows and spears of sunlight in a haze of memories of both her friend and her husband. The flicker of shadows and light reflected her inner landscape, sadness and the subdued joy she felt at being among friends, at having known Angelica, even if for a brief a time.

Peering through alleyways to the valley below as she walked, she noted how the intense green of the trees embraced the silver thread of river. Small fields—sprinkled in open spaces among the trees—lay partially harvested. Thin arms of tomato, basil plants were dying, falling in tangles to the earth.

Was this the way it would be from now on? Always beautiful, always lonely? Scansansiano had become home to her, but without Nick and with older friends dying, would she ever feel completely at home anywhere? It seemed death always found her, waiting in a corner, in the smile of a friend— or she tripped across it, as she had when she found her friend Elia, murdered in the forest.

On this simple walk through the piazza, she felt a loss of substance, as if the wind could slice through her, the light shine through her body, transparent now, dissipating in air.

When Leah entered the bar early the following morning, she found it crowded with townspeople having morning coffee and brioche. Idrissa called her name from the table by the window.

Like Leah, her younger Senegalese friend preferred the spot where he could relish the heat of the sun through the long glass window. Leah knew that for Idrissa the warm sun elicited memories of Senegal, where his family still lived, and she knew that he suffered a painful homesickness, the price he paid after surviving the perilous trip through the desert, across the sea, and into a foreign land. He had spent years as an immigrant, struggling to earn enough to keep his parents and siblings in Senegal alive and safe.

Leah took a seat across from him, relieved as a swimmer who has found a shore. They took hands.

"I'm so happy to see you, Idrissa! You were back in Venice for a while, with the Signora, yes?"

"And I'm happy to see you, but your face is sad. What's happened?"

"I was the one who found Signora Piras; it's brought back memories, or warnings… something, but the worst thing is Arrammundu won't open the door, and I'm worried about him."

"Warnings?"

"Maybe that's the wrong word."

"I understand. You are still standing close to the border of what my people call the spirit world. I'm sure you did well. You were a friend; she had a good burial and can become an ancestor, partially because you were present at the passage. You should be proud to have had that moment. Don't be impatient with Arrammundu. The funeral's only just happened, so I'm sure he needs time." Idrissa paused. "Let me distract you. I was just remembering something too, but my memories were of those days when I laid out my fake Gucci bags on a blanket on the street, and you bought coin purses from me."

His kindness touched Leah. Tears rose in her eyes, but she laughed and waggled her finger at him. "You never did convince me to buy one of the knock-offs, but I do still have the little leather purse—the one your father made—and I treasure it. I always will. The others I gave to friends. But what about you? How are things going? You look as if you're thriving."

"I'm good, thank God. The Signora has taught me much about material, about what the women and men in town like to wear, and how to buy and bargain. And by the way, after you bought the little purse my father made—it seems so long ago now—I asked him and my uncle to make more, and I sell them in the shop, along with the material."

"I started a fad? I have to come to the shop and see them. I'm ready to send more presents to my American friends, and they'll make perfect gifts."

"Thank you, Signora Leah. You're like a sister, and the Signora's like one of the old women in my village; she moves straight through the world with no hesitation and is full of wisdom. I owe her a great debt and will soon owe her even more."

"Don't let her hear you say she's like an old woman from your village! She won't like it!"

Leah regarded Idrissa's quick smile, his smooth dark skin and high forehead. He held himself with dignity, had a strong sense of humor, and since his work with the Signora, had developed an easy confidence and assurance that charmed the people who met him. These characteristics alone made him a perfect businessman. Leah knew adding to his personal qualities, he was fair and affable with customers and took with aplomb the rare—but given the perversion of some people's hateful nature, unavoidable—racial slights. Tall, handsome, a skilled musician, good son, hard-working provider, he laughed easily, and could display passionate anger and great joy. She felt lucky to know him, although there was a time when she had been afraid of him, and she never quite forgot.

"Why the wily smile, Idi?

He broke into a laugh, leaned across the table, and whispered. "Very soon I'm sending for my bride."

"What good news!" Leah clapped her hands together.

"Yes. My own family." He stared through the window, as if he could see Senegal from where he sat; as if he could see his beautiful bride packing her suitcase, and his mother folding the brightly patterned wedding camisole, pagne, and headdress.

Leah saw a tinge of sadness touch his eyes.

"But others in your family won't be able to come?"

"It's too expensive. We'll need all I have to make our own house and to continue sending money home."

He changed the subject, as if he might curse his plans by talking about them. "I'm sorry about Signora Piras. The last trip, I brought her threads from Venice. She seemed happy with the colors."

"She told me you were the only one she trusted; you brought the best and always had a fair price."

He smiled. "I'm glad she was pleased. The last day I brought her thread, I heard something that upset me."

"From Angelica? I'm surprised."

"I had delivered her thread, and then I passed her later that same day. She was sitting at the fountain with a friend. I greeted them, then as I left, bent to tie my shoe, and I couldn't help but hear her friend talking about a grown woman she knew who had been beaten."

"Did she say who?"

"No, she didn't say who it was or the name of the one who attacked her. But I didn't like the sound of it. The attack seemed particularly brutal, and it sounded like it was here, in town."

Leah had a flash memory of Baccia Mura standing at the door to her apartment, arm in a sling, face bruised.

"It's unimaginable to think it's happening right here. The Lieutenant…"

"For sure, he'll be on top of it. But you know, people have to make complaints, or he can't do anything."

Chapter Eight

Leah was working at her desk when the phone rang that afternoon.
"Signora Leah?" The voice on the line was deep, rough.
"Arrammundu, is that you?"

"Yes. I wanted to let you know I'll be out of town for a while. I'm going back to the farm for a week or so. Mamma always wanted to go back…"

"And you're going for her. What a fine idea."

"A few of the families she knew are still there. And I'm going to hunt for the cave where Mamma and her family hid the Jewish family. She spoke of it so often, I think if I wander around in the Dry Forest, I can find it, and if I do, I'll take you there someday."

"Your mom would be happy to think of you carrying her stories forward and weaving your own stories with hers. I hope you'll come and tell me about it when you get back."

"I will, Signora, I will."

Driving toward the land his mother had known in her youth, Arrammundu was startled to feel a twinge of joy, as if his sadness, his anger, like a curtain, had opened for a moment. He took the rutted, single-lane backroad toward the farm, maneuvering around potholes, taking pleasure in the overhanging trees that made a tunnel of the narrow road.

At the border of the regional forest lands, the road became gravel and then dirt, winding up and down the hills, crowded on both sides by thick clumps of raspberry bushes, wild roses, and a dense ground covering of ivy that, snakelike, rose and wrapped around the trunks of the maples, hornbeam, firs, poplars, and linden growing in dense ranks throughout the area. It felt good to escape, to be doing something that would have pleased his mother.

He passed the Brigand's Trail, said to be the trail followed by the infamous outlaw Tiburzi in the early twentieth-century, and bounced slowly along until he came to the state highway. Following the highway to the intersection with Valentano, he turned upward on another gravel road running past open fields and leading to the farm where his mother had lived with his father.

The house was a beautiful old casa colonica, well-maintained, but not modernized as many in the area had been. It was high and rectangular, with four windows across the top of the front, a wide arched doorway in the center below, and larger windows to each side of the doorway. Around the house to the right, Arrammundu could see a shed and yard for chickens and, beyond that, what looked to be a pig pen and outbuildings.

He stopped at the top of the long lane in front of the house. A man and woman had come out the doorway and were approaching the car. Arrammundu stepped out to be warmly greeted by Maria Teresa and Antonio, whom he recognized as older versions of the couple his mother had described. They had been waiting for him.

The two were dressed as they might have been in the 1920s or 1930s. Antonio wore loose, homespun work pants held up by a wide leather belt, a long-sleeved cotton shirt, a vest of thick homespun buttoned down the front, scuffed boots, and a hat, the brim of which flopped a little over his face.

Maria Teresa was his counterpart in dress. She wore a wide scarf that covered her hair except for a few wisps of gray that had escaped and curled at her ears. Her earrings were like those Arrammundu's mother had worn: hanging gold fixtures with a small glistening red stone. Her clothes too were cotton homespun: a shirt pleated at the shoulder; a full, ankle-length skirt covered with a long apron.

"Arrammundu." Maria Teresa shuffled forward, arms open.

"Yes, it's me."

"We're so glad you've come." She took his hands in hers and studied his face. "You have your mother's eyes."

"And your father's build." Antonio placed a hand on Arrammundu's bicep, "I can feel the muscles," he nodded. "We're so sorry about your mother."

Arrammundu lowered his eyes. "She was in great pain at the end. Now she's released."

Maria Teresa nodded, and the three stood quietly for a moment, until Maria Teresa spoke. "Come eat." She gently pulled him forward.

They entered a long, wide room that extended the length of the house. An open hearth stood across from the doorway, with the kitchen area to one side and a long dining table on the opposite side. At the narrow end of the room, Arrammundu could see another doorway leading to what he guessed was a storage area that must, in turn, lead to a stall and mangers for the animals in cold weather.

The rough-hewn wooden table was set with what must have been the couple's best dinnerware. A large platter of antipasto had been placed in the center. The woman gestured to a chair. Arrammundu regarded the food. For the first time since his mother's death, he felt a pang of hunger.

After the antipasto, Maria Teresa smiled and exclaimed, "I think you've been starving yourself!"

She set a large plate of pici all'aligone in front of him. Arrammundu protested half-heartedly.

"You must eat." The Signora patted his shoulder. "You'll need strength, especially today, because we need your help." She laughed.

The old man patted his wife's hand. "Shhhhh. He doesn't need to do our work. Gerardo and I will figure it out."

"You can't *figure it out*, as you say. It takes two young, strong men, and I think Arrammundu will be happy to help." She turned to Arrammundu, "Yes?"

"Of course! I'm happy to help. I've been closed up in the house, so it's a vacation for me to get out and do something. Especially something physical."

Antonio sighed with relief. "Well, if that's the way of it, it will be a big help to us. Gerardo is coming by in another hour, and he'll take you to the mow. I need lumber moved down from a high shelf so I can repair a few rotten boards. But I'm too old for the lifting and carrying."

When they heard Gerardo's Vespa coming up the lane, the three rose from their dessert and went out to greet him. Arrammundu and Gerardo shook hands and started for the mow.

Thirty minutes later, the old couple heard angry yelling. They rushed to the doorway to see Arrammundu and Gerardo punching and kicking each other, cursing at the top of their voices, until they fell into the dirt beside the barn, rolling over and over in the dust, brown as the earth, a flaying ball of young men.

"Stop!" Antonio and Maria Teresa shouted in unison, lurching toward the boys. Boys! Stop! This is no way to behave. What's wrong here? Stop and speak to us."

But their shouts were useless. Arrammundu had straddled Gerardo and was punching him in his face, already swollen and bloody. With one last punch to Gerardo's jaw, Arrammundu rose to his feet and pitched toward his car, leaving Gerardo inert in the dust and the old couple dismayed and confused.

Later, after Gerardo had stumbled toward home, Maria Teresa and Antonio sat together by the open fire in the kitchen.

"What could they have been fighting about?" Maria Teresa asked.

"What is it always about? A woman. For sure, it's a woman."

Chapter Nine

Leah spotted Arrammundu on the far side of the piazza. He gave a quick wave, then turned to walk away. Leah hastened to catch him. Coming close, she saw his clothing was disheveled, and he needed a shower and shave.

"Wait, Arrammundu! I'm surprised to see you. Did you decide not to stay long at the farm?"

"Yes, I decided to come back. I just want to keep close to home. There's a lot to do—to deal with Mamma's will and her list of what to do with her work. There's another package for you, by the way."

He evaded eye contact with her.

"I'm sorry it didn't work out at the farm, but another gift? It's too generous of your mother. Her things should be in a museum."

"They will be. I contacted the museum in Sansepolcro about her death, and they're excited to have her work."

"That's good news. After my article and interview with her are published, I'll send them to the museum and to the local papers here and in Sansepolcro. Your mother was a true master."

"Have you opened the box I gave you the day Mamma died?"

"Not yet. It's too emotional, still. I know what's in it, though."

"You're sure?"

"Yes, remember? I'm sure it's a set of curtains or the bedspread I admired. Beautiful and intricate. I'm honored to have them."

"Oh…" Arrammundu seemed distracted. "Well, she was anxious for you to have them. She kept reminding me to be sure to give you the package after… And I think you should *open* it."

"I promise I will as soon as I get my emotional courage. But for now, do you have time for a coffee? We haven't spoken much since your mom passed."

Noah, who had been lying in the shade of one of the trees, padded softly up to Leah and leaned against her knees.

Arrammundu stepped back.

"It's okay, Arrammundu. You know Noah— He's harmless."

Arrammundu glanced at his watch. "No, no, it's not that. I'm late. I'm meeting someone." He turned and rushed away.

"Another time then…" Leah called after him, watching him run away like a man escaping.

Leah walked to the bar and was surprised to find the Lieutenant sitting by the window in the corner of the bar, smiling to himself.

"You look happy."

The Lieutenant looked up. "I am!"

"Something special?"

"Lots of things. Crime, even petty theft, has slowed since the cooler weather. My sister has evaded the clutches of a distant uncle to whom she'd been promised in marriage by my foolish father. And my mother has written to say she's delighted my sister is now in love with a suitable young man studying physics on the mainland, but who comes home most weekends.

The family is at peace again; the town is quiet, and now I see you!" He blushed, and seeing him blush, Leah blushed.

From the first time the Lieutenant met Leah, he had been silently, distantly, painfully in love. Through the years after that first meeting, he kept his own counsel: she had been married. Now that she was a widow, it seemed to him she continued quietly to mourn the loss of her husband. He would not interfere.

His was a complex love. He was truly in love with her, but he was also often infuriated with her. All the months she stayed in Scansansiano, from one year to the next, she meddled in police business and terrified him by putting herself in danger. When she had been shot, he felt he would go crazy with worry. On top of it all was the irritation of her constant stream of questions about crime in the town. It began to seem she was writing mysteries rather than cultural articles.

The Lieutenant had never hinted at his deeper feelings. There was that time in the coffee shop when he had taken her hands, and she had not resisted. But he was determined he would never be too open with her unless, by a miraculous answer to his fervent prayers, she indicated she felt the same.

For the present, he grasped what moments he could, retained a reserved demeanor, and hoped he appeared to her to be self-possessed, urbane, debonair.

"Espresso?" he offered, "and then you can tell me about the American West you love so much."

"An espresso would be welcome, thanks. And why do you want to know about the American West? Are you going to visit me when I'm back in the States?" She smiled. "I'd like that. I could show you beautiful places."

The Lieutenant shuffled in his seat. A sudden fantasy had popped full-blown into his mind. He and Leah were riding horseback into the mountains on an early fall day. They came to a cabin by a wild mountain river. Nightfall was fast approaching. After building a campfire near the river, they cooked cowboy stew. He wasn't sure what cowboy stew meant, but in the fantasy, it would be delicious. The moon was full, they were nestled together against the cold, and soon they were on a rug in front of the cabin's fireplace...

"Lieutenant?"

A flush crept over his face. "I'm sorry; I was distracted for a moment. Visit you? I don't know. Maybe someday. I'd like that."

"Distracted by a new case?"

"No! No, not that. Are you going back soon?" He stumbled on the words.

"You're changing the subject. Is there a new case?"

"You're impossible!"

"Lieutenant?" Sergeant Montaro stepped through the doorway.

The Lieutenant sighed in relief. "Yes?"

"You'd better come."

"What is it?"

The sergeant tilted his head toward the street.

Leah leaned forward with an expectant look and touched his forearm.

"No, Leah! You can't come. It's police business."

"I won't say anything, I'll just listen."

"No! I don't even know what it is yet, and look at you, ready to meddle." He stood and took his hat from the table. "Come on, Montaro."

Through the window, Leah could see them talking with their heads together. Only a minute passed before they set off across the piazza at a fast walk.

She jumped up from the table and shouted at the barmaid, "Pay you next time, okay?"

The barmaid brushed her hand through the air, and Leah ran out the door.

On the far side of the piazza, near the Lieutenant's old Alfa Romero, a middle-aged farmer stood waiting for the two officers. Leah circled around and stepped behind the corner of a building within earshot of the three. She heard the man say, "… in the first cave, about a third the way up the via cava."

It was enough for Leah. Racing across the piazza to the trailhead on the north side, she stepped onto the narrow pathway that descended into the valley. Just above the river, the trail turned downstream toward the via cava.

Leah pecked her way with nimble steps along the slippery path, rushing to be there before the Lieutenant and Montaro.

Who was in the cave? Doing what?

Chapter Ten

"You've got to stop this, Leah! The odds are against you; one of these days, you'll get killed. And besides all that, damn it, you're interfering with police business."

The Lieutenant's face flushed a livid red. He paced the room. Leah sat in the chair in front of his desk, aware of the light, spicy smell of his aftershave, intensified by the overactive heater at the side of the room.

"I had no idea there would be a body, Lieutenant. And no idea it would be Cecco…that brutalized face…"

"No more! It's bad enough you went into the cave and probably, damn it, compromised the scene; it's bad enough you sneak around listening to conversations when you shouldn't. Don't you have any sense of the law or of minding your own business? And you'd better be quiet about what you know. Why can't you…why can't you just… be good!"

His exclamation elicited the memory of Leah's mother's exasperated admonitions for her to behave. Leah tried, unsuccessfully, to stifle a laugh.

"You see! You're laughing!" He jabbed his finger at her. "You could have been killed, and you're laughing."

Surprised by the Lieutenant's anger, which seemed to be verging on actual tears, she stopped laughing and hung her head.

"Get out of here! Go home! I don't want to see you. And if you say a word to anyone about what you saw, I'll have you in jail."

"But I can…"

The Lieutenant clamped his index finger against his lips as he would to a child, pointed toward the door, and shouted. "Out! Get out!"

Chapter Eleven

The day after the Lieutenant had given Leah a thorough dressing down, Leah ran into Arrammundu outside the grocery store.

"Mio Dio, Arrammundu! What happened? You look like you've been sleeping rough."

"I'd rather not talk about it."

"But you're…"

"I really don't want to talk about it, and I have to be somewhere." His fists were balled as if ready to fight.

She watched him limp away.

"What'er you lookin at?" Lodoletta appeared at her elbow.

Leah swung around, "It's you!"

"Sor-ry. What'er you looking at this time? The sky again?" She grunted a laugh.

"No. I was talking to Arrammundu; he looked rough, like he hasn't slept or changed his clothes."

"So what else is new?"

"You mean he's often like that? I've never seen him so bad."

"You're clueless, you know that? How long have you known him and his mom, ahhh years?"

"Angelica never said. And anyway, how do you know I've known them for several years? I just met you."

"Angelica wouldn't say anything about Arrammundu. She was a good person, and a great mother." Lodoletta's voice quavered.

"Sounds like you knew her well."

"Duh! Arrammundu and I are sort of an item. Anyway, we were until I started messing with some farmer down by Valentano. But his mom was always nice to me."

"You and Arrammundu?"

"Why so surprised? You think he wouldn't be interested in a loser like me? Anyway, we've gotten it patched up, I think."

"I didn't say you were a loser. It's just I never knew about you and Arrammundu."

"Mio Dio! There's so much you don't know. I guess ignorance is a great shield." She shook her head. "Forget it. I stopped because I wanted to thank you for not telling my mother how rude I was to you the other day when you were looking at the sky and nearly knocked me down."

"I wouldn't have said anything. But I couldn't figure out why you gave me the finger."

"No reason, I was just in a shitty mood, and I took it out on you."

"Why were you in such a bad mood?"

Lodoletta laughed. "You can't say it, can you?"

"Can't say what?"

"Shitty."

"It's not a word in my vocabulary… but tell me anyway, okay? Why were you in such a bad mood?"

Lodoletta released a loud guffaw. "I was in a lousy mood because of my shithead of a dad. He thinks it's fun to beat the crap out of me and my mother and brother, and it was my turn that day. Pretty sick of me to hope it would be my mother's or my brother's day instead of mine, isn't it?"

Without waiting for an answer, she turned away, calling back over her shoulder. "But that's just the way it is."

"Wait! Lodoletta…" Leah called, but Lodoletta wouldn't turn back.

Chapter Twelve

"I can't stand and talk, Leah. I have to go over to Chieto again. There was a death, and I still have some questions. Besides, I don't want to talk to you. You're nothing but trouble."

The Lieutenant motioned for Montaro to wait in the car. When he left, the Lieutenant pulled her into the entryway of a deserted shop. "Just stop interfering, would you?"

"C'mon Lieutenant, I know you're angry," Leah pleaded, "but haven't I been good about the cave incident? I didn't say a word to anyone about who it was or how he was killed until you'd made it public that it was Cecco and you'd given details. And even though I'm crazy with curiosity about how the case is going, I'm not pushing you. I have ideas, but I'm not saying a word." She made the gesture of a zipper over her lips. "Just tell me who died in Chieto? Was it murder?"

"You never let up! People die, and it's not always murder. I have to go!"

"Just curious… I know a laceworker there."

"It's not a laceworker; it was an old man with heart trouble named Giacomo Martelli, a peasant who worked hard all his life and deserves to have died in peace without you hovering at the edge of his death trying to make it a murder!"

Leah sighed. "Am I really such a vulture?"

The Lieutenant caught the flicker of distress in her eyes. His heart softened, and he leaned toward her. "You're not a vulture; you're just exasperating."

Her face brightened; she flashed a grin. "I like 'curious' better—and haven't I been useful in the past?"

"Impossible! You should be contrite, instead you're proud of yourself. Balance how useful you are with how many times you've almost gotten yourself killed."

"Three…and I didn't get killed."

He gritted his teeth. "Three times too many! I've got to go! You won't give up until you wheedle it out of me."

Leah stood in front of him, looking up, into his eyes. "Wheedle, what out of you, Lieutenant? Something about Giacomo Martelli? What is it?"

"Nothing, damn it!"

He grabbed her by the shoulders, pressed her to him, kissed her on the lips, and, blushing furiously, stalked away, hating yet again that he could never get it right with her.

Leah watched him go, wondering if she had imagined what had just happened. It was quick, but more sensually powerful than she wanted to admit to herself. She stared at the empty space where he had just been and felt a vivid yearning mingled with the sadness she always felt when they left each other on angry terms. Or, it now occurred to her, perhaps she was simply experiencing sadness because he was gone, and she wanted more of him, more of his arms around her, more of everything.

She turned toward the fountain, wondering if she and the Lieutenant would ever be able to communicate with any clarity. She sat down on the bench that circled the fountain. When she looked up, she spied the Signora, called to her, and waved in greeting.

The Signora came toward her with her usual slow, graceful approach. "It's good to see you, Leah. What are you doing sitting here? The article finished?"

Leah laughed. "No, Mom, it's not. I'm enjoying the day and thinking."

The Signora straightened her shoulders. "If you're going to be smart-alecky and condescend to my interest in your work, I'll leave you to do whatever it is you are doing!"

"I apologize, Signora. Please don't go. Please. Sit, and we can talk for a while. I've only seen you once or twice since I got back from visiting Sara and Jonathan."

Leah scooted to the side and smiled when she saw that although the

Signora's lips pursed in annoyance, her eyes sparkled. As if to prove what Leah had guessed, the Signora sat beside her. After a moment of silence, she patted Leah's hand and spoke.

"I've trained Idrissa, and he's learned well—almost too well—the store is busy all the time. He reads the tastes of people like the back of his hand. I help out as much as I can, but soon we'll have to hire someone younger. At my age there are other things to attend to—and too often that means funerals. Just recently another one: my friend's husband—in Chieto…"

Leah's head jerked up, "Martelli?"

"How did you know that?" The Signora's mouth dropped open.

Leah blushed. "I was just speaking with the Lieutenant. He said he had to go back to Chieto because a man named Martelli had died, and he had a few more questions. Was it a normal death, Signora?"

"Only you would ask that!" She shook her head back and forth in quick little jerks. "I never saw anyone so interested in murder. It's uncanny you ask. According to the doctor, it was a normal heart attack. But when I spoke to her on the phone, Martelli's wife says he was in good health except for a very slight heart problem he'd lived with for years, one that would never—and had never—caused an attack." She raised her finger. "I trust her evaluation."

"What does she think caused his death?"

"She thinks he had some kind of shock, but doesn't know what it could have been. Giacomo, her husband, made a point to keep his life calm, uneventful. My friend insisted they don't go out, not even to a movie or to see friends. 'He's practically a hermit,'" she said—and repeated it several times. The poor woman. She also kept repeating, 'a heart attack is not believable, not possible.' She told me she's angry with the doctor and with the Lieutenant because they won't listen to her."

"Did Martelli have visitors that upset him?"

"Leah!" said the Signora, exasperated, "I told you, he's reclusive… he was…"

"I wonder what the Lieutenant thinks."

My friend says the Lieutenant listens to the doctor. She says she's not going to let it go, but I don't know if she can hold on. She's devastated."

"Do you know any more about Martelli? Did he know if he knew Cecco?"

"Here you go again! The answer is I don't know who Martelli knew. And don't ask me again!"

Leah laughed. "Okay. Don't get your dander up. I'll try to stick to my new article."

Leah waited an hour and then drove to Chieto.

"Yes?" Signora Martelli poked her head around the door, which she had opened only a few inches. She stared inquisitively at Leah. "May I help you?"

The woman's eyes were bloodshot, and her face had a pale gray cast as if she were malnourished or had spent months indoors without the benefit of the sun. She wore a flowered housedress with a stained, dark green apron. Strands of her gray hair had slipped from the pins with which she tried to control her wild curls, and her eyes betrayed both fear and sadness.

"Signora Martelli. My name is Leah Contarini. I'm living in Scansansiano and would like to talk to you. Do you have a minute?"

Gesturing at the black wreath on the door, Signora Martelli responded gently, "It may be as an American you don't understand…"

"I do understand, Signora. I had the same wreath on my door just a few years ago. It's about your husband's death that I want to speak to you."

Signora Martelli uttered a nearly inaudible "oh" and stepped back to allow Leah to enter, indicating the living room, a large, west-facing, sparsely furnished area with a comfortable chair, divan, television, and little else.

Bright afternoon sunlight filled the room, giving a harsh cast to Signora Martelli's pale face. "Signora Contarini, if I have met you before, I don't remember you. I'm sorry. I can't imagine what you might have to say about my husband's death. The doctor and the police have been here again, and they insist it was a simple heart attack."

"The Signora told me about the decision of the police and the doctor, but I gather you're not certain."

Signora Martelli shook her head from side to side; words tumbled from her lips as if a dam had burst.

"What the Signora said is true. I'm certain his death wasn't caused by a simple heart attack. My husband was careful, overly careful, most people would say. Practically reclusive. At his insistence, we lived a particularly isolated life. He'd had three stents, but many people his age have stents. There was no reason whatsoever he would have a heart attack! He ate modestly, he exercised, he stayed to himself, hardly drank wine. I'm convinced only some horrible shock could have caused it."

"You mean some outside force?"

"Yes, I know what the Lieutenant thinks: It wouldn't be possible if he were so reclusive. And I know it's rare for people to die of shock, but it's not unheard of. Some outside force, or fear, some trauma."

"Had he had visitors?"

"It's possible I suppose, sometime when I've been out to the store. But as far as I know, no one," she repeated, "no one ever comes to the house. He forbids it. If I want to meet my friends, I have to meet them in the bar."

"Did your husband know a man named Cecco?"

"The one they found in the cave?"

"So you've heard?"

"Of course! You surely must have experienced the grapevine of Scansansiano and it's the same here. So many of our little towns are connected by family and friends. Sometimes I've heard more than I've wanted."

They both laughed and for the first time, Leah saw her smile.

"But your question. He may have known Cecco or maybe his father, I don't know. I remember once he was upset about some gossip concerning Cecco, but he didn't tell me why, and he only mentioned it once. It seemed at the time he was upset about gossip in general rather than about Cecco being a victim of it. I didn't pursue it. He seemed to get over whatever it was. With my husband, it's difficult to judge. He worried about many things."

"Where did your husband work when he was younger?"

"He was an assistant manager on a farm."

Leah leaned forward, "Do you know whose farm it was, Signora?"

"No, it wasn't around here anyway. And I don't understand all these questions. Giacomo is gone. What could possibly be your interest in someone you've never met." Her face flushed in frustration. "I'd like to be left alone, to grieve by myself in peace."

"I'm sorry, Signora. It's true I never met Giacomo, but when the Signora told me about your husband and about the way you were certain it wasn't a simple heart attack, I had a hunch."

Suddenly, Signora Martelli sat up. "I understand now! I'd forgotten your name. You're that woman from Scansansiano involved in those earlier murders. You think my husband was murdered?"

"I think a wife knows her husband."

Tears welled in Signora Martelli's eyes. She brushed them away, wiping her fingers across her cheeks. "You're one of the few who believe me. I won't go so far as to say murder; I hate to think that, but I do know it's not as it seemed to the police."

Chapter Thirteen

The Lieutenant's face flushed when he looked up to see Leah brush past Signorina MacCleod and stride through the doorway to his desk. His heart pounded at an unsettling pace from the conflicting emotions of fury at her temerity and delight that she had come. The memory of kissing her flashed across his mind. He stood abruptly, catapulting to the floor a sheaf of papers he had arranged in alphabetical order just the moment before Leah appeared. He bent to pick them up, chastising her as he squatted over the papers.

"What are you doing here, Leah, and why have you barged in like a bull in the China shop? It's ill-mannered; I won't have it!"

He stood, papers askance in hand, his face beet red.

"I'm sorry, Lieutenant. Please don't shout. I have a hunch I wanted to tell you about."

"You have hunches every day; your mind is like a popcorn maker; a new kernel bursts every minute, all day, every day. Even if I wanted to hear your hunch, any interest I might have had fades in light of your rudeness to me and to Signorina MacCleod."

Leah turned. Standing in the doorway with her hand on the doorknob, Signorina MacCleod smirked.

Facing the other woman directly, Leah apologized. "I really am sorry, Signorina. I didn't mean to be so rude."

The apology was heartfelt and done. Leah turned back to the Lieutenant. "May we speak in private, please?"

The Lieutenant tipped his head at the signorina and saw that the apology had been too quick to appease. She made a face, backed out, and slammed the door behind her.

"Sit down," he ordered Leah.

"But I did mean the apology."

She dropped into the chair across the desk from the Lieutenant. "I know you're busy, but this is important. Signora Martelli believes her husband suffered some sort of shock, and that was the cause of his death. So maybe there wasn't a heart attack, but a deadly shock. She doesn't believe it was a normal heart attack."

"You went to see her?"

Leah blushed.

"My god, what have I done to deserve your presence in Scansansiano? I must have committed some grave sin, and you're my punishment. If I arrest you for interfering, it will only be worse. Oh god…" Elbows on the desk, he dropped his head in his hands.

"I didn't know you were a believer, Lieutenant, and…" she hesitated, "considering your behavior in the entryway of the shop, I thought perhaps you liked me being here."

He raised his head with a jolt, anger in his eyes, his face red. "I'm not a believer, damn it. And forget about the other. It was impetuous, born of frustration. I'm at the end of my rope with you. I want you to stop interfering! Stop talking to people. Stop looking for clues. Stop getting shot, or getting kidnapped, or chased by a maniac in the middle of the night… I'm not an idiot!"

Leah leaned forward and touched his arm. "Lieutenant, I never said or thought you were an idiot. I have great respect for you."

He shoved his chair backward.

"Then why don't you act like it? I was at the scene, remember?" He poked his chest with his index finger as he spoke. "*I know* what Signora Martelli said. *I know* she thinks some outside force caused the attack. *I know* what the doctor said."

"Do you always poke yourself when you're frustrated?" She asked, truly curious.

He dropped his hands with a brusque movement. "A shock or trauma can, yes, cause a heart attack, but it's rare, *rare*, Leah, and according to Signora Martelli herself and to the neighbors—I did question them—Martelli never saw anyone. He was reclusive, a hermit."

"But there's got to be something we're missing. And I think Martelli knew Cecco. I think their deaths are connected."

The Lieutenant sighed heavily. "There's no 'we' Leah. And don't make trouble where there isn't any. We've got enough trouble without fabricating more. There's no reason to think the deaths are connected. One is murder. Martelli's death is simply a heart attack in an older man with a weak heart. Leave me to my job. Please." He clasped his hands as if praying and shook them slowly up and down, forcing the words out of his mouth, hoping she would go, hoping she would stay.

"Alright, I'll leave, but Lieutenant…" She stood.

It was the first time he had seen her appear the least contrite.

"I didn't do anything to start trouble. It has just happened."

The Lieutenant emitted a loud groan and watched her disappear through the doorway. As soon as he was certain she had crossed the piazza and would not see him, he left with Montaro in tow.

Chapter Fourteen

An hour later, after she had just finished a difficult paragraph, there was a knock at Leah's door.

"Do you know where Diego is?" Secondo looked up at her from the bottom step, worried.

"I don't, Secondo. I'm not friends with him at all. What's happened?"

Secondo dropped his head, "They're looking for him to tell him about Cecco."

"Nobody's told him his son's dead! The Lieutenant didn't say…" Her voice trailed off.

She motioned Secondo to walk along with her, and they headed up the narrow street toward the piazza.

"They can't find him. Baccia doesn't know, and the kids don't know, nobody in the bar knows, and the friends he plays cards with said he hasn't shown up for their game for a few days. The Lieutenant's asking."

Leah frowned. "I saw the Lieutenant earlier; he didn't say anything about Diego."

"He's mad at you, and he's got a crush on you." Secondo threw back his head and laughed loudly.

"He's just mad. He doesn't like it that I have hunches."

"You have good hunches, but you're not very smart about what to do with them."

Leah laughed. "You're right. My hunches have created a lot of trouble. Do you know where the Lieutenant is now?"

"I think he's down by the waterfall, but he's mad at you, so you better not go."

"I want to tell him something."

"What?"

"I need to tell him first."

"Why can't you tell me?"

"First, the Lieutenant."

"That's not a good idea."

"Why not?"

"He'll get mad, and he doesn't like to get mad at you. Plus, it puts him in a bad mood for the rest of us."

"Come with me? Maybe if you're there, he won't get mad."

"Okay, but first coffee and a cornetto."

"Now?"

"Why not?" Secondo looked at her with sincere puzzlement.

Leah laughed again. "Secondo, I missed you when I was in Montana."

They sat at the table by the window, warmed by the sun. Cinzia, the waitress, set the coffee and cornetto in front of Secondo, smiled, and stepped back to the bar.

"Did you miss Joel while we were away?"

The question startled her. "Of course! He's my friend; I missed you both."

"He missed you *a lot*. He and the Lieutenant will have to have a duel!" Secondo hooted.

The others in the bar turned to stare at them.

Leah leaned close to Secondo. "What are you talking about?"

"Joel wants to marry you, but the Lieutenant does too. But nobody knows who you want to marry."

Leah flushed bright red. "Joel and the Lieutenant are my good friends, just that. I'm not marrying anyone at the moment."

"Will you marry one of them if he asks?" He grinned. "I'd like that, but I'd like it better if you married Joel because he's my real live relative and then you'd..."

Leah cut him off. "Let's go find the Lieutenant."

"It's too late. I have to go to the doctor's for my medicine."

"You rascal. You just wanted coffee and a cornetto."

Secondo grinned without embarrassment.

They stood to leave. Leah put her hand on his arm. "Secondo, I'm just friends with Joel and the Lieutenant."

Once again, Secondo howled with laughter, then turned away and dashed down the steps into the piazza.

Leah watched him go, grabbed her coat, and rushed to the north edge of the piazza, where she stepped onto the dirt trail that switch-backed down the side of the narrow valley. Following the snakelike trail, she threaded through thick clumps of bamboo, through the narrow tufa walls of the Hillock of the Dogs, along thick brambles and vines to the river, where downy and turkey oaks, cousins in the forest, reached toward the sun and acacia trees, white with blossoms in an earlier season, now stood dark, blending in with the other trees and foliage. On the lip of the ridge, holm oaks bowed like old servants.

Leah stopped, took a deep breath, held it, and slowly exhaled. The Lieutenant would be angry again, but she exasperated him no matter what she did, and, befuddled by the frustrated look he'd given her in the office, she had neglected to tell him that Diego and Giacomo may have known each other. Strange: Giacomo and Cecco—perhaps on the same day. She would find the Lieutenant and tell him. He could do what he wanted with the information.

The mill sat on the far side of the river, a brilliant white against the green of the forest trees and lush undergrowth. To reach it, Leah followed the trail a quarter mile west, to the road, climbed the steep berm, crossed the bridge, and turned back east on the northern side of the river.

Deserted, eerily quiet, the woods closed in as the trail tapered to a single track barely a foot wide. Sunshine filtered through the leaves of the trees, painting a dappled pattern across Leah's face and clothes. She moved carefully, her eyes adjusting every second to the flicker of light and shadow. Faint bird songs rose from the limbs above her. She thought of what Secondo had told her.

A sudden rustle to her left in a stand of manna ash arrested her. In the next instant, a swish of the thick brush around an ash tree sent her stumbling backward, flaying her arms for balance.

A small sounder of wild boars emerged, moving forward with hesitant steps, weak eyes in a perpetual squint, their long snouts goading the air. Leah knew the worst time to encounter them was in broad daylight, and the worst thing to do was startle them. She righted herself and froze.

The females and young males of this group—thank god there were no squeakers or juveniles—had not heard her coming, and by the way they prodded the air and moved cautiously, Leah understood they were curious rather than angry. Still, she recalled coming across a sounder of boars when she had discovered Elia's body on a via cava years before. That time, the sounder was larger. They had surrounded Elia's body, sniffing and rooting at his arms and face. She had no choice but to attack them, screaming and waving her hands in hopes of driving them away.

Now, she turned her head from side to side, scanning the trees for one she could climb if she needed. The manna ash close by was surrounded by brush with too thin of a trunk to climb.

A loud, unusual sound might scare them, as it had before. Leah puckered her lips for a whistle, but fear had made her mouth dry. She gently cleared her throat and, in a raspy voice, belted out the loudest, most raucous song she could think of:

She's my darlin, she's my baby
She's bowleg-ged and she's crazy;
She's my black-eyed beauty on the hill
Oh she took strychnine and died
And I hope she's satisfied
Cause she done the whole darn thing
Against my will.

The boars' heads popped up, and they stood staring in Leah's direction, each with one hoof raised mid-air.

In the next instance, they swiveled and fled, crashing through the undergrowth in a wild flight from whatever beast stood before them making a terrifying sound.

Leah threw her head back and laughed crazily, part for fear, part for the sight of the fleeing pigs. In the next instant, she wilted onto a stump next to the river, drawing breaths in deep gulps.

A few minutes passed. Trying to remember the breathing exercises she had learned in her failed attempts at meditation, she watched the shallow water burble past on its way to the Tyrrhenian Sea.

Finally calm, her pulse returned to normal, Leah stood, listening for the sound of the boars or the voices of the Lieutenant and his search party.

Silence.

She stood and went on.

Chapter Fifteen

The three-story, white-painted grist mill had been built just below the shallows of the dam. Leah spotted the remnants of the sluice gate, weir, and the mill race. The stream sparkled in the sun, and she could hear the plash of water over rocks in the stream.

The mill had been the business and home of the miller for decades, but had been abandoned when stores began to sell packaged flour. With the new convenience, it was no longer necessary for women to carry their wheat down the long pathway, wait for it to be ground, then hoist it to their shoulders and wrangle it back uphill to their kitchens.

Leah examined the damp earth at the door of the mill. Only faint tracks. The Lieutenant and his men had not yet come this way.

She mounted the few steps and gently pushed the door. It swung open, releasing a musty smell of animal scat and mold. She zipped her jacket and drew it up over her face to block the sickening odor and stepped into the high-ceilinged room.

A tattered mattress lay in a corner, dirty cotton stuffing bulging from a tear along the side. Two beer bottles, half full, sat at the head of the mattress, and empty whiskey bottles were scattered haphazardly around the floor.

On the far side of the room hunkered the mill's giant bed stone with its runner stone askance atop it.

How could they have moved it? Leah wondered.

She looked up to see the machinery, still intact but dented, broken in places as if someone had beat the metal with a hammer. In the ceiling she spied the slot with swinging doors through which the grain sacks attached to a pulley were hauled to the floor above. Through a break in the wall, she could see the water wheel, broken blades gently jostled by the stream's flow.

Leah moved to the stairs and, testing each step, started upward to explore the higher floors.

The body lay sprawled near the hopper, a knife sunk to the hilt in Diego's bloated chest. His skin, wrinkled with age when he was alive, was now swollen and taut. Leah guessed he had been dead some days. His eyes were open and blotched with tache noir along the bottom edge of the whites.

The gorge rose in Leah's throat; she took several deep breaths to calm herself.

Voices outside. The Lieutenant. She rushed to the small window, banged on the glass, and called to him.

"Damn it, Leah! You…" His voice trailed off.

Leah watched the Lieutenant pace back and forth from the corpse to the window. Here she was again, as she had been in, if not the same, at least similar circumstances too many times before: found hovering over a corpse when the police arrived, while a dead body, murdered in one way or another, lay splayed on the floor, and the Lieutenant paced back and forth above her, yelling.

The Lieutenant's men huddled in a group at the bottom of the steps. They could hear him above, cursing, berating Signora Contarini. They stood whispering to each other while they waited for him to finish yelling and giving them orders.

Behind the gauzy sensation of fear and nausea, the absurdity of the situation redux was bubbling upward, and Leah knew if she didn't act contrite and be very quiet, the Lieutenant might actually put her behind bars just to keep her out of the way. She also knew she had to stay long enough to tell him what Signora Martelli had said.

"It was circumstances, Lieutenant. Really, just circumstances. I came to tell you something Signora Martelli told me about Diego and Giacomo, and I'd forgotten to pass it on to you. I knew you were searching for Diego down this way, so I thought…"

"*Thought!* You *don't* think! You never *think*! And circumstances! It's always circumstances with you."

He was poking his forehead with his index finger and now turned the finger toward her, jabbing the air between them. "You just barge ahead! You don't care about yourself! And you don't care that others have to watch out for you all the time! Don't you get it? You could be killed."

He stopped prodding the air, ran his hands over his face, and stared at her. "Go away! Go back to town. Come to the office later and I'll take a statement."

Angered, Leah stepped toward him. "I've never asked anyone to watch out for me! I don't *need* anyone to watch out for me. I… And do you realize they all were probably killed on the same day?"

The Lieutenant noticed the word "all," but he let it pass. The insult to his intelligence and his skills infuriated him. He threw his arms, palms out toward her. "Get out! Go!"

Leah stumbled forward toward the stairs, then turned back to look at him. He was bending over the corpse, studying it carefully.

She shook her head, descended the steps, and without a word walked through the silent group of policemen who were gathered in the lower room.

Chapter Sixteen

The town buzzed with gossip of the deaths. Women, on their way to market, lingered in the piazza to speculate on who had killed the father and son, perhaps on the same day. Only the coroner's report would tell. Until that report was issued, the talk turned to Baccia's broken arm, Lodoletta's bruises and scratches, and injuries Cecco's women wore as regularly as their clothing.

Everyone had seen the evidence of beatings, but no one had spoken, except behind doors or at the fountain, when they whispered their suspicions. Openly, they passed on the excuses Cecco's women made themselves: a motorbike accident, a fall on the stairs, a book cascading from a high shelf…

Women at the fountain or gathered near the vegetable stand at the market, in a manner similar to their husbands and fathers sitting together at the bar, voiced support for the mother and daughter and for Pagolo, even though he had assumed some of the same behavior as his father and grandfather. Cecco and Diego condescended to women, and everyone knew the two men had used a few of the unsuspecting, vulnerable daughters of the town and then left them in trouble and shame. Thus, secretly, because people feared the men's power, they cheered Baccia and Lodoletta, whichever it was, or both if that was the truth of it, for their resolve, and they wondered about Pagolo, who always wore long sleeves but had never shown any marks on his face or neck.

The Lieutenant brought Baccia in first for questioning. She took her seat on the straight-backed chair at a table in the interview room, her head bowed. The Lieutenant moved to take a seat across from her. As soon as he was settled and facing her, Baccia spoke in a soft, calm voice.

"I killed them both."

Mouth agape, the Lieutenant stared at her without speaking.

"I killed them, Lieutenant. Life for Lodoletta, Pagolo, and me had become unbearable, and we were sick of making excuses. Cecco and Diego were two halves of the same disgusting whole. They were abscesses with a slow leak, spreading infection. They beat us, raped us, humiliated us, and tried to teach Pagolo the same way, first by beating him, then by trying to corrupt him with alcohol and money. The older he got, the more they pushed him. And the women! Young women's lives ruined. Cecco and Diego were pigs."

She began to cry, but spoke through her tears.

"Pagolo's been so confused he doesn't know which way is up. Tender to us one day and cruel the next. They delighted in trying to ruin his heart anyway they could. What was left for me to do? What I should have done long ago! What I've been too weak to do until now. Lodoletta deserves freedom from this evil Lieutenant, and Pagolo deserves a chance to be the good man he is. What was left, Lieutenant? I hate myself, not for killing them, but for waiting so long to kill them. I'll take the consequences."

The Lieutenant bowed his head. "It's not as easy as a confession, Signora. And I'm afraid I'll have to keep you for now. Step by step, we'll clear this up."

He turned to one of the policemen that stood near the door. "Take her to the cell, and give Lodoletta and Pagolo open visiting rights. Make sure she has plenty of blankets and good food—and I mean full meals with wine."

"But Lieutenant…"

"Do as I say!"

The Lieutenant had heard gossip about the abuse for years. He had talked to Baccia many times, but she had refused to file a complaint, and without a complaint, there was nothing he could do. Now he could act—and now he didn't want to act.

"If I had my way," the Lieutenant told Montaro after they had taken Baccia to the cell, "I'd give her the key to the city and make a celebration. The whole town is better off."

Montaro nodded in assent. "I feel the same way, but we have no choice, Lieutenant. We're the law. The judge and the court will understand the situation and go easy on her, but she's got real motive. You know she does. There are plenty of people who hated them and might liked to have killed them, but hating someone is no motive."

"What about Pagolo? And Lodoletta?"

"I've already checked. The neighbor said during those two days—or only one day, depending on what the coroner says—Pagolo was helping him in his cantina. It seems a tight alibi."

"I know Baccia says she did it alone, Lieutenant, her broken arm… Lodoletta?"

"We have to see what the coroner says. He'll be able to tell which arm was used."

"Still, it doesn't seem either Baccia or Lodoletta could have done it alone. Anyway, Baccia doesn't seem strong enough, and with only that one good arm."

"Lodoletta is definitely strong enough."

"Mother protects daughter? Or could they have done it together?"

"My god, I can't think of these two women…" The Lieutenant's voice trailed off and he shook his head, "And what about the two different MOs? A beating and a stabbing? The beating, I can understand. A taste of his own medicine. Still, not the usual woman's choice, and it hardly seems possible. But the stabbing?"

"One does one, and the other does the other?"

"She confessed to both."

"It's difficult to believe. I mean, the consequences. She'd be away from the children for years. Did she say anything about that?"

"She looked at me as if I were five years old and said, 'Which is worse? Lodoletta and Pagolo are nearly adults. They're able to cook and care for the house, and they will visit me. Can that be worse than what's been happening with that demon in our house and his father at the door?'"

"I told her I couldn't imagine worse. I know people here will help out. I only wish she'd spoken to me earlier and made a formal complaint. Then she told me what a good man I was and that she hoped she'd never again confuse what she wished for with what was real. She said it was impossible to wish an evil man into a good man.

"I told her we'd talk again tomorrow and to let the guard know if there was anything she needed. I also had to let her know that Lodoletta wasn't yet in the clear. She just nodded and said, 'You're very kind. The only comfort I need is knowing my children are safe, and I believe now they are.'"

"I don't believe it, Lieutenant," Leah said it for the second time, and the Lieutenant shook his head.

"She confessed."

"That doesn't mean it's true."

They looked at each other; both of them blushed.

Leah had detected a shift in the mood between the two of them. The Lieutenant seemed calmer, more accepting of her ideas, as if something had ameliorated the tension between them.

"You're right. It doesn't. I had the same feeling, but I can't think of who else would kill either one or both of them. By all accounts, everyone in town knew what was going on. There are witnesses of the abuse, and Baccia's descriptions of the crime fit."

Leah's face flushed bright red, "I may have talked to her a little about the crime scenes."

The Lieutenant's jaw dropped. "No!"

Whatever progress had been made between them was erased.

"I'm sorry. I thought it was just a natural interest. She's his wife."

"So if she isn't the killer, she can readily seem like she is…down to the details and can claim shock for forgetting anything."

"I'm sorry."

"You don't look sorry enough! Now I'm in for it, and you'll need to testify that you told her the details."

"That won't work. She'll say I was repeating what she already knew and that she was simply pretending to be innocent."

"Damn it to hell." He glared at Leah.

"Lieutenant?" Montaro stuck his head in the door of the Lieutenant's office.

"What is it, Montaro?"

"The coroner is here; he wants to talk to you."

"Send him in," he swiveled in his chair toward a file cabinet, his back to Leah, "And you go home."

"But…"

"Goodbye, Leah."

"Not staying?" Signorina MacCleod smirked as Leah passed.

Leah hesitated a moment, then stepped to the signorina's desk.

"Signorina MacCleod, I think for a long while you and I have had trouble communicating. I'd like us to change that—together, if you feel the same and would like to."

Leah thought to say that she knew it was partly her fault, but decided to offer simple friendship instead, with no blame on either part. "Would you like to take a short break and have a coffee with me?"

Startled by Leah's offer and uncertain how to respond, the signorina emitted a slight "Ehh" and stared at Leah a moment before answering.

"Yeah, sure. Just let me tell the Lieutenant."

She knocked lightly on the Lieutenant's door and stuck her head in his office. Leah heard her say, "Lieutenant, I'm taking my break now; Leah and I are going for coffee."

"What!" the Lieutenant shouted, "Wait a minute, come…"

Signorina MacCleod gave a little wave of her hand, retrieved her purse, and joined Leah.

Chapter Seventeen

They sat at Leah's favorite table in the bar on the piazza. While the signorina stared out the window at the passers-by, Leah motioned Cinzia for two coffees. Cinzia tilted her head toward the signorina and made a face of surprise, but Leah waggled her finger, warning the barmaid not to say anything.

Sitting across from each other, Leah listened. The signorina's voice betrayed mistrust. "Why did you want to have coffee with me? I thought you'd hated me all these years."

"No, I know it must have seemed that way, and I didn't like you much, but it hit me this morning how stupid I've been. We just haven't paid any attention to each other. I tend to get mired in and excited by my own thoughts, my own plans or interest and then plunge ahead, single-mindedly. I don't want to do that anymore."

"You're not just trying to use me to get at the Lieutenant, are you?"

"You're right to be suspicious; it could be tricky being friends with each other, because you work there and I'm—well, I'm a big pain in the Lieutenant's neck. Still, I think you and I should give friendship a go."

"I thought you were in love with him; he sure is with you."

Leah blushed. "I'm not sure where I am about men. I lost the man I loved a few years ago, Signorina." Leah interrupted herself, "Do you mind if I ask your name? It's awkward to keep calling you 'Signorina.'"

"As long as you don't laugh."

"Why would I laugh?"

"My given name is Freya Aurora, and you know the MacCleod."

"Good Scottish names! They're beautiful. Aurora is 'dawn,' isn't it?"

The signorina nodded. "Yes, and Freya is Old Norse for 'noble lady' but also for the Norse goddess of love. 'MacCleod' is from the Dalriadan Clan, the west coast, and the Hebrides."

"You sound proud of the heritage."

Freya laughed. "I am proud of it. My father named me. He was a wonderful man and I miss him, my mother too."

"She was Italian?"

"Ummhumm. I got her eyes and his hair."

Leah studied Freya's long, thick red hair. "How fortunate you are! What name do you go by with friends."

"I use Freya. I had a boyfriend once who liked Aurora better, but he was the only one who ever called me that."

"How did you end up here?"

"My mother. She was from the South and she came north as one of the mondine, the women rice workers.

"*Oh Bella Ciao, Bella Ciao, Bella Ciao, Ciao, Ciao...*"

"You know the song!"

"Yes. I think first it was associated with WWII and the partisans…"

"Yes, and later with the rice workers, which is how I think of it. My mother was one of them, and just as political as the rest. Anyway, she was riding her bike with the others one day, and the chain fell off. She had to stop to fix it, and she got behind. Even as capable as she was about mechanical things, she couldn't get the chain back on and was ready to give up and push the bike back to their barracks when a big Scottish guy came out of a stand of trees and offered to help her. That was my dad, and that was the story."

"But what was he doing in a stand of trees?"

"He was traveling through Italy on foot and that's where he'd camped. It was her good luck!"

Leah wanted to ask if Freya's mother knew Baccia, but didn't want to be perceived as using Freya rather than offering real friendship. Perhaps a general question. So your mother must know other mondine."

"Of course—and don't be afraid to ask Leah; your questions won't ruin our budding friendship. I'm happy to tell you what I can, but I have to disappoint you this time. My mother didn't know Baccia. I think Baccia worked in Lombardy; my mother worked in the Veneto. Different crews. And Mamma's been gone for several years."

"I'm sorry. It's difficult to lose a parent. Thanks for not being angry. I don't mean to pump you for information."

"We *need* to talk about it. There is no way Baccia killed Cecco and Diego. I know her, not well, but enough to know she's not a killer. The Lieutenant is crazy to carry on with a case against her."

"How to convince him of that? I think he's caught between a rock and a hard place. He's the law, so he has to take her confession seriously, no?"

Freya nodded. "You're right, of course. I think what's needed is proof against whoever did kill them."

Leah noted that Freya believed there to be only one killer.

Leah left the meeting with Freya gratified for the exchange and wishing she had approached Freya earlier. She had little considered Freya in previous years and yet had proven to herself how easy it was to change perspective simply by making the first move toward opening a window on someone else's life. She knew there would be more of Freya's story, more to this Scottish-Italian woman, and she guessed Freya's story would play a part in that of the town. Perhaps in that of the recent murders.

The sky was a gray bowl overhead, with a slight breeze through the trees that lined the piazza. It seemed a simple, overcast day, and Leah sighed at the momentary pleasure of the breeze and the dim light of the clouds.

Outside the bar, a group of the older townsmen sat with coats on, wine glasses, and snacks in front of them, in their usual spot, talking and laughing together, waiting for the mid-day meal, which their wives were home preparing as the men sat gossiping. These habits and the similarity of days soothed Leah, giving her a sense that as long as friends talked to friends and the days of the town fell like regular footsteps, troublesome, even horrific, times would pass, and peace would be restored. Customs gave life a sense of certainty, of normalcy, exactly what was needed when the shadow of murder rent the fabric of community.

At the edge of the piazza, Leah leaned against the stone wall to look out over the ravine and forests below. Restless, agitated, she felt certain there was a connection between the three deaths, no matter what the Lieutenant said. What did the father and son share and what did they have in common with a man long made reclusive by heart trouble?

Leah headed toward her apartment, passed it by, and descended to her car. She would go see Giacomo's wife once again.

Chapter Eighteen

"Who is it?"

"Signora Martelli, it's me, Leah Contarini. I came by the other day."

Beatrice Martelli opened the door, but didn't stand aside. "Signora Contarini, I've told you all I know. I appreciate your concern, but I don't think there's anything to be done."

"You may be right, Signora, but I trust your instincts. Please let me come in for just a few minutes?

The Signora pursed her lips, but moved aside and gestured for Leah to come in. They sat in the living room across from each other.

Leah could see the frustration in the Signora's eyes. "I know I'm frustrating you, Signora, and at a time of deep grief, but I do trust your instinct, and I can't ignore it. From what you say, Signor Martelli was extremely careful with his health, and his heart was not so bad that he should have died. May we go over the day he died? You said you had gone out to get groceries and were gone a little longer than you expected because you met friends. What was Signor Martelli like when you came home?"

"Well, strange. He seemed angry, but he was close to tears. Upset. When I felt his forehead, his skin felt clammy, and he was sweating and anxious, as if he were waiting for something to happen. I convinced him to drink water and lay back on the pillows, but I could see that his pupils were enlarged, as if… oh, I don't know… I asked him if anything had happened, if anyone had come and bothered him…"

"As if in shock."

"Well, yes, as if in shock, but what shock could he have had? He sits here all day by himself. No one comes, and he doesn't go out. He said nothing had happened, but it was evident something had."

"Have you asked the neighbors? Perhaps they saw someone and forgot to mention it."

"No. The Lieutenant was thorough about questioning the neighbors, and nobody saw anyone coming in or out."

"Is there a back door to the apartment building?"

"Of course, but the back door is always locked, and it takes the keys of the apartment owners to unlock it. We use the back door only to carry out the garbage, or to sit in the little garden area at the back of the yard, or, when it's sunny, to hang out laundry."

"Could someone slip in when a tenant is emptying garbage?"

"You're grasping at straws. The tenants here are old and cautious, perhaps not as much as my husband was, but nearly."

"Then the shock could only have come from a phone call or from a message on the computer, perhaps?"

Signora Martelli laughed. "The phone, possibly, but Giacomo didn't even know how to turn on the computer. I'm the only one who uses it. Don't you see? The symptoms are those of shock, but how could he have gotten a shock? It makes no sense."

"It doesn't make sense *yet*. Perhaps with time it will; we just have to keep going over and over that day. Some detail will pop up that will help us understand."

"I appreciate your efforts and your tenacity, but I've accepted the Lieutenant's and the doctor's conclusion." She sighed.

Leah stood. "Please don't give up yet, Signora. Trust your instincts; I'll help in every way I can." At the door, she touched the Signora's arm and bade her goodbye.

Outside the apartment, Leah walked slowly toward the entrance of the building, but as soon as she heard the click of the lock at Signora Martelli's door, she turned back and stepped quietly down the hallway to the back of the apartment building. She tried the back door; it was locked.

Chapter Nineteen

Leah worked on her article for the rest of the day, took a break at sunset to eat a bowl of the pasta fagioli she had made the day before, then glanced at the article once more and, with relief, sent it off.

She had come up with an idea for the next piece: an overview of Tuscan mysteries for the cultural section of *The Wild Blue*, a new airline magazine. She made a note to herself and underlined the last reminder: research after I figure out these murders.

Her notebook back on the shelf, Leah took advantage of the last light to sit in the hammock swing at the back of the garden behind the apartment. From the swing she looked across the ravine to the grassy slope on the far side where sheep were slowly grazing their way upward.

Within minutes, the gentle back and forth of the swing lulled her into semi-consciousness. Leah could feel herself descending into a peaceful, heavy-limbed darkness where worries faded, and one could rest, free from the bewildering hodgepodge of thoughts trailing through the mind.

Suddenly, she sat up straight. "Laundry! The laundry!"

A loud knock sounded at the front door. Discombobulated by her sudden illumination in near sleep and the knock on the door, Leah sat unmoving, excited by her idea.

The knock sounded louder.

"Alright! I'm coming."

Joel Stein and Secondo stood on the steps smiling.

"Have we come too late?" Joel asked. "You look a little sleepy."

"It's only sunset!" Secondo reprimanded.

"I know it's only sunset; I was resting in the hammock swing at the back of the garden."

"Like a little girl," laughed Secondo.

Leah nodded. Never able to resist Secondo's bright, childlike perceptions, she flashed a broad smile. "Yes, like a little girl. It's a pleasant swing, and I can look out over the ravine."

"We're not here to disturb you, Leah," Joel explained. "We're going on another hike tomorrow morning early and hope you'll come along."

Leah hesitated.

"We thought your article was probably finished, and we could celebrate with a hike and a picnic."

"It is finished, and I sent it off, but…"

"Then come!" Secondo shouted.

Leah laughed. "Alright, I'll come; just let me make a note of something."

Joel smiled. "Meet us in the piazza at 7:00. We're doing Via Cava Santa Madonna."

"Will it be light by then?" She quipped.

"Just, but it's the longest via, plus we haven't done it for a long time, and after all our visits with family and all the food we ate, we need the exercise. By noon, it will be warm enough to sit in the grass, so we're bringing a picnic lunch—fruit and vegetables!"

Leah quipped, "And bread and cheese…"

"Yes!" Secondo shouted again, "And gorgonzola cheese, dolce! And chocolate."

"See you tomorrow then."

When the alarm sounded at 6:30 a.m., Leah wished she hadn't agreed to go on the hike. She wanted to convince the Lieutenant to go back to visit Signora Martelli.

She forced herself to repeat Signora's advice out loud: *You get the chicken by hatching it, not by smashing the egg.*

Chapter Twenty

In the gray light of early morning, Joel, Leah, and Secondo wound down along a short via cava at the edge of the city to the river. From the bank, they stepped carefully forward on each of the stepping stones someone had placed to create a precarious bridge. On the far side, Via Cava Santa Madonna ascended sharply through the high tufa walls toward the ridge above them.

Impatient at their slow pace, Secondo moved ahead, surefooted, singing 'Let It Be," a Beatles song he had learned when he visited his new family in New York. Strong and rich, his voice floated along the tufa walls through the forest, and a male mourning dove that had been persistently calling its deep-throated message, stopped its call, making Secondo's the only voice in the forest.

Joel and Leah stopped to look in one of the many caves that pocked the tufa walls of the trail.

"I've never seen a cave this large, or this well chiseled," Stein said, walking closer. "I don't remember it from last time." He stepped inside. "Come look, Leah, it's huge; it must have been for a large family and their animals—and look at the rhythmic, sweeping cuts of the chisel. A beauty of its own, particularly where one workman was right-handed and one left-handed. I wish I could have even a brief look into the life of living Etruscans."

Leah stepped into the cave. "You're a romantic. You know these trails weren't this deep when the Etruscans were here. A Roman family, or a medieval family, probably lived in this cave. Or maybe it was a shop that sold vegetables to the passersby, or a leather worker."

"Say what you want. I'm going to say it belonged to an Etruscan family."

Leah laughed. "Okay. I won't contradict you. *Someone* started chiseling the tufa and creating these strange superhighways."

"More 'superhighways' as you call them, then than now. We have only a few ways to leave town; in the time of the Etruscans, there were at least ten! But Leah, I don't want to talk about superhighways or vie cave…"

He came near.

Leah stepped back.

"Joel, you and I are good friends, and we had to overcome a lot of suspicion to become good friends…"

"Wait a minute there." He laughed. "You mean it took *you* a while to overcome suspicion."

Leah blushed. "Okay. True. It's just that I don't want the friendship to change. I like things the way they are."

"Does that mean you have no feelings for me? The kiss we shared before you left didn't seem like it."

Leah remembered the moment they had shared an impetuous kiss just before she had left for Montana.

"I meant it, and it was delicious, but I didn't mean to start a whole relationship. I was leaving, and it was an emotional moment. There are so many things you don't know, and kissing you that way was imprudent on my part."

"Can't you be imprudent again?"

She laughed, but in the next instance turned serious. "Don't tempt me, Joel. When I get involved again I don't want it to be just because I'm lonely, which I admit being at times. I want to get involved when I'm ready to have someone else in my life, for the rest of my life, and right now I'm not ready. I'm content, more than content, to be single for now."

"I won't push it, Leah. But I can't help but wonder if part of it has to do with the Lieutenant. Just know that I care about you, more than care; I would like to love you and be with you, and I'll wait…for as long as I can."

"Please don't say these things, Joel. Like I've said, there's a lot about me you don't know, and I'm not ready to talk about those things."

"What things?" Secondo stood at the opening of the cave, staring at them.

"Lunch." Leah said the first thing that came to mind.

"You're goofy!" Secondo laughed, "We can't have lunch; we just started the hike."

The next morning, Leah walked to the Lieutenant's office, hoping his anger had abated.

Freya was in her usual place at the reception desk. She had left her long red hair untethered, and it hung free down her back and around her face in thick flowing curls. Above her bright blue sweater, Freya's hair gave startling accent to her eyes, and Leah wondered why, although Freya smiled, in the midst of her unusual beauty there was profound sadness.

Freya leaned forward toward Leah and whispered, "He's calmer today; in fact, he's in a good mood. But he still thinks Baccia probably did it."

"Do I dare suggest another idea?" Leah whispered.

"You're brave. All I can say is, go slowly." Freya tilted her head toward the door.

The Lieutenant answered Leah's knock with a gentle, "Enter."

She turned the handle and walked in. The Lieutenant sat behind his desk. The room was hot and Leah saw the Lieutenant had removed his jacket and hung it neatly on a chair at the side. He had loosened his dark navy tie and opened the collar of his light blue shirt. Above the blue his face looked tanned, smooth, as if he had been long in the sun. He watched her approach but said nothing. His eyes held a tender curiosity.

"Hello, Lieutenant. Have you been to the beach?" The words escaped her mouth before she could catch them, and she mentally kicked herself for the foolish question.

"The beach? This time of year? And at any rate, does it seem to you I would have time to go to the beach?" He made a little grunt and indicated the chair in front of his desk.

"Of course not. Sorry. It's just that you seem particularly tan. It looks very well on you."

He blushed. "I've been repairing the terrace; I'm hoping my sister will come to visit from Sardegna."

Leah was surprised at this personal information. "I'd forgotten your sister, the one happy with the new beau, or do you have other sisters? I don't know much about your family."

"There are many things about me you don't know."

Leah looked away, embarrassed she'd given rise to a slight but defensive response. "That's true, Lieutenant. There are many things I don't know about you. Many things we don't know about each other, I imagine."

Now she was being defensive.

"Not yet, but I hope that will change."

Leah tensed. Remembering what Secondo and Freya had said, she felt herself skating on the thin ice of emotions. "Friendships don't happen quickly."

"No, not quickly, but we've known each other for what, a decade at least, no?"

"Yes, Lieutenant," she quickly segued back to her message for him, "and because we have known each other for so long, I'm hoping you've forgiven me for the other day. I'm always so anxious to tell you what I'm thinking that I behaved badly. I have something to tell you today, too, but I want to do it calmly…"

The Lieutenant interrupted. "But…" He caught himself. He could no longer find his way back to talk of the more personal things he'd hoped for. "Not about Signora Martelli's ideas, I hope."

"Well, yes. About hers and about a thought I had while I was sleeping in my garden swing."

"Another hunch…." He shrugged, a sign he had resigned himself to hearing her out.

"Signora Martelli described her husband's symptoms to the doctor, and the doctor agreed that they were the same symptoms as those of shock. And Lieutenant, I agree…"

"Well, that's good of you to agree with the trained professional."

"Don't be sarcastic please, and anyway, I agree with the trained professional because for a while I served as a first responder in my community in Montana, and I saw shock many times. I know the symptoms first hand. Obviously, I didn't see Signor Martelli in shock, but his wife's description reads like a classic checklist of the symptoms."

"Why are you speaking so fast?"

"Because I'm afraid you're going to kick me out of the office before I tell you what I want to tell you."

The Lieutenant threw back his head and laughed aloud. His teeth were perfect and brilliant white; Leah had not noticed before.

"I'm not going to kick you out. Sometimes I do, but it seems I always let you come back in. And medical training is another thing about you I didn't know. Go ahead. Tell me what you want to tell me."

"It wasn't in-depth medical training, Lieutenant. First responders are people who get some very basic training and then make initial sense of a site of human disaster."

"Okay, okay, go on; let's suppose he did die of shock. How did it come about? He was alone, he never went out, no one came in, he didn't use the computer, and there had been no phone calls. He was a recluse, Leah."

"I agree. We all agree on that. But I was sitting in my hammock swing, and I had an idea."

"So it is another hunch."

"Yes, it is. But hear me out."

The Lieutenant nodded and leaned toward her in a way that startled Leah by its unexpected sincerity.

"Well, okay…," she faltered. His attitude was different from the two days before; she could not make sense of it.

"Go ahead," he spoke softly, which unnerved her even more.

"Okay. There is a back door…"

"That's always locked."

"Yes, always locked, except when it isn't…"

"When people take out the garbage, yes."

"Lieutenant, I'm glad we're on the same wavelength now, but could you please stop finishing my sentences for me and let me speak?"

"Of course."

He smiled again in that disconcerting way. Leah wondered if he were condescending to her, or simply trying to show agreement.

"They do more than take out the garbage, Lieutenant. Signora Martelli says there's a swing in that backyard, and most of the tenants put out a drying rack for their laundry on the days they do laundry. My bet is that there's at least one woman in the building who does laundry habitually on a given morning.

The Lieutenant broke into song:

Monday wash day, Tuesday ironing, Wednesday mending, Thursday market, Friday baking, Saturday cleaning, Sunday church.

"Like my mother. Okay, Leah. I noticed the swing and I asked about laundry, if anyone had been out putting up laundry. The swing—a long shot given the tenants' ages—was put up for some grandchildren of an earlier tenant. As for laundry, someone actually had put out laundry that day, but they locked the door each time they went in or out."

"Right. And I think it is almost always locked each time. Almost. Here's my guess. And it's just a guess based on the way I do laundry. I put the wet clothes in a basket, so I have the basket of clothes and the wooden fold-up drying rack to take outside. I have to carry them to the doorway individually because it's too cumbersome to carry them together. So, I get the basket to the doorway, go back and get the rack, carry it to the doorway, then, from the door, I do the same thing. It only takes me a minute to take the rack out and set it up, then I go back, get the clothes, and take them out to arrange them on the rack. I'm careful about arranging them, because I know that if I shake out the shirts and slacks and skirts, it means no or only a little ironing. Arranging them takes somewhere between five and fifteen minutes, depending on the load. That's not long and certainly not long enough, I think, to bother locking the door. So I might just put a little stick in the door to prop it open for just those few minutes when I do go back inside and lock the door behind me. Now, Lieutenant, I haven't been out in that back yard, but my bet is that there's a sweet spot to set the rack, a spot where the sun shines perfectly and where there might be a little breeze. The spot may even be at the corner of the building, and I bet in those few minutes, a tenant with her back turned wouldn't notice someone who'd been watching slip in the door and once inside be free to act like any visitor, and go up to Giacomo's apartment without being noticed, or even seen."

"Why wouldn't the tenants tell me about something like that?" The Lieutenant asked.

"Who would even think about it? It's such a short time, and for sure, any tenant would have locked the door when she reentered. I'm sure all the women you asked were telling you the truth. To them, the time hanging clothes was an instant, and anyway, the door would have appeared to be locked. Even a tiny pebble would have kept the door from locking."

"This means, Leah, that someone would have been studying the habits of the tenants. It would have been planned." He cupped his chin in his hand and leaned his elbow on his desk, thinking. "The timing would have to be perfect."

"Not so perfect, really. Someone putting out laundry, perhaps singing while they do it…"

"Is that what you do, Leah?"

Her face flushed. "Well, yes, why not?"

"That wasn't an accusation. It creates a charming image."

Leah ignored the comment. "What I mean is, whoever was sneaking in just had to be extra quiet. Once inside, they could go to Martelli's apartment without being seen, and if they were seen, they could have said they were lost and couldn't find their way to the front entrance."

The Lieutenant ran a finger up and down his cheek. "Evidently, they weren't seen. I'll need to go back to the apartment and find out if any of the tenants do their laundry regularly and on which days, and if they do it as you describe."

"You agree with me?"

"It's not a matter of agreeing. It's an idea, a possibility if Giacomo were actually killed. I'll follow it up."

"Can I go with you, Lieutenant?"

"No!"

"But…"

"No, Leah! I appreciate your idea; I take it seriously, but there has to be a line."

"Why?"

The Lieutenant laughed and shook his head. "Just because I said so. Now go home."

"Okay, I'm going. But Lieutenant, since you're amenable to this idea, try on another one: all three murders are connected."

Chapter Twenty-One

Instead of going home, as the Lieutenant suggested, Leah went to sit by the fountain, her favorite spot in the piazza when she was alone. A round stone structure with a giant vase-like centerpiece surrounded by a pool of water, the fountain had been constructed with a stone bench around its circumference. The fountain was a meeting place, a thinking place, a grieving place. While friends met on the south side, warmed by the mid-fall sun, a person alone could sit quietly and read on the east side without being disturbed by the gentle murmur of voices.

In this way, the fountain held many of the stories of the town: the story of Secondo's father, a wounded American soldier who, injured and exhausted, had stumbled to the fountain for water and was rescued from the curious townspeople by the widow who was Secondo's mother; or the story of Grazia's husband cowering below the concrete bench while his wife beat him with a bucket; or the story of the tender advice of an old woman to a younger; or the place of the joyful reunion of a father and his daughter. Directly or tangentially, Leah had been a part of all these stories since she had lived in Scansansiano, and it was as if, as she sat on the bench with the water singing into the pool behind her, Leah could feel the stories whispering around her. She closed her eyes, the play of falling water tinkling behind her.

"What are you thinking behind those closed eyes?"

Leah looked up at the first sound of the Signora's voice. Smiling, she rose and kissed the older woman lightly on both cheeks. They sat down together.

"I was thinking about stories and about the Lieutenant."

"And what about him, poor man."

"Why poor man?" asked Leah, startled.

"Because he's so in love with you, and he keeps wanting a response from you, but all he gets is a fistful of flies. He doesn't know which way is up. He's got these murders, and you keep interfering, so at one and the same time, he wants to send you away and to keep you close because he thinks you'll do something irresponsible and then get hurt—and we all know you will."

"Not this again! From what they say, I have two men in love with me, and I keep saying I simply want to be on my own, doing my own little work."

"Joel's the second?"

"Yes, backed by Secondo. I'm a woman of discrete age, for god's sake."

"First of all, I don't believe you when you say, 'Oh, I just want to be on my own and do my work!'" The Signora had imitated Leah in the voice of a little girl whining. "It's pathetic that you try to push that one on me! And second, you know nothing about being a woman of discrete age, as you call it. You are a long way from that. You are an attractive woman in her late thirties, early forties—you've never shared that information with me—anyway, if you would only listen to me, you would be truthful with yourself and know that your age is one of the most sensual of ages, and Joel and the Lieutenant are sensual, handsome men, each looking for a mate, and both look at you with mullet eyes. It's pathetic, but that said, their pursuit is perfectly normal. Don't make war against May."

"What?"

"It means youth is wasted on the thick-headed young, particularly those like you. It means don't complain and resist the normal drives of the world, like love." She hesitated. "Responsibly, of course."

Leah laughed. "But Signora, I don't! I believe in love; I adore being in love, but I'm not in love right now."

"Then why did you kiss Joel?"

Leah's head jerked. "How did you know about that?"

"And I'm betting you've kissed the Lieutenant several times! He seems to be in the lead."

"I…"

"Oh, hold your horses."

Leah burst into laughter. "Hold my horses? What is this, the 1800s?"

"Alright then, just calm down. I know lots of things and you kissing Joel is one of them, and my instinct, which is almost perfect, tells me you're not innocent as far as the Lieutenant either. Way less innocent in fact."

"But how did you...?"

"Do you know me to be a person who tattles?"

"No."

"Then don't expect me to tell you how I know. I just think you should seriously consider what it means to choose a life alone, a life without a partner. For myself, I love it. I love the freedom, I love doing what I want, when I want. But it's not for you. You're a different character, my dear. You need the challenge of a relationship; you need love, and you need a love that will take the edge off your impetuous behavior."

"I'm afraid even a love won't change me, Signora. I was no different when Nick was alive, sadly for him."

The older woman laid her hand on Leah's.

Leah smiled at her. The Signora was a generous, thoughtful woman who silently and effectively supported, with money and with attention, dozens of people in the town and surrounding countryside. Her wealth was common knowledge, but her background was unknown territory. She was good-naturedly teased behind her back about her fur coat, all while she was loved and respected for her quiet philanthropy.

"I haven't thought about what it will be like as I get older, Signora. I'm almost middle-aged, and I just can't see how to fit someone else into my history, my memories, without confusion and misunderstanding. I've had years of experience a new person in my life can never understand or know."

"Love is a misunderstanding between two fools, my dear. The saying is true. But it's also true that having the courage to enter, and re-enter, that forest of misunderstandings and unknowns is the only way to learn. I think with you, it's not that you don't want love. It's that you're afraid."

"Don't you think my hesitation is reasonable?"

"You surprise me! You're a woman who chases a killer alone on isolated trails, you get shot, and yet you always go back for more. You're impetuous, bull-headed, fool-hardy, reckless, rash, heedless of real dangers, and yet you're hesitant to love?"

"But I have loved."

"And that will never end. And a part of you will always be saying 'Come back' for the rest of your life. But your heart is big enough to hold that plus new love. They're not mutually exclusive."

"You sound like a woman who knows."

"Don't try to evade the subject; we're talking about you. I think you'll choose the way that best suits you. I just want to remind you that you are at a crossroads if you actually care for either of these men. It's a question of choosing a life alone—with friends and family, of course—or choosing a husband, as opposed to a lover, which I don't think either of the men want to be. It's not right to keep a man who loves you dangling. I understand your need to feel free. You're manic as the day is long; you're erratic, you're all the things I've said before, and you know it. But quite truthfully, I think you should stop being a 'scaredy cat.' Fish or cut bait my dear."

Leah had listened quietly. What the Signora said was true. Still, she balked at the idea that she was afraid.

"Tell me about your history. How you handled love."

"Evasion again." She shook her head and patted Leah's hand. "There will come a time when I tell you my history, but not now, and I see there will be no more milk from this cow, meaning our talk about the Lieutenant and Joel. Is that the idiom?"

Leah laughed. "Yes, you have it, more or less. And you're right. Let's get back to me telling you what I was thinking about the Lieutenant."

The Signora nodded.

"I talked to Signora Martelli because she doesn't think, and I agree with her, that Giacomo's death was a simple heart attack. She thinks he died of shock, a shock someone else had to cause, and I agree with her."

"Why would you agree or disagree? How could you know?"

"He showed all the signs of shock; I talked with her about it, and I trust her instincts. And my own knowledge."

The Signora looked skeptical.

Leah sighed and rolled her eyes. "I'm not so scatterbrained that I've never done anything, Signora. I was a first responder for a few years; I know how to recognize shock."

"You surprise me yet again, even after all these years. Did the Lieutenant listen to you?"

"About Giacomo, yes, but only after I told him about being a first responder. And I've proposed the idea of the three murders being connected, but I'll have to work on the Lieutenant for that."

"I sense trouble again. Cecco and Diego I can understand, but Giacomo?"

Leah wanted to avert any discussion of the trouble she was infamous for causing.

"It's an unformed idea."

The Signora grunted.

Leah switched subject, hoping the Signora would drop it. "How is Idrissa doing? I thought his bride would be here by now, but I haven't seen him lately."

"I understand: change of subject. He left. He's gone back to Senegal to bring more leather goods from his father and to finish up business on that end for his wife coming. There's the bride price, the passport, gifts for friends, all the things involved in a big wedding."

"I'm confused. The last I saw him, she was coming here soon."

She laughed. "That was his hope, but from what he said, there are more forms and regulation requirements to take care of than they anticipated. It's not as easy as buying a ticket and getting on the plane. He was sanguine about it, though, and by the time he left, he was giddy, happy, worried, excited, and nervous all at once."

"I'm surprised it all happened so suddenly, and that he went without saying goodbye. Strange."

"Don't let it worry you, Leah. He also said he was happy to be leaving for a while because he'd heard terrible arguing below his window the few nights before he left, and it scared him."

"Who could be on that trail? It was closed days ago because of falling rock."

CHAPTER TWENTY-ONE

"I don't know, that's just what Idrissa said."

"And no idea of what they were saying?"

"I think he was too frustrated to listen carefully. Lots of cursing and threatening, and strangely, laughing. He also thought he heard Cecco's name, but he said he didn't wait to hear it all. He yelled at them, slammed the window shut, and put cotton in his ears. He said the last thing he wanted to hear was anything about Cecco. Evidently Cecco and Diego caused him a good deal of trouble last year at the city council."

"What about?"

"Oh, it's over. He can tell you about it later."

"Did he at least tell the Lieutenant about the noise below his apartment?"

"I don't think so. It was the night before he left. I saw him early the morning he left, and I don't think there was time before his bus left for the airport. He told me he'd get to the Lieutenant when he got back."

Leah let the new information sink in for a few minutes.

"Have you gone to visit Baccia, Signora?"

"Of course. I took her fruit and the chocolate *tozzetti* I know she likes—I prefer the rustic ones. And I've had Pagolo and Lodoletta to dinner, but there's little to be done for Baccia. The Lieutenant seems convinced."

"The Lieutenant has a blind spot. Baccia is terrified one of the kids will be blamed, and now they're both confessing because they want Baccia to be released. But their confessions don't hold water. It's horrible that their love has to be manifested this way. Unfair." Her voice trembled slightly.

"Stop mouthing cliches, Leah. You sound unschooled; it's not like you."

Leah fell silent, embarrassed by her bubble of emotions.

A few minutes passed before the Signora rose.

"Well, my dear, I'm on the way to the pharmacy. Be kind to Joel and the Lieutenant, and for the sake of all of us who love you, stay out of trouble just this once. Please."

She scuttled away without a goodbye.

Leah watched the Signora cross the piazza. Several people stopped to give a short bow and mutter, 'Buon Giorno, Signora,' as she walked by. The Signora nodded in return and continued on to the pharmacy.

"Gentle obeisance to a real queen of a woman. And rightly so," Leah thought.

Chapter Twenty-Two

Leah sat watching the townspeople come and go on their various errands. Some carried fresh bread from the bakery, others, late to shopping, pulled their rolling carts, rattling at a fast walk over the street stones. She felt warmth and love of community for the people in Scansansiano. Many had accepted her and Nick, had shared their lives and festivals, wine, olives, meals, tragedies, and their joys.

A flicker interrupted her attention. She turned. Arrammundu was crossing the piazza toward the bar. She hadn't seen him for a few days and was shocked by his slovenly appearance. It looked as if he had been sleeping rough. His hair was greasy, tousled, and his clothes were dirty and wrinkled. One shirt sleeve was torn at the elbow. The flap of plaid material hanging off his wrinkled shirt fluttered slightly in the breeze.

The loss of his mother had hit him hard. Leah called to him. "Arrammundu."

He lifted his head and raised his hand in a weak wave, but continued toward the bar.

"Arrammundu, please come say hello." Leah rose and walked toward him, her palms extended.

He watched her approach, a look of resignation on his face. "Salve, Signora. It's good to see you." His voice belied the words.

"What's happened? You don't look well."

"I haven't been able to sleep lately; it's taken a toll on me and on the daily things—like bathing."

"Can we sit and have a coffee?"

"Oh, okay." He tilted his head toward the bar, but it was evident he preferred to be alone. With Angelica in mind, Leah persisted, and they walked together into the bar.

Instead of coffee, Arrammundu ordered two tuna and tomato sandwiches. They were cut in the traditional triangle shape regularly served in local bars, and he ordered a spritzer to go with them. Leah had coffee and watched as Arrammundu finished the sandwiches in little more than two bites each.

"Arrammundu, how long has it been since you've eaten?" Leah raised her fingers to Cinzia to signal two more sandwiches and olives to go with it.

Finished, Arrummundu wiped his mouth. "Thank you, Signora. I haven't been feeling hungry, but I guess I am now that the food was put in front of me."

"I'm happy to see you eat. Have you been away? I've stopped by, but you weren't home."

"I may have been sleeping. My days and nights are mixed up, so I take the chance to sleep whenever I can."

"And wherever?"

Arrammundu shrugged his shoulders.

"Arrammundu, I hope you can find some balance and take care of yourself. I've been worried about you. The last time I saw you, you were black and blue, as if you'd been in a fight. I don't know what's happened, but I do know grief is a difficult terrain to navigate. If you experience it anything like I did, you're remembering all the things you took for granted and only now are realizing that you didn't pay as much attention to your mother as you wish you had. I just hope you won't let it drag you down."

"Didn't pay enough attention?" he shouted.

The room fell silent, and people turned to stare.

Arrammundu flushed. "I'm sorry," he spoke in a lowered voice. "I didn't pay attention at all! She needed me to help out, and I took and took and took…"

He punctuated each word with a slap against the table as if the wood itself were the offending party. I'm sick of myself. Sick of my squirming little courage that came late, sick of my ego, sick of the way people treat each other, hurt each other, and yet go on living, laughing as if they were just normal, good people who'd never done a wrong thing in their lives. My girlfriend…"

Shocked at his vehemence, Leah moved closer and put her hand on his arm. "Arrammundu, stop and think for a minute of your mother. Think of what she would want for you. The grief will never go away, but you will walk through the emptiness of it and 'hang photos on the air,' as they say. You'll have memories, and they'll be sweet."

"Signora, I will have memories alright. I have memories now, plenty, but they will never be sweet because my part in them was smoke, tricks, because *I* wasn't in those memories. Oh, I was physically, but I never even asked my mother her story, and if we don't know each other's stories, what good are we? You probably know more about my mother than I do. I never asked her, not about daily things, and not about her love for my dad, what troubles they went through, how she lost him so early; nothing about the twenty-four-hour day of every seven-day week and thirty-day month and on and on and on. What good was I to her? What the hell did I know about love? If we only laugh with our friends and family and take them for granted, and ream out of them all of the good we can get from them, and yet never understand the inner wars of even the ones closest to us, what good are we? How do we live with lessons that come too late? Why didn't I know things? What have I done? My god, what have I done?"

He jolted to his feet, knocking against the table. Leah caught it just before the cups and plate slid off.

"But, Arrammundu, what do you mean? You were a child, and you grew into a responsible man who loved and aided his mother and gave her solace."

"Solace! How could I have ever given her a tenth of what she gave me? And what good is the puny amount I've done for her now, after her death? Papers and business. I'm going crazy. I'm going crazy with my own ineptitude, my blindness for my mom, and for my creep of a 'girlfriend.' I have to go. I have to get away."

He rushed from the table, stumbled, and fell down the steps into the street. Pushing himself quickly to his feet, he ran in an awkward, jagged gait across the piazza toward home. A trickle of blood ran down his arm.

Chapter Twenty-Three

"Hi, Freya."

Freya was bent over, reading a paper on her desk, deep in concentration. Leah spoke gently not to startle her. Freya looked up and smiled. Dressed to provocative perfection, she wore a form-fitting sweater of warm green, a tight black skirt, and high black boots. The sweater accentuated her red hair, which she had let flow over her shoulders and back, making tendrils of long cinnamon curls at her cheeks. For jewelry she wore a single string of what looked like very expensive pearls, which made Leah wonder how she afforded them on a secretary's income. The thought crossed Leah's mind that perhaps there was a wealthy lover in the background.

"You're just the person I was hoping to see." Freya smiled.

"Then I'm doubly glad I came. What's up?"

"I wanted to ask you to visit Baccia again." She brushed a long curl away from her face. "I know you've come before, but she's so down I'm worried about her. About her safety."

"That bad?"

Freya nodded. "The Lieutenant's worried too. He's keeping her here in town so Lodoletta and Pagolo can visit, bring food, and sit with her while she eats. Otherwise, she won't eat, not very much anyway."

"He won't be able to hold her here for long, will he?"

"That's the worry, but it seems he has some sort of pull, because, for the moment, there's no pressure. The danger comes from her. We've got to do something before then. Have you had any new ideas?"

"None. It's all confusing. These murders. And on top of everything else, I just had coffee with Arrammundu. He's in terrible shape over the death of his mother. He's beating himself up, thinking he didn't do enough for her, didn't treat her well enough. He looks like he's been sleeping rough, and I know he hasn't been eating because he wolfed down four sandwiches in the same number of minutes."

"Scuttlebutt is that his girlfriend left him too. But I don't see how…" She stared out the window.

"How?"

"Oh, nothing. I just didn't understand he was particularly tight with the girl, that's all. But what I started to say is that after they grow up, lots of children of single parents feel that way. They look at the children they were and judge those children by the adults they've become. It's unjust, but I think they can't help it, and they have to get through that stage before they can let themselves remember the really good things. If they make it that far, then they can simply love and respect the parent for the person she was." She shook her head. "Everybody carries guilt about something."

"You too?"

"Of course! And you, as well, I bet. Someday, we'll get into all that, but for today, it's Baccia and her predicament."

"You're right; I just meant that Arrammundu's hurting himself he feels so guilty, and I don't know how to help him. Angelica would be sad to see him thinking this way. He's let himself go. He hasn't washed, he hasn't slept, and he's not shaving so he looks scruffy, plus, I think he's sleeping rough."

"Yeah, you said. But he has the apartment, and I bet he'll go back when he can't stand being dirty anymore.

"Okay. Today, Baccia. You and I were actually on the same wavelength. I came because I wanted to see her. I was afraid I'd have to fight the Lieutenant to get the chance; I'm glad I won't."

Freya nodded. "He's afraid for her; I think everybody is."

They walked to the back of the building to a large metal door. Freya unlocked it, and the two stepped through into an aisle bounded on both sides by cells, their bars reaching from floor to ceiling. The jail presented a dissonant scene. The city offices, including the office of the carabinieri, were located in what had been an Aldobrandeschi family palace. The town jail, at the back of the palace had once been a beautiful stone hall, with giant archways, Medieval stone pillars with foliate and ionic capitals. Now, the space was a jail with cells, all empty, except one in the middle where Leah could see Baccia sitting on a narrow camp bed reading a magazine.

Baccia stood and moved to the bars, gripping them with both hands. "Leah! So good of you to come."

Leah turned to Freya, "May I sit with her inside the cell?"

"It's contrary to regulations…"

"I know, but just this once. I'm happy to have you search me."

Freya barely hesitated. "I don't need to search you, but the Lieutenant is coming back in an hour, so I'll have to move you out before he gets here."

"Thanks."

"And, thanks from me too." Baccia put her hand to her heart.

Freya unlocked the cell and checked her watch. "Okay, I'll be back in fifty minutes."

Leah took a seat on the edge of the bed with Baccia.

"Where's Lodoletta? I thought she might be here?"

"She's gone home to shower. And she'll draw it out as long as she can. She hates these cells."

"Are you two getting along?"

Baccia laughed, "Of course. We get along fine, but she's young. Since I'm here, she feels tied down. Even at home, she never stayed; she's always going somewhere, always in a rush."

Leah nodded her head. "Everyone's worried about you, Baccia, I want you to know that. And I want you to know that people are rooting for you."

"I wish they'd rooted for me earlier." She spoke without rancor.

"You have good reason to wish it."

"I know that before anyone else, it was my duty to do something, so I don't blame anyone. I guess I was afraid he'd kill me—or us."

"Let's not go over it, Baccia. We're living now, yes? And I want to know if there's anything I can do to make things easier for you?"

Baccia laughed and looked Leah in the eyes. "That's the first time I've laughed in weeks. I forgot how good it feels. And yes, we're living—if that's what you call this!"

Leah looked puzzled.

"It's difficult to understand why I'm laughing, I know. It's just that the response to your offer was, "Let's see…what would make things easier for a woman who lived with physical and psychological abuse for decades, watched her son and daughter be abused, lost all self-respect, lived in fear almost every hour of the day, has committed murder and will probably spend the rest of her life in jail? Hmmmm. Let me think about what I need to lighten my load?"

There was no cynicism in Baccia's voice. Under the pressure, she saw humor in her situation. Leah thought this denoted a sort of deep-seated health, an amazing attribute in a woman beleaguered and threatened with years of jail time over a murder that bordered on being a justified act of self-defense.

"Actually, there is something, Leah. Take care of Lodoletta and Pagolo in whatever way they'll accept. I know Lodoletta has been rude—to say the least—but at base she respects you. She's talked to me often about you and delights in telling me about you standing in the middle of the piazza looking up at the sky. She thought it was 'cool.'

And Pagolo—he's a profoundly angry young man. It's my fault for not protecting him. Cecco, and Diego too, were rough on him." She began to cry. "Physically when he was younger: spankings, hard spankings, a cuff in the face, all of it, and then when he was twelve, they started introducing him to things he shouldn't have had to know. Bastards. They were both bastards. And now it's like Pagolo is in the boxing ring with himself. He can be violent and then can seem totally defeated and do nothing but sit around all day."

Her shoulder shook under the sobs. Leah held her and let her cry. Several minutes passed before Baccia pulled away. "I'm sorry." She wiped her eyes with the back of her hand. It's overwhelming, and the worst is that I've been a coward. I should have done something sooner, before it got so bad."

"You're not a coward, Baccia. You never were. You suffered a situation too many women have suffered. I know you can't magically get over it in an instant, but Cecco and Diego are gone and can't ever hurt you or the kids again. The task now is Lodoletta and Pagolo, yes? We'll do as much as we can, but you're the one they need. You're the only one who can help them into their futures."

"I won't be in their futures. I'll be in jail, with maybe some time off for good behavior." She looked at Leah as if expecting Leah to refute what she was saying. "And if I'm out early, that will be only after years."

"Don't think that way. You know you're not guilty; you know it, and so does everyone else. And neither are your children guilty. We just need to find out who killed Cecco and Diego."

"If they don't take me, Leah, they'll take, or try to take, Pagolo or Lodoletta. We're the only ones who have motive. I can't stand the thought of Pagolo or Lodoletta suffering like that; they've suffered enough. I deserve prison, whether I killed Cecco and Diego or not, and I'm not saying I didn't kill him, but they don't deserve all the interrogations and a jail cell. They're children. They have no guilt in any of this."

"Baccia, I have to ask a question. I don't want to ask, but I'm compelled."

Baccia lifted her head and looked into Leah's eyes. "It's okay."

"I know you didn't kill them. Tell me straight, could it have been Lodoletta? Or Pagolo?"

Baccia burst into tears and leaned against Leah. "Never!"

Freya locked the cell, and she and Leah stepped back into the front reception room just before the Lieutenant came through the outside door.

"What are you doing here?"

Leah stepped closer and looked up at the Lieutenant. "I came to visit Baccia. It seemed alright. Freya said you'd been worried about her."

His face softened. "I am worried about her; I'm glad you're here."

He took her elbow and guided her into his office. Freya watched them go, a strange look on her face.

The Lieutenant closed the door and indicated the chair in front of his desk. "Have a seat. How did Baccia seem?"

"She's a mother who fears for her children, a mother who is guilt-ridden for not doing something sooner, and a mother ready to spend her life in jail, so the children don't have to suffer police scrutiny. She's devastated, determined, and she spent most of the time crying."

"I thought I couldn't keep her here much longer, but it turns out I can. I may even be able to let her out, if she promises to stay in town and report in. We're breaking all sorts of precedents to make it possible, but it would be better to solve it."

"Only you, Lieutenant, would go to these lengths."

The Lieutenant gave a wane smile. It eased his homesickness and made him feel that perhaps there was a slight crack in Leah's resistance.

Chapter Twenty-Four

Frustrated by the inability to make things happen and grasping at straws, Leah decided to wait for nightfall and go to the spot below Idrissa's house, hoping whoever had been there would come again. If they were coming, she reasoned, they would come after the town was asleep. She could be there at first dark and be safely in hiding by the time they arrived.

The afternoon passed slowly. She took notes on her next article. Sauteed zucchini for the risotto she planned for supper, and cleaned the bathroom sink. She read the next chapter in Alessandro Barrico's new book.

Hour by hour the day passed. By 5:30 she'd finished eating, cleaned the dishes, and shed the clothes she'd been wearing in exchange for a black t-shirt, black sweater, black pants, and dark running shoes. From the hanger by the dresser, she took a black wool beanie and black rain coat and hung them on the handle of the outside door.

Determined to wait until seven, when most people would be off the streets and at home preparing their evening meal, she sat in the stuffed chair by the window, took five deep breaths, and let herself sink into a state of semi-consciousness, visualizing herself on the trail, hiding in a clump of bamboo, safe and still.

Leah woke a few minutes before seven. She rose and looked out the window. The streetlight made a dull circle of yellow on the cobblestones. She heard a loud clank of dishes.

The men who had met below Idrissa's apartment were sure to wait to return there until midnight or after. To be ahead, she would go out to the trail as soon as people had finished eating and were sitting in front of their TVs with the volume high. She hoped tonight would be a night the men, whoever they were, would come back to that isolated spot.

Out the door, a cold wind swept up the sleeves of her coat and down her neck. She turned back inside to take another dark sweater from her drawer, eased it over her head, and stepped out again, locking the door behind her. In the shadow of the overhang on the steps, she waited, listening.

Two women walked by, but failed to notice her standing there, just three feet away from the street. Leah held her breath and waited.

A man and his wife came up the steps just off to the left of Leah's tiny porch, chatting about their late supper. He would fix the salad and she would make the *tonno con panna*, tuna with cream. They said something Leah couldn't catch, and both laughed, passing her by as if she were no more than a stone. They had not seen her.

Within minutes, the street fell silent. There was no sound of footsteps, no sound of voices, no laughter. She eased off her little porch and quickly, quietly jounced down the steps to the road, turned to the right, up the road for a few feet, and bent low to slip under the plastic ribbon that alerted people not to enter because of falling rock.

The narrow trail rose sharply uphill, with a steep descent to her left and the sheer tufa rock on which the city was built to her right.

The ambient light of the apartments high above faded before reaching the pitch dark of the trail. She switched on her small solar-powered flashlight, thankful for its dim circle of dark yellow, which spread only enough light to detect dangerous holes in the path or rocks large enough to make her slip. There was nothing to protect her from loose rocks in the tufa above, but Leah knew she would have to take that chance.

She moved slowly upward, gauging the distance to a spot under Idrissa's window, where the men—she assumed men—had met. She had walked this trail many times in daylight and figured they would meet at the wide spot, where the clump of bamboo ended and there was a little patch of grass off the descent side of the hill, just at the steep drop to the ravine.

Placing her feet carefully at each step, she shined the flashlight low to the ground, hoping to be unseen by anyone who happened to look down from their window.

Every few feet she stopped and looked up, her sight following the sheer rock wall from which the apartments rose. Excepting one window fifty yards ahead of her in the lowest apartments, there were lights; the darkened windows were Idrissa's apartment.

Leah headed on, slowly, carefully, stopping every few steps to listen, to gauge the distance to the spot below Idrissa's apartment.

The ravine side of the trail was lined with clumps of bamboo, Scotch broom, and stunted oak tangled with vines. If she fell and rolled downhill, Leah knew it would be trouble. She smiled. Photos of Tuscany often showed rounded hills of waving grain and cypress planted like soldiers, leading to a beautifully refurbished casa calonica, isolated and graceful at the top of a gentle hill. Fewer tourists thought of wild Tuscany, the forests of tight trees, thick and impassable except to cinghiale. The brush and vines that could capture and bind any hiker who wasn't careful. If she fell, Leah knew it would be at the least uncomfortable, and at the worst, possibly deadly.

She raised her eyes and glanced upward. In just a few yards, she would be directly below Idrissa's window. She stopped to listen.

Voices. They were coming up the trail. Much earlier than she had anticipated. Her heart began to beat hard. She swallowed. Her mouth went dry.

She bent low, extending her arm toward the trail, so the circle of light was no wider that six inches. Creeping quickly forward, she released her breath in low exhales and drew breath silently between her lips.

The voices grew louder.

Leah stepped into the opening, now shining her light around the grassy area, looking for a place to hide. Over a small cliff was a sharp drop. From below, on the steep side of the ravine, a clump of giant bamboo shot straight upward. To her right, a thick tangle of Scotch broom allowed no opening. She turned to the right again and scanned the rock wall. A few steps up the trail, she could see a darker spot that denoted one of the remnants of an Etruscan cave, but her memory of being trapped in a cave with a killer some years before stopped her. She refused to take the chance of it happening again.

Turning again she saw a narrow opening in a thicket level with the patch on which she stood. She stepped between the culms of the bamboo, gritting her teeth at the soft rustle. Just as she disappeared, two men rounded the curve to the open ground.

By their light Leah could see that both were of the same height, and both wore wool beanies and neck warmers that obscured their faces and their voices.

She stood rigid and waited, hoping they would pull down the neck warmers. Why would they hide from each other?

It wasn't as she had hoped. They stood close together and spoke in little more than a whisper. She caught fragments of a sentence, but the rest of their words were swallowed by the night.

A drug deal?

A slight sound came from further up the trail. An overturned stone. And another. Someone was fast approaching.

The man holding the flashlight flipped it off. The other one hissed, "The bamboo!" and they stepped backward directly into Leah's hiding place.

Rooted, rigid, Leah held her breath. Their backs were within inches of her face, separated by only four or five thick culms of the sturdy grass. The three of them waited.

They heard sniffing and a low whine.

One of the men burst into laughter.

"It's that damn dog! The man stepped from the cane and shone his light on the dog's pure white pelt. Seeing the men, the dog moved forward to be petted.

Noah! The name blossomed in Leah's mind.

The man Noah had approached brought his leg back and kicked Noah full force. "Get the hell outta here! Go on!"

Noah cried in pain and bared his teeth, but the second man had joined in kicking and yelling, befuddling Noah, who snarled but didn't know which way to turn. The men laughed, enjoying their own cruelty and relieved that it had not been a human on the path.

"Leave him alone, you bastards!" Leah charged from her hiding place at a run and, in one powerful leap, threw herself on the back of one of the men, jerking his shirt front against his windpipe.

He twirled from side to side, hands grasping at his neck, gasping and squeaking, "Get her off me," but the other man was teetering at the edge of the cliff, the prisoner of Noah, who had cornered him.

In one final twirl, the man threw Leah from his back. She landed near Noah at the edge of the cliff, and as she struggled to rise, the man who had thrown her bent to shove her back to the ground, distracting Noah just long enough for the first man to run toward the trail. Noah bounded after him, latching onto his leg with his teeth, growling low and angry, tearing through the man's pant leg and into the flesh.

"Ahhhhh!" He cried in pain, kicking his leg in jerks like a wooden marionette, "Get off me, you bastard!"

Leah struggled again to rise, but the man punched her in the face, and she fell back. The other man had reached the trail, dragging Noah behind him. When Noah loosened his grip for an instant, his prisoner limped quickly away down the trail, pumping his arms to help his running limp.

Noah turned and bounded toward the man bending over Leah. The man glanced over his shoulder, saw the dog coming, and in one swift movement, put his hand to Leah's shoulder and thigh and pushed her over the cliff into the thicket of bamboo that grew like spiked grass trees on the steep descent of the ravine.

Noah leapt toward the edge of the drop-off, staring into the darkness. The man grabbed the flashlight from the ground and struck Noah across the forehead just above his eyes. With one whimper, Noah dropped to the ground, stunned, and the man escaped.

A wind came up, sweeping through the trees, whispering through the culms of bamboo. Noah, still dazed from the blow to his head, dragged his way to the right and then to the left, whimpering as he moved to the edge of the cliff. Exhausted, he peered over the edge, raised his head, and howled into the wind.

When no one came, Noah barked and then howled again in wordless, high-pitched sounds of distress and anxiety. Like a siren from the animal world, he called and called all night long to alert the townspeople that Leah was lost.

The lights in the windows went on and off, and the townspeople, who did not know the language of dogs, poked their heads out the windows that dotted the cliffside above to yell at him to be quiet. They could believe a dog bite could impregnate a woman, or a dog walking between a courting couple meant the wedding would be canceled, or stepping in dog poop with your left foot meant good luck, but they could not read a howl that meant, simply, "Help!"

Chapter Twenty-Five

Leah woke shivering and sore. Above her, she could hear Noah's whines and tired, muted howls. He had kept watch over her throughout the night. She tried to roll over, but grunted in pain and lay back. Blood had congealed on the leg of her pants, and her hands were cut. She imagined her face, too, was cut and bruised, but her second sweater and jacket had protected her from serious cuts to her torso.

She looked up through the giant culms of bamboo. Above her, the sky was a pale gray-blue. Either it was cloudy, or it was first light, not yet dawn.

"Noah," she spoke barely above a whisper.

Noah whined.

"It's okay, Noah, go down the trail, go on, go now. I'm coming."

He whined, but stood to all fours.

"Go on. I'm coming."

She heard a few clinks of rocks from above. Noah pattered away.

Mustering her strength, Leah pulled herself up by a thick culm, whispered "thank you" to the bamboo, which like all worthy experiences had cut her to shreds, but had also broken her fall as she was catapulted over the cliff. She stumbled down the cliffside to the trail along the river below, where she could meet the trail leading upward to the piazza.

Noah was waiting where the two trails crossed. He slowly approached and sat next to Leah's leg without touching her, as if he knew she was wounded and could not bear the pressure.

"C'mon, Noah," she said, running her hand gently over his head. "Take me home, and we'll eat."

After a slow, torturous ascent, Leah reached the piazza and started gingerly across, followed by Noah padding wearily behind her. At the bar, she turned into the narrow street that led to the lower part of the old town, thankful no one was yet up and about, hoping she could make it home without being seen.

Past the bar, a door opened and Pagolo came out, turned to lock the door, then stepped into the street directly in front of Leah.

"Signora Contarini!! What happened to you?"

Noah growled and bared his teeth.

"Quiet, Noah. It's only Pagolo. Quiet."

She patted the dog's head. Noah sat obediently on his haunches, but continued to make a deep growl in his throat.

"I was out walking, and I had a fall."

"Musta been a bad one! But you still look good." He stepped toward Leah. Noah sprang toward him.

"Noah! Stop!"

The dog jerked back.

"Noah, come here!" Noah slinked back to Leah and crouched at her feet.

"Well, thanks for the concern, Pagolo. I don't feel so good."

"You don't get what I mean. You're in good shape for your age, trim, and when the scratches heal…"

He looked her up and down, and his lips curled in a crude grin.

As exhausted as she was, Leah burst into laughter.

"Pagolo! You're a kid. What are you doing looking at me like that and insinuating such things? It's ridiculous."

His eyes went dark, and his hands balled into fists, the knuckles white. He glanced down at Noah.

"Don't tell me I'm ridiculous!" he screamed, "Someday, I'll show you who I am and what I can do. And you'll love it, Bitch!"

Leah felt a frisson of fear, but angered by his threatening stance and words, she stood her ground, Noah growling beside her.

"Don't do something stupid just because you're upset. I'm not making fun of you; and it's ludicrous to make fists over such a small thing, especially when so many people care about you and love you."

"What the hell do you know? You have no idea how strong I am and no idea who does and who doesn't love me. And look at yourself. Out wandering around in the middle of the night, all scratched and bruised. You're a crazy woman, a nosy old foreigner, and you should stay out of other people's business."

"You're right on at least one count, Pagolo. I am a little crazy. My vanity won't let me admit to being past my prime, as you seem to think, and perhaps I don't—or perhaps I do," she paused and leaned slightly toward him, "have an idea how strong you are. Maybe even strong enough to push a woman over a cliff, do you think?"

Pagolo averted his gaze, and Leah went on, "And I see we are *both* out in 'the middle of the night,' as you so strangely call the dawn..."

Pagolo stiffened.

"...so, if you intend to hit me, please land the punch where I'm not already cut or bruised, if you can find such a place. Someone, or two someones, have already had a go at me, so a bit more won't hurt. I wonder if you might know who those someones were?"

She smiled, walked away a few paces, and turned, "Go visit your mother and sister. Those two need you, Pagolo; they need a strong, *good* man who knows better than to get them all in trouble."

She had spoken with more bravado than she felt. Pagolo had used the phrase *in the middle of the night.* Had it been merely a colloquial saying, or had it been a slip, indicating he was one of the two men, perhaps the one who had pushed her over the cliff? But why would he have? And who could he have been with? Was it a drug deal?

She was too tired, too bruised and aching to think about it.

At her door, she turned the key in the lock, stepped in, and called Noah to follow. Thankful for the heat of the room, she filled a bowl from the sack of dog food she kept on hand for Noah and scrounged through her cupboard for another bowl to fill with fresh water.

Once Noah had turned several times in circles and settled in the blankets next to his bowl, Leah went to the bathroom, slowly undressed, and showered, pressing a soapy sponge against her wounds to wash away the blood, wincing as the hot water splashed over cuts and bruises and finally eased the deep chill that had imprisoned her body after the night in the cold.

Out of the shower, wrapped in a warm green bathrobe, she was halfway through a cup of tea before she felt completely warm. She set the cup on the table beside her cushioned chair and leaned back to mentally review the events of the previous night, struggling against fatigue to remember details. As she fought to recall a face, a jacket, and the sound of a voice, she was soon lulled by Noah's rhythmic snores and fell into a deep sleep, legs akimbo in the chair. She slept, woke to eat, and slept again until full morning, when she woke sated with dreams of wandering through a bamboo forest arguing with Pagolo about visiting his mother and sister.

Chapter Twenty-Six

The Signora gasped. "Leah! What happened to you! Your face is a mess!"

"Yes, Signora. I did look in the mirror this morning; you don't need to remind me what I saw."

"Well, what happened?" She shook her head in frustration that, Leah noted, carried a tone of real concern.

"Please let me ask Cinzia to make a cappuccino when she finishes with the customers at the table; then I'll tell you the story." *If not all of it,* Leah thought to herself.

Cinzia, the barmaid, set the steaming hot, frothy coffee on the table and greeted Leah with a quizzical look, but didn't ask about her wounds. Leah gave her a short nod of thanks.

After drinking half of her coffee, Leah turned to the Signora, who had been waiting patiently.

"I literally fell off a cliff into a clump of bamboo while I was walking on one of the trails last night.'

"*Sei pazzo*! Truly crazy. I don't know why we all love you so much! You ignore our concern and blunder ahead with no care at all!" The Signora was exasperated, near tears, and angry at the same moment. "Why were you out on a trail at night? And why do you do these things! One day, we'll lose you if you're not more careful."

"Don't worry, Signora, please." Leah felt a touch of guilt. "Here I am in front of you with just a few scratches, some minor aches and pains, and no broken bones. Sometime, I'll tell you how often I've been bucked off a horse."

She touched the Signora's hand. "And last night's was a very small fall," she lied.

"I don't care how small it was; it's obvious it was dangerous. Were you knocked out? And where was this, and how did you get home without help? And why, why, in the first place, did you go walking on an isolated trail at night!!"

"Please, Signora, let's forget the fall and my scratches. I'm happy to tell you why I went out and where I went." *Just not how I happened to get pushed over the cliff.* "Would you like another coffee?"

"No, what I need is a spritzer with plenty of prosecco!"

Leah laughed and motioned to Cinzia, mouthing "spritzer," indicating large, and tilting her head toward the Signora.

When the drink came, she waited until the Signora had taken her first delicate sips.

"I went out because of something you said about Idrissa."

"I'm sorry I said it, if it sent you over a cliff!"

Leah ignored her.

"You said that the night before he left, he heard what he thought were two men arguing below his window, and he was frustrated because he wasn't able to sleep. I thought about that and began to wonder why two men would be meeting late at night on that trail below the apartments, so I went up early to find a hiding place where I could listen to what they were saying. I thought it might have something to do with the deaths. It was a long shot, but why not?"

"Why not! Because you could have been killed, and as it was it looks like you almost did kill yourself." She shook her head in irritation. "Well, did they come?"

"No," Leah averted her eyes.

"You're lying to me, Leah."

Leah blushed. "There are things I just can't tell you now, Signora. Please don't press me. There are things I have to think about first."

"You know me well enough to know that I won't press you to tell me who they were or what they said, but you *must* tell me if you actually fell, or if they pushed you."

"I was pushed, but it would have been much worse if it hadn't been for Noah."

"The dog!"

"Yes, he's the one that actually saved me."

"*Figuriamoci!* What else would one expect of you but to go out alone on a dangerous trail, chasing after two potentially dangerous persons, be pushed over a cliff, and then have a dog save you. Perfectly normal. You may not want to tell me, but you must tell the Lieutenant!"

"I can't, n—"

"Must tell the Lieutenant what?" The Lieutenant appeared beside them.

Startled, the two women looked up and cleared their throats simultaneously.

"My god!" the Lieutenant yelled, "What happened to your face?"

The other people in the bar turned to stare.

"Please sit down and stop yelling, Lieutenant," Leah squeaked, glancing over her shoulder.

He remained standing and stared at her.

"Why aren't you at work?" Leah tried to sound accusatory and stern, but the words came like a plea.

"I'm not at work because I haven't yet had coffee, but instead of a hot cup of coffee, I'm here, looking at your swollen, sliced-up face, certain you've been in some sort of trouble and certain that whatever it was is going to cause *me* trouble."

"My face is not 'sliced up'! I have a few scratches and bruises, that's all."

The Signora intervened. "It does no good for the two of you to argue about Leah's face, and I imagine it's her arms and legs and torso as well. Sit down, Lieutenant. And after you get your coffee, take this woman to the station and make her tell you what happened. It's like loving a child. She's recalcitrant and irresponsible, and she should be in jail. Failing that, you must give her a very long interview—no, a very long interro-gation. And please don't let her off easy just because you're in love with her! She doesn't deserve your love today; she deserves a good spanking!"

Blushing furiously, his mouth agape, the Lieutenant watched the Signora swipe her coat from off an adjoining chair and storm out the door.

The Lieutenant and Leah did their best to evade each other's eyes. The Lieutenant coughed and cleared his throat in awkward attempts to regain his composure, and Leah turned from side to side, looking out the window, then toward the bar, anywhere but directly at the Lieutenant.

Realizing it was useless, the Lieutenant looked straight at Leah. "Let's forget what the Signora said and get on with it. What happened?"

"I think the Signora was right. We should go to the station," she glanced around the room, "where there aren't so many people."

Chapter Twenty-Seven

"Uh-oh, looks like you're in trouble again, Leah." Freya spoke as Leah and the Lieutenant approached. "What happened to you?"

"Never mind," the Lieutenant said. "We'll be in my office and please don't disturb us, no matter how crucial it seems."

Freya looked at Leah, turned both palms upward, and raised her eyebrows. "Okay."

As she passed the desk, Leah whispered, "Later," and followed the Lieutenant into his office.

Rather than sitting behind his desk, the Lieutenant took a notebook and pen off his desk, pulled a chair toward the seat Leah had taken, sat down, and looked her in the eyes. "Okay, tell me everything." He seemed unusually calm.

Going slowly to remember each detail, Leah recounted what she had done the night before, beginning with dressing in black and heading for the trail at a little after seven p.m. The Lieutenant listened closely, took notes from time to time, and asked her to repeat certain parts, making sure he understood.

Most difficult to remember in the sequence was the part when the men began to kick and beat Noah. Leah remembered that she had lunged from the bamboo, leapt on the back of one of the men, but then it had been a free-for-all, a tangle of bodies, voices, barks, and groans.

"Height of the men? Build? Could you recognize a voice? Any particular smell—like of aftershave or soap? Anything?"

"I'm sorry. It's pretty much a blur. I do remember thinking the guy who pushed me over didn't seem much bigger than I am. I mean he was definitely taller, but he was slight of build."

"Okay. Then?"

"Well, then I went over. I remember feeling I was falling for a long, long time and was being tossed back and forth. I think I felt like that because I was bouncing back and forth. The culms of those big bamboos are thick, so I must have hit one, been tossed against another, and then another. Anyway, I have bruises on all sides. And having the culms pitch me back and forth like that broke my fall. Like switch-backing through the air. But I think for certain I must have been unconscious when I hit the ground, because I don't remember the final blow.

"Noah stayed there all night; I know that because I overheard some people in the bar saying how a dog was howling all night in the ravine. I wasn't aware of it, but when I woke—at first light—I heard Noah above me, whining.

"I was terribly cold, exhausted, and sore. Hoping he could alert someone, I told Noah to go and meet me lower on the trail, there where it ascends to the piazza. He did, which surprised me a little, but I guess he understands. I turned over, got slowly on my feet, and made my way to where the trails meet, and Noah was there, waiting. We shuffled up to the piazza together, crossed it, and turned toward my apartment. That's when Pagolo came out of an apartment near the wine store and locked it. When he saw me, he seemed shocked, maybe even a little concerned, but whatever sort of concern it was, his remarks soon turned into a sort of a pick-up line. It would have been farcical in any situation, but it was even more so at that moment. If I had had the energy, I would have laughed even harder. As it was, I told him he was being ridiculous. Which infuriated him. He told me I didn't know how strong he was, that I was a bitch, and then he stalked off.

"I went home, fed Noah, gave him some water, showered, had tea, and fell asleep. When I woke, I went to the bar, ran into the Signora, and then you. And that's the story."

The Lieutenant stared out the window without speaking.

Leah waited. She had anticipated anger, but he hadn't raised his voice or reprimanded her; he seemed simply to be thinking.

"I can't control you."

Leah sat bolt upright, "Of cou…"

"Just calm down and let me speak before you leap into angry defenses of your independence, would you?"

Leah drew a deep breath and nodded.

"I can't control you. You meddle in my cases; you're headstrong; you act impetuously; put yourself in danger; and keep all of us who love you worrying about you whenever there is a murder in the area, which unfortunately is more often than any of us like. You're to murder like a fly is to honey…"

"Do you love me too, Lieutenant?"

A bright red crept over the Lieutenant's face. It was a serious question, and he knew he could not joke his way out of it.

"This isn't a time for that question. I was speaking generally about the way people here care about you. For now, I've made a decision. I want us to work together instead of always working at odds."

"Do you mean it? And what do you mean?" She scooted forward in her chair, face bright.

"Yes, I mean it, but with certain restrictions. I understand that your curiosity leads you to some very important information and some perceptive observations. What I want is for you to share these things with me…"

"And will you share information with me, as well?"

"Yes, but sharing information with you is on the condition that you won't misuse it and go off on your own before we can talk. I know you're impetuous; the question is, can you just have a smidgeon of patience to talk to me or at least let me know where you're going, before you run off to follow some cockamamy 'instinct.' Can you agree to that?"

His unusually calm manner and the sudden offer of working together discombobulated Leah.

"Well, I can promise to try; I can't really promise I'll succeed." She paused, "But yes, I promise I'll try."

The Lieutenant sighed. "Not the best answer, but I'll take it—for now. And I'll begin: it looks like Pagolo has been dealing, not just marijuana, but cocaine and heroin, and it seems like some of it is laced with another substance we haven't yet identified. Lodoletta may or may not be involved, but we do know that for a long time, she's been smoking, and probably dealing, marijuana at least. Baccia doesn't seem to know about any of this, or else she purposely refuses to know about it. I have the sense that admitting this to herself, on top of admitting she's allowed the abuse to continue for so long, would drive her over the edge. Plus, the three of them are bound together as a tight circle of victims against Diego and Cecco."

Leah had listened carefully. "I agree about Baccia and am not surprised about Lodoletta. Pagolo, I don't know. He seems to have taken on the behavior of his father and grandfather. Although I've seen a compassionate, gentle side of him too when he's around his mother."

"That's the question." The Lieutenant nodded. "How far has he gone in becoming like the other men? I have the feeling he, like other young guys his age, could go either direction. Maybe he's already become too much like his dad and grandfather. They both have a history of shady deals, but they were slick as oil; I haven't ever been able to pin anything on them. Both of them had a part in ruining the lives of some silly young girls who fall for fast cars, vacations on the beach, and fine meals and then find themselves in some home for unwed mothers in Rome, too embarrassed to come back, too young and inexperienced to find any decent work. Pagolo may be in a war with himself under the influence of such a gentle, generous mother and such a bastard of a father."

"So the men on the trail could have been Pagolo and one of his clients? Or Pagolo and another dealer, is that what you mean?" Leah asked. "I don't think it could have been anyone much older; the ones on the trail were just too strong and agile, I think, and when I jumped on the back of the one, he felt slight. But why push me over a cliff just because I might have guessed they were making a drug deal, if that was what was happening?"

"Like I said, Pagolo's into not just marijuana. He's moved onto heavy drugs, jail-time sort of drugs, if I can ever find evidence, and he has an explosive anger, which makes me think he could have killed you before he even realized what he was doing." Fear flashed across the Lieutenant's eyes.

"Yes," Leah said, remembering the hands against her back and side pushing her body to the cliff's edge. "But Lieutenant, if Diego and Cecco got Pagolo alone or Pagolo with Lodoletta, involved, both those kids could be so messed up by the conflict between what their father's influence and what their mother is that they're suspects. From what Baccia has told me, Cecco and Diego did their best to mess with Pagolo's mind. And who knows what they've done to Lodoletta."

"Exactly. I'm thinking the kids may have been enticed into doing some horrific things they didn't want to do. Maybe Diego or Cecco threatened one or both with more beatings, or worse, they could have threatened even harsher beatings for Baccia. That could scare the kids badly enough to commit parricide.

At this point it's all guess work. I have no proof that it was Pagolo, Lodoletta, or both. It's all hearsay and conjecture, and I can't get anything on Pagolo since he has an alibi, Lodoletta is refusing to talk about anything, and Baccia insists she did it, even though we all know she didn't. Not to sound insensitive about what happened to you, but I was hoping you could provide another piece of the puzzle."

"What a mess drugs make! I wish I could help, but I can't. The night was too dark and the fight and my fall happened too fast to catch any useful detail. All my attention was on saving Noah, and then suddenly, I was at the bottom of the cliff. Are you sure Pagolo has a watertight alibi? He does have a slight build."

"I doubt if you've seen a tenth of the damage drugs have done around here, and yes, I'm sure Pagolo has a tight alibi, according to the neighbor anyway. He says Pagolo was helping him in the cantina, and Arrammundu says he passed by and saw Pagolo working. And, do you know how many young men around here have a slight build?"

"Could the neighbor just have forgotten about Pagolo taking a break or going back home to get something, or running off to do an errand…?"

"I'll ask again when he gets back; he's gone to some relatives in Lazio. But Arrammundu was certain he saw him working there."

"Yes, but Arrammundu can only attest to at most a few minutes, if he was just passing by. He can't attest to Pagolo being there the whole day, no?"

"That's true, but the neighbor can, and it seems Arrammundu was there about the time of the killing, according to the tentative time set by the coroner. He won't be sure until tests come back."

"But what about Diego?"

"I'm thinking they had to be the same killer. And if Pagolo has an alibi for one, that lets him off the other."

"Lieutenant, what's the real reason you've asked me to work *with* you?"

He regarded her for a minute before answering.

"It's not like asking you to be part of the police force, Leah. I just want to talk with you more often, listen to more of your ideas. I'm tired of being angry at you, tired of fighting with you, and most of all, tired of worrying about you. I want to keep you safe."

It was Leah's turn to blush. She interrupted, "But…"

"And it's not only personal. You have a way of blundering into things, of finding out things, or—what shall I call it—bringing certain truths to the surface, especially because you're so stubborn and have no sense of danger. I know you're not going to change; I know you'll still act impetuously. I can't change that, and it's one of the… never mind. What I mean is, what you are has helped us.

Leah smiled.

"Don't be so happy about it. You're a troublesome element in the mix. You make situations froth and explode like that volcano experiment of baking soda in vinegar we did in grade-school. Or maybe a better metaphor is you're a detonator. You walk through town; you just *exist* and you create explosions and…well…I want you where I can keep an eye on you."

Leah made a face.

"I'm not sure what I think of your metaphors, Lieutenant, and I'm not sure I can be of any use to you, but I do know I don't like being, and *won't* be, corralled, so I'm not sure I want to enter this agreement. It's an honor for you to invite me, but I don't want anyone to "keep an eye on me," as you put it, not since I was a little girl. The ideas come to my head, and I'm compelled to follow them, just like a dog chases a squirrel. Are you sure you don't want to reconsider?"

CHAPTER TWENTY-SEVEN

He emitted a loud laugh.

"I know all these things from personal experience, and I can imagine them in you as a little girl. And no, I don't want to reconsider. If we agree to talk more, and if you can keep quiet about the information I give you, at least I might be a step closer to working with you instead of against you and maybe even closer to solving some of the crimes that seem to plague Scansansiano."

"We understand each other then. So okay, I'm in."

She held her hand out toward him. He reached for her hand and, in a powerful but gentle move, pulled her onto his lap and kissed her on the mouth.

Leah put her hands on his chest to push him away, but all of her strength left her. She raised her hands to the sides of his face and gently, insistently, responded with a fervor she thought had faded and left her long ago.

When she reluctantly broke away, she stood looking down at him as if she were surprised to see him sitting there.

The Lieutenant's voice was jagged. "I guess I'm sometimes impetuous as well."

He stood, turned away, and stepped around his desk. Without raising his head, he muttered, "Let me know if you remember any more details."

Chapter Twenty-Eight

Freya raised her head when she heard the Lieutenant's door open. Leah stepped out, looking dazed.

"*Santo Cielo!* What did he say to you? I don't see any new bruises, but you look like someone just knocked you silly."

"He did." She bit her lip and stumbled toward the door. "Later, Freya."

Freya watched her walk to the outer door and struggle to push it open.

"Pull, Leah. Pull!" she called.

Leah walked into the piazza and across to the southern side of the fountain, where she was hidden from those passing on their way to shop at the COOP on the hill above. It had become a habit for her to sit there, to regard again, as she had many times, the five arches of the aqueduct and the beautiful Fountain of the Seven Spouts with the broad faces of men and a lion's head in the middle.

The plash of water falling into the pool that surrounded the central fount usually soothed her, but today with thoughts of human tragedy and horror mixed in her mind with the vibrant memory of the Lieutenant's lips and his warm scent, Leah realized she couldn't sit; she felt a compulsion to be active. She needed a hike on the vie cave.

The yearning the Lieutenant's kiss had aroused bewildered her. For months, she had dismissed the tangle of emotions she felt when she was near him. Those emotions muddled her thinking, twisted the words in her mouth, and made her sweat.

And what had he actually meant by offering to "work" with her? That he simply wanted to keep her close so she wouldn't ruin his investigations?

The idea infuriated her. She was not a dog, not a child to keep from danger.

She shook her head. Memories crowded her mind: memories of being attacked and pushed off the cliff, of Baccia's mournful face, of Cecco battered beyond recognition, of Diego's bloated, dead face at the mill, a face that in death showed the true age of the man who had worked so hard, so piteously to appear young in life; a face which still held the horror of his last seconds of life.

She didn't want those visions to interfere with the sweetly painful and evocative yearning of the kiss.

A voice called to her from a few yards away.

Abruptly, Leah stood and strode away, away from the voice, away from people toward the north side of the piazza, to the trail that led down the side of the ravine, through tall stands of bamboo, down to the river. She followed the trail west, crossed the road by the bridge, and hurried on toward the via cava that threaded up through the forest toward the ridge and flatland above.

It was a cool, sunny day with no sign of rain. Within a few paces along the trail, Leah had forced from her mind all thoughts except those of the forest around her. Someone had said, "Trees are always a relief after people."

It was true, Leah could feel her spirits rise and her head begin to clear. Across the small meadow, she entered the tight space between the high walls of tufa stone and slowed her pace to a steady walk, moving upward, bending by instinct under the overhanging rock although the overhanging rock was a good 6 feet above her, at the entrance to the proper trail. She moved at an even pace, watching her step along the rough tufa stone, aware of the rustling of holm oak at the top of the vertical walls, which hugged tightly to either side of the trail. A chill settled on her back and arms, but within minutes, she was warm again from the exertion of her gentle but steady ascent.

She took a deep breath and, with renewed concentration, allowed the murders to sift back into her mind.

What were the essential questions? She began a mental list: Could Baccia, even with her broken arm, have killed Diego and Cecco because they were ruining Pagolo's life by enticing him into drugs and licentious behavior? Could Lodoletta have killed them because they had not only beaten her, but perhaps in acts of pure evil, raped her? Could Pagolo have killed them for both of those reasons and because of the drugs. How depraved were the men?

It was ludicrous to think of the two women killing them together: Baccia with her broken arm, Lodoletta enticed into violence by her mother. Leah could believe Pagolo might have done it, but not the women. She shook her head.

"Why are you shaking your head? There's no one else here."

Startled, Leah's head jerked up.

Secondo was standing in front of her.

"I was trying to answer some unpleasant questions."

"I've had those. What were yours about?"

"The murders. I don't understand what happened so I let the questions go through my mind and then get rid of what seems impossible answers."

"You don't know a lot of things. Are you on the trail because you want to think about answers?"

"Yes. And you're right, Secondo. I don't know a lot of things."

"The Signora says that if you want to understand something like a murder, you have to understand what happened before the murder, and you have to find out people's secrets. She says it even works with all kinds of questions. Remember, Joel and I didn't know we were half-brothers until he found out the secret about our father being here during the war and living with my mom. That was a story and a secret my mom didn't tell me. And that was something that happened before, a long time before, we found out. And as soon as we knew those things, we knew we were brothers, or half-brothers at least, but that's the same. And everything was clear."

Leah smiled. "You're right. Half-brothers can be just the same as whole brothers. You and Joel are just like brothers."

Secondo grinned and straightened his shoulders. "Yes, and now I'm a nephew and a cousin and a sort-of-another son. Way more things than I used to be."

"You're right. Maybe I need to find out more stories and more secrets about more people before I can understand why the murders happened, and maybe if I can understand, I'll stop being bothered so much by all the questions."

"You're stewing in confusion; that's what my mom used to say. That's a sort of saying. Just go find out."

He brushed by her and walked on down the trail, whistling.

Leah laughed. Secondo was right about almost everything. Leah continued upward, making a mental list. What was their history? Diego and Cecco were abusive, were in some form or another into drugs, and they had ruined the lives of at least a few of the young women in town. But what lay in their pasts, beyond their lives in Scansansiano?

If what Secondo said was right and she needed to look at the history and discover secrets, there seemed to be no secrets about their lives in Scansansiano. Everyone knew they were degenerates and abusive; there was no secret in the men's treatment of family and of some of the young women in town. Everybody knew the history and, sadly, had accepted it.

For this reason, it seemed too obvious for Pagolo, Lodoletta, or Baccia, or any combination of the three, to have killed Diego and Cecco.

Leah stopped to lean against the tufa stone to cool herself. The reasons for the three to kill Diego and Cecco were there, but it didn't feel right. Baccia was a gentle woman who loved her children, and regardless of his bravado and tough-guy act, Leah had seen Pagolo behave tenderly toward his mother, and joke and laugh with his sister in an equally gentle way. They may have been wounded by the abuse, but they weren't killers.

There had to be something, someone else.

Leah walked on. There had been three deaths, not just two. Did the three deaths have something to do with each other? An old man and his son, a recluse who didn't know them, who never left his house, and whose death had been professionally certified as simple heart failure?

At the entrance of the little park area with a picnic bench just a few yards from three dromos, Leah turned in. After wandering by the dromos, she took a seat at the picnic bench. Two of the dromos were now filled with water and brambles, only one could be entered.

The one still accessible was the one in which she'd been trapped by a killer the first time she came to Scansansiano; the one when, for the first time her little silver whistle, a gift from Nick, had saved her. It saved her again when she had discovered Elia's body some years later.

She reached and pulled the chain at her neck, bringing the whistle to her hand. Nick had saved her life many times, in many ways.

She sat and, breathing deeply of the cool air, stared out over the forested slope of the valley and down to the river, which wended its way like a liquid silver chain southwestward toward a larger river and finally to the Tyrrhenian Sea.

The Lieutenant had kissed her, for the second time. An abrupt, gently passionate kiss. And she had responded with equal passion.

What was she doing? He thought he knew her, but he didn't. Nick had been the only one capable of living with the chaos of her character. Many men had been attracted to what some of them had called her "wildness," what others called her "energy" without understanding it was a two-sided coin or, more appropriately, a double-edged blade.

She had desire, yes, but no desire to relive years of the pain her barely controlled energy and wildness caused in intimacy with a man, and, like the Lieutenant and Joel, she had no interest in being a casual lover.

She rose, stepped back onto the trail, and hiked hard to the top of the ridge, where she crossed a field to the road and turned onto the berm for the long walk back to town.

She would put the Lieutenant out of her mind and would concentrate on discovering the histories of the murdered men. "All three," she whispered defiantly to herself.

Chapter Twenty-Nine

Leah stayed in her apartment the next two days, reading and writing. The evening of the second day, when it turned dark and she heard the clank of pans and laughter or arguments at the tables of her neighbors, she dressed in a warm sweater and jacket and walked quickly toward the back steps leading out of town down to the trail by the river. From the end of the trail, she crossed the road and, using her flashlight, headed up the via cava that began above the ditch and twisted steeply upward to the spot where she had discovered the body of her friend Elia. It seemed to her to have happened a lifetime ago.

She stopped at the spot remembering how the body—she hadn't yet known it was Elia's—had been surrounded by a sounder of wild boars, sniffing over an either dead or unconsciousness man. She could see only the bottom of his shoes.

As she watched the boars in the sounder, it had started to rain. She wanted to turn and run back to town, but in order to save the man, who might still be alive, she had seen no alternative but to attack, with hopes of startling the animals.

Taking and releasing several deep breaths, she eyed the group of wild boars, shook out her arms, and ran full speed into the sounder, screaming and waving her arms wildly above her head.

To her relief, the sows, little ones, and wide-tusked boars had turned tail and scattered back into the forest.

And there on the ground was Elia, murdered and dragged to this isolated spot. Elia who, with his wife Anna, had treated Leah like their own daughter.

Friends and advisors, now gone.

Standing there, remembering, Leah thought of the others in her life and felt herself to be a part of the community of both the dead and living: Elia and Anna, the Signora, Secondo, Joel, the Antoninis, the Lieutenant… Their griefs had mingled with her own, their joy and her own, their festivals, their funerals. She was as much a part of Scansansiano as she had been a part of her town in Montana.

She turned from the spot where she had discovered Elia and went on into the cold, but exhilarating darkness of the forest trail. The climb was clearing her mind. The memory of her last meeting with the Lieutenant had scrambled her thoughts, convoluted enough before that encounter.

It would be exciting to work with the Lieutenant in a professional sense, to follow her curiosity about Pagolo's conflicted character, to discover who had pushed her over into the stand of bamboo, to be part of a murder investigation. And she would pursue those things. But now, as she hiked through the darkness, she decided she would let it all go for some days, let go of all the threads of her interests and curiosities, and concentrate on more research into Angelica's background. Angelica's parents' love story was enough to make a good piece itself, and if Leah could find out more about Angelica's childhood and those walks to the cave, it would be exciting and might even make a book.

By the time Leah reached the top of the trail and came to the road leading in one direction to field after field of vineyards and in the other direction back to town, she had decided. She would work on Angelica's story, a tribute to a fine lacemaker. The first thing to do would be to visit the farm where Angelica's parents had lived and Angelica had been raised. Arrammundu could tell her how to get there, and the people still living on the land may have known Angelica's family.

The Lieutenant would be happy; he could continue his investigation, and she would be out of the way and safe.

Chapter Thirty

By the time Leah was twelve kilometers east of Scansansiano, headed south toward the farm, the road had dwindled from pot-holed asphalt to a rutted, rocky, narrow dirt trail. The few farmhouses in small clearings gleaned from the thick forests of the area were set back from the road, and although the weather had been good, there was no sign of anyone working in the fields or pastures. Great, thick stands of tangled raspberry bushes crowded the road, scratching the sides of the car, forcing Leah to the middle of the track. She felt herself draw in her shoulders to become smaller.

From time to time the forest opened to hillside pastures dotted with small flocks of sheep. It seemed to Leah she and the sheep were the only living beings in the area besides the hare, deer, porcupines, wolves, hedgehogs, owls, nightjars, salamanders, pheasants, and wild boar that crouched and scuttled, glided, crept, and wandered through the stands of brush and trees.

Dirt rose behind the car as she bumped and rattled along. In places, vines had covered many of the trees, and she wondered if any of them were Married Vines, wild grapes that long ago had climbed elms and shown the Etruscans their first vision of viticulture.

Leah was content to be moving slowly. This was deeper into the forests of Tuscany and Lazio than she had ever been. A century earlier, she knew, she never would have entered here. This area was then the territory of such brigands as Domenichino Tiburzi, famous or infamous depending on who was telling the legend, writing the book. He had lived, and killed, and robbed from his hideouts in these forests for twenty-four years after his escape from prison. A Robin Hood figure, who killed a man for being disrespectful to a woman, some said; an extortionist who demanded protection fees, others said. Finally, he had been caught and killed by authorities near Capalbio. His body had then been propped up and tied to a tree, gun in hand, hat on head, so the police could take the only photo ever taken of this little five foot two-inch crook and killer whose life and purpose continued to be disputed.

Leah laughed aloud. *Crime.* She couldn't escape it. But today, she was only on the trail of a story, an in-depth story about Angelica, so she might write an article that would pay homage to one of the finest lacemakers in the area, one of many women who continued to practice their art in even the most difficult of times.

After flipping a coin and the toss luckily indicating the left hand of a forked road, Leah drove along a narrow creek, upward into cleared land, and came at last to a spot where the dirt road joined asphalt and she could head in the direction of Valentano. At the intersection in the highway, she turned away from the hilltop town and instead headed toward the Dry Forest, which surrounded Lake Mezzano.

The short stretch of asphalt ended abruptly after a quarter mile, and again the Fiat jounced along a dirt road, climbing upward, dust rising in giant puffs behind her. Four miles forward, Leah came to an open area bordering the forest. There, she spotted a long lane that led to a casa calonica attached by a broad archway to an outbuilding. Through the archway, she could see a wide inner dirt yard bounded by graneries, barns, and what must have been, in the time of the mezzadria, workers' housing.

Leah wished she had been able to find Arrammundu to ask for specific directions, but he had not been at home, and she had been impatient to get going. From his earlier description, this looked like the place. She moved slowly up the lane.

Approaching the house, she expected to see a big Maremma Sheepdog come out barking. Any dog in this countryside would not be like Noah had become; here, the dog would be a guard dog and possibly a vicious protector. She pulled close to the house, turned off the motor, and waited.

A few minutes passed. No one came from the house, and no dog appeared.

She waited.

The door opened. An elderly woman, wizened by the sun and hard labor, stepped out and came toward her, wiping her hands on a long apron that covered an even longer skirt, a simple, but pristine peasant blouse, sleeves rolled to the elbow. She wore her gray hair tied back by a simple cloth scarf of blue, and her face was bright with a wide smile, as if she were happy to see Leah, although she could not possibly have anticipated her arrival.

Leah stepped out of the car and greeted her formally. "Good day, Signora."

The woman laughed. "Come, come. It's good of you to address me so carefully, but here, we pay no attention to that. Come into the house and have a little vin santo and one of my torcetti. When you're refreshed, you can tell me how I can help you."

As she walked in, Leah could feel herself relaxing into the simple but elegant grace of Tuscan hospitality. It had been a long drive, and she was here. From the earlier farm Arrammundu had described, this had to be the place.

They entered a long, wide room. An open hearth stood across from the doorway, with the kitchen area to one side and a long dining table on the opposite side. At the narrow end of the room, Leah could see another doorway leading to what she guessed was a storage area that must, in turn, lead to a stall and mangers for the animals.

A rough-hewn, wooden table served for dining. It was now set with a beautifully simple glass carafe of vin santo and a plate of torcetti. Leah opened her eyes in surprise.

"It's not magic, my dear. We have a clear view of the road, and I saw you turn into the lane. I knew whoever was coming would need a little refreshment. Please..." she gestured toward a chair at the table. When Leah was seated, she poured wine into one of the glasses, which seemed almost too delicate and beautiful to hold.

"I see you like the glasses and carafe. I'm glad. They were a gift to me from my friend, Angelica Sanna Piras and her son Arrammundu Piras. I cherish them greatly, the people and the glass set."

Leah's mouth dropped; before she had even taken a drink, she set the glass back on the table.

"What is it? How have I startled you, dear?"

"It's actually about Angelica that I came to speak to you."

"Oh." Sadness clouded the older woman's eyes. "If you've come to tell me that she's gone, it's alright." She reached to pat Leah's arm. "Her son Arrammundu was here, and we had heard about it even before he came. She was a gem among gems, just like her parents, Beatrice and Lorenzo, and like her son, Arrammundu."

A look of pain flashed over the woman's face.

"I knew that you had heard, Signora. I came for another reason. My name is Leah Contarini; I'm a friend, I was a friend, of Angelica's and I hope to be a support to Arrammundu."

"Ahhh. You're the writer Arrammundu mentioned. Perhaps he also mentioned that my husband, Antonio, and I were friends of Angelica's family from the first moment Lorenzo brought his beautiful little Beatrice home from Sansepolcro."

"He did. And you're Maria Teresa, yes?

Maria Teresa's lips curved in a warm smile. "Yes, and now *we* are almost friends. Tell me how I can help you."

"I've come because, yes, I am a writer, working for a magazine that wants more of my articles on Italian merletti. I've interviewed Angelica at length about her work…"

"She was one of the best. Perhaps only Beatrice was better."

"I have many photos of Angelica's work, and she also told me the story of how her mother and father met. The article on her merletti work is finished, but I want to add a second installment about her parents' story and life here, under the mezzadria system, including how her family—and, as I understand it, others of you as well—helped hide the Jews of Scansansiano during the German occupation. I'm moved by the bravery of you all, and I think the story should be told.

Angelica agreed that I could write about it in one of the articles, but I wanted to add more depth to the article by hearing more not only about the Piras family, but about the rest of you as well. I think you and your husband may be, if not the only ones left from that era, two of the last ones. I'd like very much to hear the perspective of someone who knew the family and, in some respect, lived through the same experiences."

Maria Teresa had listened carefully, nodding her head slightly.

"Those were terrible times and, as you understand, dangerous times. Most of us did what we could. Not all, mind you. There were fascists here, too, ready to turn in Jews, ready to sneak around to find Jews in hiding, ready to hand over their own neighbors—their own neighbors!—to the Germans because their neighbors had given some little Jewish children something to eat. Some would demean themselves lower than pigs to ingratiate themselves with the Germans. They fawned and shuffled and grinned themselves silly. Oh yes, it was a way to stay alive, but such an ignominious way it was better perhaps to die."

"I hear bitterness in your voice."

"Oh yes, Signora. A part of me *is* still bitter. Our farm manager and his son and their assistant were fascists. They weren't so bad before the war, but once the Germans came, we lived in terror not only of the Germans but of those three. You can't imagine how we had to plan and hide and be quick on our feet to keep them from knowing that we helped the Jews. Unlike the men who owned the fascist shops, the Jews were decent and understood poverty, they always added almost double to our groceries or clothing materials when we paid for only single, they let us buy on credit with no fee until harvest, and taught our children in the evening after work. If the fascists turned us in, it meant the destruction of our houses, the rape of the women, and too often the death of the father."

"It must be impossible to forget."

"Of course. And I keep a photo of those three, so I don't forget! I want to remember what they were, who they were, and because it gives me great pleasure to understand that for all the evil they did, they lost. The goodness of people prevailed, at great cost, but it did prevail."

"The way of truth and love have always won," Leah muttered.

"No!" Maria Teresa shouted, and Leah sat bolt upright, ashamed of having mouthed a platitude.

"Truth and love don't always win. Truth and love are brutally beaten; they take the best to the earth. They rarely win, but they do *prevail*, if wounded and in terrible pain. Do you think one side *won* the war? Can you forget the dead and the lost, the gas chambers, the broken families, the haunted eyes?"

She stood and stepped to a chest behind the table, opened a drawer, and pulled out a photo, tossing it onto the table in front of Leah. Her voice was soft, but firm.

"Take a good look. This is the face of fascism: three nice-looking, smiling, well-dressed young men, assured of their place in the world, neither landowners nor peasants, but men of the in-between state ready to grovel before their enemies to keep their spot in the hierarchy, smiling and shuffling. I want to remember! I want to remember that if good prevailed, these men still are always around; if dead, they simply rise up from the grave in some other man's or woman's form; they are always, always here."

Maria Teresa saw that her words had shattered Leah's face. The younger woman was staring at her as though mesmerized.

"And then draw to mind Angelica's face, and imagine her mother, who had the same face, and Angelica's dark eyes and hair, so much like her father. Imagine their patched, but always clean clothes; imagine their bravery. Those walks Angelica took at night carrying bundles of food and clothing to the Jewish children and their families. Jews crouching in a cave because there are people like this." She tapped the photo with her finger. "That too is what I remember, and that's what keeps me in balance while I feed the chickens and make bread, clean this house, and cook the meals. Remember that both are in the world: good and evil; don't ever try to make excuses for the evil.

Leah had been unable to take her eyes away from Maria Teresa to look at the photo. The older woman had spoken with the spirit of youth. She had opened her whole soul with these words; and Leah recognized the great wisdom she possessed always to remember, always to be on the lookout for evil, no matter how good the times seemed.

"Look, Signora! Look at the photo. See what is hidden behind those starched shirts, well-pressed pants, and wide smiles."

Averting her eyes from Maria Teresa's face, which was flushed and vibrant by her convictions and courage, Leah looked down at the photo she held in her hands.

"Oh, Dio!! Maria, may I take this photo with me? May I?" Her words came loud and jolting.

Maria gave her a strange look. "If it is so important, you may *borrow* it, but I'll need it back. It is my memory."

The Fiat bounced and rattled down the lane away from Maria Teresa and the farmhouse. The older woman watched the car pull away; Leah, driving much too fast. She could not understand what had happened to the young woman when she looked down at the photo, but she had seen that look on other faces. It was a look of sudden understanding, of determination. She had grabbed her coat and hurried way, asking if she could come back to hear more of her story.

Maria Teresa had called, "Of course, whenever you like."

It took all Leah's strength and concentration to maneuver the Fiat over the bumps and holes in the road that led to the state highway below Valentano. Once on the asphalt, she drove wildly, pressing the accelerator to the floor, passing on curves, flying northward on the longer but faster route past the grand and beautiful Lake Bolsena.

Chapter Thirty-One

Freya's head jerked up at the sound of the door banging against the wall.

"Leah! What's happened!"

"Is the Lieutenant here?"

"No, he isn't. He's out on a call. Good grief, come sit down and calm yourself. Has someone else died or been murdered?"

"I can't sit right now, and yes, three people have been murdered."

"Three?"

"I can't wait. Where is he?"

"He didn't say, only that he would be back, but maybe not until tomorrow."

"Damn it! Okay. I'll come back."

"But…?"

"Don't worry, Freya, I'll explain everything." She turned and left.

"A coffee; I need a coffee," Leah muttered to herself. Hurrying across the piazza toward the bar, she looked up and saw Arrammundu staring into the fountain in deep concentration.

"Arrammundu!" she called to him.

He groaned. He didn't want to see her or to talk to her, or to have anything to do with her, but for his mother's sake, he responded.

"Hello, Signora. It's good to see you. How are you?"

"Arrammundu…"

He interrupted her, hoping for a short chat. With nothing else to say, he mentioned the gifts again. "I hope you've opened my mother's gifts; she would be happy to know you had."

Leah waved her hand through the air. "I will soon; I do know what they are, and I just haven't had the emotional courage yet to do it. I promise I will soon, and I'll let you know. But I have something else to ask."

She reached for her purse and carefully extracted the crinkled photo of three men.

"Do you recognize these men?"

Arrammundu held the photo close, studying it carefully. I'd say these two," he pointed, "are Diego and Cecco as younger men. The third one," he hesitated, staring at it intently, "I don't recognize. Sorry." He cleared his throat with a jagged cough. "Why do you ask? They're dead, right? Diego and Cecco, I mean."

"All three are dead."

Arrammundu shrugged his shoulders. "Is the photo important? It looks old."

"It doesn't matter, Arrammundu." Leah looked past the fountain toward the other side of the valley, then turned back to him. "How are you getting along?"

"Fine. You know I cooked for us almost all the time while Mamma was ill, and I clean as well, so things go along."

"Well, please call if you need anything. It's good to see you." She nodded and turned toward home.

Leah made tea and sat at the table with the photo propped in front of her. The three men stared out from the photo, self-assured, cocky, certain of themselves and their futures. Now, all of them were dead, murdered before their natural time.

The photo was tantamount to proof. It would be impossible for the Lieutenant to refute her theory.

Chapter Thirty-Two

"I didn't bully my way past Freya. She trusts what I have to say is important, and she said you were here."

"Well, I'll have to speak to her then. It's early morning, I have several things to finish before my day even actually begins, and I don't have much time."

"I thought we were working together, and I've discovered something."

Leah withdrew the photo from the plastic bag with which she had covered it and laid it on the Lieutenant's desk in front of him.

He picked it up. A look of surprise crossed his face. "Diego, Cecco, and Giacomo. I saw a photo of the young Giacomo on Signora Martelli's mantel."

"Yes, and this photo was taken when he was about the same age. The fattore, his son, and the fattore's assistant. They knew each other; they worked together, and they all died at about the same time. It's not two murders and a simple heart attack, Lieutenant. It's three murders. It's got to be. And if we're looking for motive, it has something to do with these three men and their relationship."

The Lieutenant regarded her, his head cocked to the side. "How did you come by this photo?"

"I went back to the farm. I think I told you I was writing about merletti and the women in this area, who, by the way, are the real masters. Angelica was one of them, and Arrammundu had told me about the farm where she was raised, so I went back to see if there was anyone still living who remembered her and her family. Angelica had told me many times about the romance between her mother and her father and something about Jews hiding on their land during the German occupation, so I saw a possibility for another article. I drove down there yesterday and talked to Maria Teresa, a wizened little woman who did know the family. We got sidetracked talking about the German occupation and the fascists, and she pulled this photo out of a drawer. They all worked together, Lieutenant. It's impossible to imagine that their deaths are not all connected. Don't you see?"

"Because they were fascists and informed on the family?"

"I don't know. I just don't know. I felt from the beginning, I mean from the time the Signora told me Signora Martelli's misgivings about her husband's death being a simple heart attack, that it must have been murder, in one way or another. I felt the woman knew her husband better than any of us and so, it couldn't have been so innocent."

The Lieutenant sat quietly, looking at her.

"What?" Leah turned her palms upward. "Can't you see what I'm saying?" She made a face and, with the palms of her hands together, bounced her hands up and down in a gesture of frustration.

"Of course, I can see what you're saying," he responded, but he had actually been thinking of how beautiful she looked when she was excited. "It's wonderful work, Leah. And it indicates a motive, but what *is* the motive? Even if they knew each other then, not long after those pictures were taken, from what I understand, Giacomo went his separate way, Diego and Cecco ended up here, and they haven't been in touch. Anyway, Signora Martelli seemed to know nothing about them except a brief mention."

"Maybe it was something that happened long ago. Maybe something to do with them being fascists. You should have seen Maria Teresa's face when she spoke about them. If I didn't know better, I could believe she could have killed them. She was incensed, as if they were still the farm managers and still had influence in her life."

"The angers and injustices of the war days are long-lived, Leah. War wounds endure. Not just the physical ones, but the loss of children, spouses, parents, and friends; homes left in ruins; sexual attacks; living in terror for months on end. People don't forget. But you're right; I doubt it could have been the Signora at the farm who had the wherewithal to kill the three men."

"So where do we go from here?"

"I'm not sure. And I always go by the old saying, 'If you don't know what to do, stand still.' We probably need to think about it for a while. Let it roil around in our minds." He paused, "I'm glad you came to talk to me without going off on your own. Maybe we will be some sort of odd partners yet."

"That would be a great pleasure, Lieutenant; I like the idea of being an unofficial cop. It would give my reputation a certain flair, don't you think?"

"Your reputation has plenty of flair as it is. But it might help people understand that rather than being overly curious and nosy, you're working on a case."

Leah slapped his desk with the flat of both hands. "Do I have the reputation of being overly curious and nosy?"

The Lieutenant laughed aloud. "Go home, Leah, and work on your article. I've got work to do, but let's talk about this at more length. We've got to come up with some ideas about motive and more on how the killer could have gotten into Martelli's apartment. I'll ask Montaro to come too, and Freya; she's been coming up with good ideas lately."

"What a motley crew."

"I wouldn't care if we were a crew of monkeys and wild boars, if it would help us solve the case."

Leah laughed. The Lieutenant saw how beautiful her throat was when she tilted her head back.

Leah didn't notice his look. "By the way, where's Montaro been? I haven't seen him around lately."

"I had to loan him out. He's been in Sansepolcro. One of their officers has cancer and is out, so all the stations in surrounding areas have made a rotation to help out."

"Will he make it, that officer with cancer?"

"No, it's terminal, and he doesn't have much longer. They've hired a new man, and Montaro is back."

The Lieutenant noted a flash of sadness cross Leah's face. "I'm sorry, Leah. It must remind you of Nick every time you hear about a loss to cancer."

Leah nodded. "You're right. It does. Hearing about someone else's loss and knowing what they suffered even before the loss does bring back memories, but after that first sharp jab, the really good memories come back to me: laughter, riding horseback together during the fall round-up in the mountains, skiing, long talks about Nick's books and my articles, things we did together with Sara…" Her eyes teared. "I'm sorry, Lieutenant. I shouldn't in front of you."

He came around the desk and took her in a gentle embrace. "There's nothing to be sorry for. You'll never "get over" losing Nick, and you should never be sorry for not getting over it. You'll love him forever; that's as it should be. He was your husband and the father of Sara. But Leah, you're the kind of woman who can cultivate grief and make it grow into something good, something compassionate. I think you can even turn it into new love, if you let yourself. I know that about you. We all know that about you."

He tilted her head upward, "Now, we've got work to do. We'll be at your place at 7, and see if four heads are better than one."

Chapter Thirty-Three

Home, Leah set out wine and snacks for the others, then sat down to rest, took up a book, put it down again, and went to the little cupboard where she kept chocolate. She started to unwrap a piece of dark chocolate truffle, but quickly rewrapped it and put it back.

Arrammundu's reminder to open Angelica's gift popped into her head, and Leah decided now was the time. She opened the wide, tall doors of the armoire, reached to the top shelf, pulled down the largest of the boxes, and sat down in her cushioned chair next to the pellet stove. The wrapping was simple and slipped off easily. Carefully taking the lid from the box, she looked in to see, just as she had guessed, the curtains with edgings of beautiful lacework equal to the best of any she had seen in all the research she had done. The gift of Angelica's hands.

Leah stood, set the box on the table and picked up the top curtain, shaking it gently to fall full length. She laid it across the sofa, lengthwise to admire its delicacy and intricate work. Looking at it, she remembered a quote by the writer Iris Anthony:

"...lace is formed from the absence of substance; it is imagined in the spaces between the threads. Lace is a thing like hope... If faith...was the substance of things hoped for, then lace was the outline—the suggestion—of things not seen."

"The outline...of things not seen": this was Angelica's work. A thing like hope, the outline of things not seen. A mystery.

Leah drew the other curtain from the box, shook it out and laid it on top of the first, smoothing them both with her hand. She would show the Lieutenant, Freya, and Montaro when they came. Holding the delicate edging in her hand for one last look, she laid it back down and went to close the box and put it away.

There was an envelope with her name on it in the bottom of the box. A message from Angelica.

Dear Leah,

If you are reading this, I am gone, and you are, perhaps, holding in your hands the curtains you've so admired. I planned from the first to give them to you because I knew how you would appreciate and care for them; and I know that after reading this letter you will care even more and understand with even more depth, the spaces between the threads, the life I refused in life to tell you.

Thank you for being a friend, for loving the details of my work (most people take scant notice of the simpler arts), for allowing me the pleasure of telling you my parents' story again and again, and for the help and solace you gave me and Arrammundu in the last months of my life. If I do indeed walk from this world into the arms of the angels, I will tell them to reach down and guard you from harm. If I go the other direction, my dear friend, I promise not to utter your name or arouse any curiosity about your impetuous, stubborn character!!

We've laughed and cried together, and I'm afraid now it must be more of the same mix of joy and tears, at least on your part. I am beyond it all.

So, the spaces between the threads: the story of my all too short, but very happy marriage and the loss that came after. I'm telling this story to you, Leah, on the condition that you never tell it to Arrammundu. It would break him. I have hopes that in innocence of my history, he will find a girl, love her, and have children of his own to cherish as I have cherished him.

That girl may be Lodoletta. I know at first she seems harsh, even bitter perhaps, and rough. Hardly fitting for Arrammundu. Her life has not been easy, but she is a young woman with unmined depth. I believe she is slowly learning to know herself and her possibilities, and I think she truly cares about Arrammundu, although she's had setbacks. Help her when you can. And please help Arrammundu too. He has suffered profound wounds, more than either you or I can understand, I think. An actual war leaves in its wake an inner war in every man or woman that took part. You understand this, I know, because of your experience of the friend in Montana you once told me about, the ex-soldier man who shot up a bar. And, since you know about Lodoletta's "war" with her father and grandfather, you can see that she and Arrammundu might make a good match. Both of them understand in some essence what the other has gone through, both are striving toward their true natures of goodness. They will both hide behind their protective bravado, but persist, Leah, they are worth it and will come through in the end.

I can't put this off any longer. Here is my story.

From the time I was a child until I was a teenager, I lived an idyllic life. You may think it odd I can say that because we were so poor, but I did not know we were poor. My parents were loving; they taught me to work hard and take pride in my chores; our Jewish friend from Scansansiano came to teach me reading and writing and brought me books. I was perfectly free in free time to run about the countryside, explore the forest and roam on the hillsides. I played by myself much of the time and with the neighbor children on the far side of the hill sometimes. We built dams in the creek, climbed trees, picked berries, chased and petted the lambs in the early spring. Do you see what I mean by idyllic?

Mattia was one of the neighbor children. By the time we were eight or nine, we were fast friends, and we played together as much as we could, but we were old enough by that age to be doing real work on the farm. One of my happiest moments was when Mamma and Babbo asked if Mattia could study with me, and our friend agreed. I was a little ahead in studying, but Mattia learned quickly, and soon we were reading books together. Our parents were proud of us because none of them knew how to read.

By the time we were in our early teens, we were working as adults.

Besides doing her regular work in the house and the weaving and lacework, my mother had been "assigned" to the big house, cleaning and cooking for the fattore, his son, and his assistant. The fattore's first wife, a spindly woman, had died young, but it would have been the duty of one of the peasants to do the housework there at any rate.

My mother worked doubly hard caring for not only our house but for theirs as well, and when I became a teenager, I began helping her in the main house to lighten her load.

The men at the main house, Diego, Cecco, and Giacomo were abrupt and rude, but except for crass remarks about me or about my mother's limp, they left us to our work. We ignored their comments, washed and ironed, cooked and cleaned with the efficiency of four hands rather than just two, and then went home to our good life with my father.

When I had just turned fifteen, my mother got sick. It was a problem with her lungs, and it took a long time for her to heal, so it was necessary for me to work at the fattore's house by myself. My father and I asked him to bring in another girl to help me, but he said that I could do it by myself. And so I did.

Initially it wasn't too bad. There were still coarse remarks, but I ignored them and when I couldn't, I quickly learned a certain sassy way to deflect them—it went against my grain to speak like that, but it was necessary.

Those boorish remarks soon came to seem only a nuisance. The Germans were coming, our little community was being split between the Italian partisans and the fascists, Italian and German. Italians who sided with the fascists were strutting around making noise, hunting down partisans. These men, some who had even been neighbors, grasped at power in stupid and demeaning displays. They forced "suspect" non-fascists to drink laxatives and soil themselves. They sneaked around the town and countryside trying to find community members "guilty" of anti-German behavior. Things were falling apart and grew worse day by day. Our Jewish friends were hunted like animals.

In the midst of all of it Mattia and I were becoming closer and more and more in love. My parents could see it; our friends could see it. We wanted to marry. We knew we were too young to be married, but the war and the occupation had turned life upside down and created in all of us a sense of urgency. The war forced us to mature quickly; Mattia and I wanted at least some life together. We never knew if we would live long.

The Germans were everywhere, sauntering through town, watching everyone; searching through the forests, making surprise visits to farms. Many of our Jews had left to find safer places, or were coming to the mezzadri in the countryside. There were too many fascists and Germans in town for Jews to stay there. Some people in town helped, but in the confining space of the town, it was difficult to hide people or to buy extra food at the market without someone noticing. Those of us peasants who did help at least had land, some wild land, around us. Some Jews who had nowhere else to go were roaming the countryside with nothing but summer clothing on their back. They slept rough, begged food, and moved from one hideout to another in order to escape the notice of the fascists, who would turn them in to the Germans. Children, Leah! Children whose parents had been taken were hiding in the winter forests with nothing but cotton dresses or a pair of shorts, and flimsy shoes. Eight years old, six years old, twelve years old—little ones whose parents hoped to save them by sending them into the forests. They wandered, sometimes alone, sometimes with a brother or sister, never knowing if, when they stopped at a farmhouse, they would be given something to eat, allowed to sleep for a night in the barn, or be turned over to the Germans.

We helped them. Many of the mezzadri helped, others didn't, and some, like us, helped while we tried at the same time to escape the eyes of the fascist fattores, like Diego, Cecco, and their assistant, Giacomo.

We knew that by helping we could lose our lives. The shattering news of the German massacre of the women and children and old people at Marzabotto was still to come, but in smaller numbers we lived a foretaste of that reality. Men and boys on farms that were found to have helped

Jews were shot straightaway, their women and daughters raped, and their houses and buildings burnt to the ground.

Mattia and I, my parents and Mattia's, and an understanding priest, allowed Mattia and I to marry. We all knew how tenuous life was for us and our friends; and our parents understood that we wanted at least a taste of what a life together could be. That one happy event and the short time of the love we had for each other gave us hope. We threw ourselves into helping our Jewish friends, and in moments we truly believed the war would end and we could live a decent, safe life again.

I've told you how, in a cave of the Dry Forest, we hid the family of the Jewish man who gave us lessons. But I don't think I told you that Mattia and I were already married then. Sixteen and married! Secretly. Only our parents and two or three of the other mezzadri knew. Both Mattia and I were going out at night to help the Jews, he on a neighboring farm and I up to the Dry Forest cave. We were both exhausted, but we were also very much in love, and Mattia and I and both our families found a certain peace in the midst of that horror.

I continued working at the main house for the fattore. Things were worse there than they had been because Cecco had started bothering me, making suggestions. As fascists, he and his father, like other fascists, were able to get things we couldn't. Sugar, warm clothing we couldn't afford, fresh fruits. He offered these things to me if I would be "nice" to him. He said he wanted to marry me. He said we could go away to somewhere safe.

Why did I keep my marriage a secret? Generally, the mezzadri went to the fattore to say they wanted to have permission to marry, and of course Mattia and I and our parents had not asked.

I told Cecco I already had a beau, that I was in love with him, and I didn't need chocolates and silk stockings. It made him angry; he turned livid and swore. He tried to grab me, but I broke away and ran from the house, and I never went back. When Diego came to reprimand me and tried to force me and to force my parents to make me go back, we refused, and he was furious.

I think it was Socrates that said no evil can happen to a good man either in life or after death. Don't believe this, Leah. All people carry good and evil inside them; a person chooses one or the other.

I discovered much later how Mattia had actually died.

The two of them, Diego and Cecco, devised a plan to kill Mattia in such a way to make themselves seem innocent. At the orders of Diego, Giacomo was sent off with Mattia one day, to help at a neighboring farm. As they approached the farm, German soldiers came from the trees. Giacomo ran away. The soldiers let him go, but they accused Mattia of being a partisan. Mattia broke free and ran toward the forest, but the Germans shot him in the back, dragged his body into the trees and left him.

We expected Mattia to be gone for a few days, so we didn't worry. When Giacomo came without him, he told us Mattia was just finishing up and would come soon.

The next day, a little boy came to tell us he had been climbing in one of the trees by the roadside and saw the whole thing. He told us how Giacomo ran away and how the Germans had shot Mattia. The boy and his father had brought Mattia's body to us in a wheelbarrow.

Grief. How we survived I don't know. It was the first part of my personal war, but I had to hold it in. There was no choice, and no time to indulge our personal suffering. The Jews were in the cave still and needed help. We had to be alert and conscious every moment for the sake of the living. And the Germans, aware of the American front moving north toward us, were more brutal every day.

I lived in a haze. Nights I went out to the cave, when I needed, but often I went simply just to wander. Nighttime was anguish; I couldn't sleep; I was filled with such hatred and despair that if it hadn't been for my mother and father and our friends in the cave, I would have run off to the partisans, happy at the thought of killing Germans.

One night I was coming back from the cave and was about a kilometer from our house when Cecco stepped out from behind a large oak.

"You're wandering around late at night, Signorina. Were you looking

for me?" He had a sickening salacious grin on his face.

Fear overwhelmed me; I was exhausted from grief and no sleep. I yelled at him "No! Leave me alone!"

But he didn't.

So much stronger, so much more well-fed, he dragged me to a grassy area in the trees.

When he was finished, he stood above me, fastening his belt buckle. "So, you're not a virgin. I don't care. My father told me this was the only way I would get you." He laughed, "Giacomo has seen you wandering at night, looking at the stars. All I had to do was wait. It was a good plan, no? All of it. And don't pretend you didn't like it. And don't worry. My father has given us permission. We'll set the banns this week.

He had been brutal. I was badly hurt, but I didn't cry out and I didn't answer him. I went home, told my mother and father what had happened, and we went on with life as it had been. When Cecco came to take me, I refused him. He could not force me; no priest could marry me without my agreement. I was a widow, and I knew before Cecco attacked me that I was pregnant with Mattia's child. When my pregnancy became visible, Diego and Cecco came again and again to try to force me, but I refused each time, and my parents, bless their memory, supported me, even though Diego had made our lives miserable. After the Americans came through and drove the Germans north, I moved to Scansansiano. Arrammundu was born here.

I'm tired, Leah. Worn out. Now you have the story. I'm sorry it's such a sad one. Just promise me you'll never tell Arrammundu. He is Mattia's son, as he's always thought. Not Cecco's!! and I don't want him to ever know how I was brutalized by Cecco. Keep Arrammundu safe from at least this grief. Arrammundu has enough grief of his own and, God willing, in his life he will find the solace and joy with a spouse that I had no chance to find with my husband in my life. Help him as much as you can.

With gratitude for your friendship and interest, and with love. I'm so very fortunate to have known you, and I am now beyond all suffering.

Angelica

Chapter Thirty-Four

eah let Angelica's letter flutter to her lap and leaned her head back against the chair. The letter had elicited a memory. A year or so previously, she and Angelica had been sitting by the fountain in the piazza. Diego and Cecco had come walking through the piazza, had seen them, and had come to greet them. At the time, Leah did not know them. Without introducing themselves, they spoke to Angelica.

"Signorina Sanna, how are you?" Cecco leered at her.

Angelica stood, squared her shoulders, and motioned to Leah to join her. "You are mistaken and seem incapable of remembering. It's 'Signora.' I'm afraid you've never gotten it quite right. But then there are many things you've never gotten right, no? Among other things, you have never understood that the Germans are no longer here."

She took Leah's arm and, with her head held high, walked slowly off through the piazza, chatting to Leah as if the encounter had not happened.

"What was that all about?" Leah had asked.

"It's nothing. Those two just like to make trouble and insult as many people as they can, that's all."

Leah had remembered the incident when she had seen Diego and Cecco talking to Joel and Secondo, and now she remembered it again, reading the letter.

This story Angelica had written in this letter, plus the photo from Maria Teresa, proved Diego, Cecco, and Giacomo all knew each other—except Giacomo's roll was unclear. The story also indicated, Leah admitted to herself with a stab of sadness, that Arrammundu had motive to murder

Diego and Cecco, at least. And perhaps, Giacomo, but Giacomo's place in Mattia's death was unclear. The Germans killed with impunity. Mattia's death on the road could have been a convergence of circumstances.

Still, the story would give Arrammundu motive only if he knew what was in the letter. Part of the story was still unclear. Had Diego and Cecco conspired to have Mattia killed, or had they conspired only on the plan of the rape?

If Arrammundu thought the men had conspired to kill his father, rape his mother, and force her into a marriage, he could have reason to believe he was Cecco's son by rape. These things would give him reason to kill, except, Leah thought with relief, he didn't know these things.

There was a knock at the door. Leah hesitated. Could she simply not answer the door and make an excuse later? She wanted to reread the letter, to think this through. There were too many questions.

Another knock, and the Lieutenant called, "Leah, we're here. Are you?"

Freya and Montaro laughed.

Leah rose and walked to the door.

The Lieutenant looked at her, "What's wrong, Leah?"

"There's new information."

The others stopped laughing and crowded into the apartment.

Chapter Thirty-Five

After Leah read the letter, they sat silent for a few moments. The Lieutenant was the first to speak.

"This gives Arrammundu the strongest motive of all. I don't see any way around it."

"But you heard: Angelica pleaded with me not tell him. Why do that if he already knew? And wouldn't she have known if he knew? Wouldn't she have seen a change in him, a hint at least that he knew, and after, wouldn't she have sensed that he had done something? He lived with her, ate with her, took care of her. It seems something would have showed."

Freya asked, "Think of how many times Sara was upset about breaking up with a boyfriend or getting involved with someone you didn't approve of, and you had no idea. Parents can be totally oblivious when the most serious things are going on. I know mine were."

Leah made a mental note to ask Freya about whatever it was she had done that her parents didn't know.

"What do you think, Montaro?" the Lieutenant asked.

"I think we'd better look for a connection between Baccia, Lodoletta, Pagolo, and Martelli. It's obvious that Diego, Cecco, and Martelli are connected in Angelica's case, and it makes sense that Baccia or one of the kids, or all three of them, would want to kill Diego and Cecco, but why Martelli? He dropped out of the threesome years ago, according to everything we know now. Baccia and the kids hadn't even heard of him. And Pagolo appears to be out of the picture, because he's got a tight alibi from the neighbor and maybe from Arrammundu too; and of course now, with this new information,

Pagolo can maybe be Arrammundu's alibi.

"So, what now?" Freya asked.

"I'm going to figure out where that neighbor is so I can double check Pagolo's alibi, and I'll get in touch with Arrammundu to go over that day with him again." The Lieutenant looked at each of them. "You'll be with me, Montaro."

"And I'm going back to the office to be the administrative assistant I'm supposed to be," Freya quipped.

"Leah?" The Lieutenant opened his palms.

"I'm going to think for a while," she pursed her lips. "I'll let you know."

The Lieutenant nodded his head.

Chapter Thirty-Six

Leah was going to think about what to do, but she intended to think about it on her way back to the farm near Valentano to see Maria Teresa. And she didn't intend to tell the Lieutenant what she was doing until she returned, and then only if she had any information.

She took the state road rather than following the slower way through the forest and along the Brigand's Trail. During the night, it had begun to rain. As she drove through the strings of the rain, which first fell gently, then harder, finally pounding with the force of a hammer against the windows, Leah slowed to a near standstill.

Turning into the long lane, Leah spotted Maria Teresa standing in the opened doorway with an umbrella. There was sure to be wine, two glasses, and a plate of freshly baked biscotti already on the table.

Maria Teresa came to the car as Leah opened the door to get out. "Come under the umbrella; you don't want to catch cold."

"But it's only a few meters, Signora!" Leah laughed.

"And the best thing one can do when it's raining is to let it rain. But we needn't get wet because of it. Come."

Leah grunted. The old woman's words rang true, but what was she to understand?

Maria Teresa led the way into the house, and, as Leah had anticipated, there were two glasses and a plate of biscotti on the table.

"Do you keep the table prepared at every moment?"

The older woman laughed and patted Leah on the arm. "Remember, I told you, I can see down the road, and I know when someone is coming. Being alert is a habit from the war. There were many people dependent on us, and we needed to be awake even when we were asleep. I've never lost the habit, only now, thank God, it is friends who come, not the Germans or the fascists. Thank God. I have the joy of seeing friends, hearing their voices, and feeding them biscotti with a glass of wine."

"I'll drink to that!"

Maria Teresa smiled at Leah and poured two glasses of the wine, which had come from Maria Teresa's and her husband's vines. The wine was gentle and smooth.

Leah wished she had come on a purely friendly visit.

"Your face is sad today, Signora Leah. Has something happened?"

"I've had a letter from Angelica."

Maria Teresa's mouth dropped open, but..."

"She left a gift for me before she died. Arrammundu gave it to me after she was gone. I knew what the gift was, but I didn't have the heart to open it until just last evening. The gift was curtains edged in her beautiful lacework. I had admired them from the first time I saw them. Anyway, when I opened the box last night and took out the curtains, I found a letter under them..."

"A letter that explained the death of Mattia and the rest of her story, yes?"

"Yes, most of it, anyway."

Maria Teresa turned her face to stare out the window at the rain. She spoke as if she were back in the days of the war and the German occupation.

"If you know the story, you know about Diego, his son Cecco, and their right-hand man, Giacomo. Fascists that they were. The photo I gave you."

Leah reached into her bag, took the photo, and laid it on the table.

Maria Teresa nodded her head in acknowledgment and continued. "I wasn't living here then. Antonio and I were just over the hill in our own little hut to be near the sheep and the large pen we had there. But we knew about those three brutal, vicious traitors that they were!" She shook her head, and Leah saw the fury in her eyes. "It was all for money, personal gain. We knew about the way Cecco bothered Angelica; if only we'd known how persistent it was! Hindsight is a torment, Leah. We even knew about the marriage of Angelica and Mattia, although we weren't supposed to know. None of us ever mentioned it aloud because we understood what it would mean for the family if Diego found out."

She turned back to Leah and bent close, staring into Leah's eyes. "Did Angelica write everything in that letter?"

Leah pursed her lips. "Yes."

"Well, we knew about that too, and because, you know, I can talk about it. Those three planned it together, I'm sure. They paved the way for that viper of a boy to brutalize her."

Tears came to Maria Teresa's eyes.

"But Cecco didn't get his way. Cecco didn't know Angelica was already married; he wouldn't have believed it, the scum. But we made sure the priests all around knew she was already married, although Angelica's mother and father never did figure out we had helped. Cecco persisted in threatening her, and he got meaner and meaner, but he didn't get his way. I hope it goaded him to the end."

"And Arrammundu?"

"Arrammundu never knew, thank God. We may have known amongst ourselves, but no one else, not on the other farms and not in town, knew anything."

"What about Mattia's death? Was Giacomo in on that?"

"I can't say for sure. I think he was a coward in it, perhaps, but I don't know if he helped plan it. I'm sure Diego and Cecco set it up, but Giacomo, I don't know; I know only he was a filthy fascist.

Her face brightened. "When Arrammundu came to see me…"

"When was that?"

"Not long ago. He said Angelica had hoped to come see Antonio and I, but she was much too weak, and then she was gone. He came in her stead. What a handsome young man he's become; he looks just like his father."

"How did he seem, Signora?"

"Well, at first, it was a pleasant visit. He had called, so I knew he was coming. I made a big meal, and I'm glad I did; he looked like he hadn't eaten in days. He couldn't eat enough, second and third helpings on everything.

We chatted for a while; then I asked if he could help move some boards. Antonio tried to stop me from asking, but I thought it would be good for Arrammundu to help, to feel useful.

And he was glad to help. We'd already asked another young man to help: Gerardo, from nearby. He came along just after we'd finished dinner. I thought it had worked out perfectly having the young men there. Antonio won't admit it, but he is too old to be lifting those boards down from the loft. He went with the boys to the barn to show them where the boards were and where they could stack them; then he came back to help me while they worked.

We finished the dishes and had just sat down for a coffee when we heard angry shouting. We ran out. Many of the boards were stacked, but the two of them were rolling in the dirt, punching each other and cursing. I didn't think they even knew each other, but either they did, or something happened between them pretty fast.

Antonio said it had to be about a woman, because it always is, and sometime later, Gerardo told us he had been dating a woman from Scansansiano, so they must have been dating the same woman. I know a woman can cause trouble, but you know what I think? I think maybe both of them wanted the fight more than the woman."

Leah nodded, a sad look on her face. "Now I understand why he was bruised and scratched when I saw him; it must have been right after that trip to see you. And I think with Arrammundu you may be right. He's been in a terrible state lately; maybe he was looking for a fight. Do you know the young woman's name?"

"It was Lodoletta. They were shouting it among all the curse words, all the blasphemy!"

Leah suppressed a smile. She had not heard that word in a long time and wondered if most people still knew what it meant.

Chapter Thirty-Seven

"I thought we were working together, Leah."

"We are, Lieutenant, and I know I should have told you, but I knew you would want to come along, and Maria Teresa wouldn't have talked freely with you there. She lives with the values and loyalties of her time. I don't believe she would have mentioned about the rape in front of you. You would have wanted to come along, yes?"

He covered his mouth with his hand to hide his smile. "I would have insisted."

Leah grinned.

"And yourself? You've talked with her about what? Twice?"

"She trusts me because she knows of my friendship with Angelica."

"Okay, a point for you. It kills me to say it, but you made the right choice. Where does this leave us? We've got Arrammundu's troubled love story, but his ignorance of what happened to his mother; we've got the tale of Cecco's twisted family: despicable collusion in the plan to rape Angelica; Cecco's and Diego's brutal abuse against their own family members; Baccia's confession to the murders, which we're certain she didn't commit; Pagolo's alibi, which seemed at first to be airtight, but is uncertain until we speak to the neighbor.

We've got the triangle of Lodoletta, Gerardo, and Arrammundu, although that has nothing to do with the murders, and Lodoletta is not strong enough to have overtaken Cecco and Diego. And we've got indications that Giacomo was in on all of it, but there's no proof of that and no certain proof he was murdered.

Freya knocked on the door of the Lieutenant's office and stepped in. The

Lieutenant and Leah turned to her.

"I just had a call from the neighbor Pagolo worked with. He got your note and said you could come anytime."

The Lieutenant jumped to his feet. "Thanks, Freya. We'll go now. Will you call him back and tell him we're on our way?" He looked at Leah, and she nodded.

Pagolo's neighbor, Signor Landi, was waiting for them. The door opened before they had reached the top step.

"Come in, Lieutenant—and Signora Contarini. Please." He gestured toward two worn but comfortable chairs in a small living room just to the left of the doorway. "May I offer you a glass of wine? It's from my own grapes, very delicate."

The Lieutenant looked at Leah, who shook her head.

"Thank you, Signor Landi, but we're in something of a hurry, so if you'll excuse us we'll get right to business."

"Of course, please…"

"I'm sure you've heard about the murders. We're trying to ascertain alibis by anyone who might be remotely connected to the murdered men. Unfortunately, this means Pagolo, among others. From what you said, Pagolo was working with you all day when Cecco—and maybe Diego—were killed. Is that right?"

"Yes. But I've told you this before. You and Montaro," Landi said, irritated. "We were clearing out my cantina. I'd been using it for storage of some old furniture and boards, and it had become unmanageable. My own fault, of course, but Pagolo said he could use the money. I knew it would take me several days, so I was happy to hire him. We worked all day; with his help I got done. He even swept and came back the next day to rearrange the wine vats."

Leah turned to the Lieutenant and opened her palms.

"Thank you, Signor. We appreciate you going over it again with us, and I hope you understand we have to ask these questions."

"Repeatedly," Signor Landi muttered.

They walked silently for one hundred meters when the Lieutenant spoke. "That takes Pagolo off the list."

"It seems so." Leah stopped and looked up at the Lieutenant. "I don't know why, but I still feel something is wrong, even with Signor Landi's certainty. The forensic pathologist's and the coroner's assessment of time of deaths are still questionable. They said so."

"Your instinct is acting up again, Leah. No one can be in two places at once. We have to pull Pagolo out of the mix and rethink things."

Leah walked along without speaking for a few minutes. In the middle of the piazza, she motioned toward the bench around the fountain. The Lieutenant nodded.

When they were seated, Leah suggested, "Maybe we should rethink Baccia."

"The broken arm?"

"One blow to stun him, and once he's stunned, repeated beating? It could be done."

"Only very awkwardly and nearly unbelievable. Even at his age, Cecco is too strong and too agile still for that to happen. It would have taken incredible luck and force on Baccia's part to land the exact strike that would stun him enough to then continue beating him. And there's no way she could have driven that knife into Diego."

"Well, if Pagolo and Baccia are both out of the picture, then Lodoletta moves to first place, and we'll need to bring her back in."

"All one hundred pounds of her! I can't believe it. She's a prickly pear; she curses and acts tough, but she's soft on the inside. I can't imagine her killing someone."

"How do you know, Leah?"

"Because she came to apologize to me. And because she not only really loves her mother, but because she loved and was loved by Angelica. Angelica even thought she would be a good match for Arrammundu."

The Lieutenant's eyes widened in surprise, and then, as if a thought had clicked into place, he stared off over the valley to the forests beyond before turning back to her.

"I see why Angelica thought they could be good for each other. Both have had a rough go of it and maybe they understand each other in a way none of us had considered."

"Arrammundu as the killer makes the most sense, but he doesn't have a motive."

"To protect Lodoletta?" The Lieutenant made a face.

"Too thin; I don't think she seems in that much danger of being charged."

"A PTSD event that threw him out of control?"

It was Leah's turn to make a face. "And he and Cecco just happened to meet up at the cave on the trail at the exact same moment? It's not likely. And why would Cecco be there in the first place?"

"We're grasping at straws. Arrammundu has problems of the heart, but no motive for murder, and I hope to God he never finds out that he does have motive for murder, even now that someone else has taken care of any possible revenge. Arrammundu can do without that story to add to his troubles."

"What story?"

The Lieutenant and Leah twisted to see who had spoken.

Chapter Thirty-Eight

"Idrissa! You're back!" Leah jumped to her feet and ran to hug him. The young Senegalese woman beside him stepped back, her eyes wide in shock at Leah's enthusiasm.

Laughing at Leah's delight, Idrissa hugged her back, flashed a wide smile, and gestured toward the young woman beside him.

"Leah, Lieutenant, this is my wife, Morido. We have been married just two weeks, and now we are back."

Morido blushed and bowed her head. She was a lithe, beautiful woman, almost as tall as Idrissa himself. Her dark-blue tribal scars angled along the tops of both cheeks, accentuating her high cheekbones. Smaller, delicate blue lines of scar emanated from the corners of her mouth. Her eyes, when she raised them to Leah, glistened with what seemed to be longing, perhaps longing mixed with a tinge of fear and anxiety her natural grace would not allow her to voice.

Leah saw that she was ill-prepared for much cooler weather. She wore traditional clothing: a pagne, and matching blouse of brightly decorated lime green and purple design, and socks that made her sandals bulge at the sides. Her black sweater and long brown coat were ill-fitting; perhaps they were something Idrissa had given her of his own, not heavy enough to warm a body so accustomed to the warm temperatures of the Senegal lowlands. Leah could clearly see she trembled, shivering in the late fall weather that seemed mild to the others, but freezing to her.

Leah took her hand and spoke to her in poor French, knowing that Morido was almost certainly, like many Africans, multilingual.

"It is very cold here for you, I think. Will you come to the next market day with me? We will buy you warm women's clothes. Until then, I'll bring you some of my winter things."

Morido's look of surprise brightened her whole face, and she responded in a gentle, almost sing-song French. "You're so kind. Thank you. I would like to come with you. I cannot make my body warm here; it will take me until summer to adjust, I think, and many more months to learn Italian. I'm so happy you can speak to me in French. You are the first." She smiled, her teeth a beautiful white flash.

"We will speak together often. It is a big adjustment to come to a new country and new language. You must miss your family and friends, but you see how the Lieutenant and I are Idrissa's friends, and there are many others you will meet soon who are our friends and will be your friends, too."

Tears rose in Morido's eyes. "Thank you, Madame. I will write and tell my mother about you. It will make her worry less to know I have a new friend."

Idrissa spoke to Morido in Pulaar. "We must go now."

She nodded, took Leah's hand once more, and walked away with Idrissa, her head high.

"So, you speak French." The Lieutenant furrowed his brow.

"Why the face? Did you think I was keeping it a secret? It's a gift of language from long ago and far away. I'll tell you someday. For now, I can only say that it's going to be a challenge to dredge it up again, but at least Morido and I will be able to communicate at the basic level. I'll probably be throwing Italian into the mix and completely confuse her."

"You sounded proficient to me."

"Do you speak French, Lieutenant?"

"No."

Leah grasped his arm and gently shook it. "That's why I sound proficient!" She laughed aloud.

The Lieutenant watched her fine profile, white teeth, and shining eyes. "If we weren't in public..." he thought.

"What's that look on your face, Lieutenant?"

The Lieutenant flushed and cleared his throat. "It's the look that says we have to get back to work."

"You're right. Where were we?"

"We were at a dead-end street. Arrammundu has no motive, or anyway doesn't know he has one; both Baccia and Lodoletta seem incapable, for different reasons, of the physical prowess it would have taken to kill either one or both Cecco and Diego; Pagolo appears to have a watertight alibi, and none of the three: Baccia, Lodoletta, and Pagolo, had reason to murder Giacomo, who we don't even know for sure was murdered. That's where we are. I'm beginning to think we need to look more closely at the men's business practices. We've gone with who and what we think is obvious, but there's almost certainly someone out there that those two—or three?—have cheated, or ruined, or maybe just fired."

"Okay, so where do we begin to look for that someone?"

"I think we use our team!"

"Our team?"

"Me, you, Freya, Montaro. We each have different networks, and I think we should find out the scuttlebutt that our friends are passing around with the pasta at the dinner table."

"I have the best informant in town, if she'll cooperate."

"The Signora? Not likely. She plays her cards close to her chest, but you can tell her what we're doing and knowing that, she might help."

Leah winked. "I think I can convince her."

"Don't overestimate your powers, sweet one. Not everyone falls for them."

Startled by the strange endearment, it took Leah a moment to respond.

"They don't? Well, I'll have to work on my powers, then, won't I?"

The words had slipped from his mouth, and the Lieutenant flushed bright red. Before Leah was finished, he turned and walked away, calling back over his shoulder, "Go talk to the Signora, Leah. I'll tell the others."

Leah laughed and called back, "Yes, Sir."

Chapter Thirty-Nine

It was nearing lunch time. Leah had a hunch she would find the Signora at the bar, where, almost daily, she had a pre-lunch aperitivo, a spritzer of Alperol and prosecco, with a slice of orange, served with a little dish of chips, olives, and salami on the side.

The Signora was sitting at the table by the window, as Leah suspected. It was the table Leah and all her friends preferred, even on the cold, wet days of winter, when gusts of frigid wind blew in with each person who entered looking for a drink or a little pre-lunch sandwich of artichoke hearts or snacks.

"I've found you!"

"I didn't know I was lost, and you know I'm almost always here at this time. So why the excitement?" Eyebrows raised, the Signora held a potato chip in hand. She took a bite, wiped her mouth gently on the paper napkin that had been placed beside the snacks, and pointed at the chair across from her. "By your fidgety manner, I gather you were looking for me, not to chat, but for information or gossip. If I do have it, I'm not going to give it to you unless you have a very good reason for it."

"The murders?"

The Signora pursed her lips. "Well, of course, that. Don't be flippant. We both know I'd help with that, as long as I don't have to hurt someone innocent. But I thought the Lieutenant was convinced somehow it was Pagolo, for all the beatings, no? His alibi was absolutely firm, then? And Giacomo is just a coincidence? We know neither Baccia nor Lodoletta would commit murder. Has he let Baccia go? If not, he should; it's ridiculous to keep her!"

"So many questions! And Baccia: you know he can't let her go; she's confessed."

"Balderdash! I wish he would assert a little authority…"

"He has, Signora. He's made a special effort to keep her here so she can see the children. She won't budge on the confession."

"Why not? Pagolo has an alibi!"

"Yes, and her worry has switched to Lodoletta. She won't yield an inch until they're both completely cleared. Anyway, we have no new leads."

"We?" The Signora's eyebrows arched.

"I mean the Lieutenant and I. He's asked me to help out a little." Leah blushed.

The Signora scrutinized Leah's face. "Oh, he has, has he? Interesting…" Her smile was one of victory. "Go on, my dear."

"Well, ah…We're turning our attention to business associates. Someone who may have gotten angry over losing money, someone who felt backed into a corner and forced to sell their business, someone hard-up over a few years of failed crops, and Cecco and Diego took advantage of their bad fortune. Those two had their fingers in so many pies it's hard to keep track. I thought you might know of something."

"Possibly; if the Lieutenant is hard up for leads, he might want to consider talking to a few of the young women in town. You've met Diego and Cecco, no?"

"Yes…"

"How did they look at you, my dear?"

"They looked creepy?"

"I asked, 'How did they look *at* you, not *to* you!"

"Oh… I know about the rumors of them and a few of the young women." Leah remembered meeting them the last time when she had run into Joel and Secondo on her way to Angelica's. "I know what you mean."

"Yes, 'oh!' And if you know about them, you know young women don't always have the same discernment as more mature women. The young act impetuously, and young women who do so often pay for it the rest of their lives. One or two of them could be very upset and might talk, particularly if they believed they would get support or if they gave the child away and have come to regret it. I think you should explore that path more thoroughly."

"Any names?"

The Signora took the last bite of her sandwich and drank the last of her spritzer. "I think that's your job, yours and the Lieutenant's." She reached across the table and caressed Leah's cheek. "I so enjoy seeing people in love. The way your eyes light up when I say the word 'Lieutenant.'" She laughed.

"But I'm not…"

"Oh, yes, you are. And we're all waiting to see what will happen with the two of you." She knitted her eyebrows. "I'm just sorry for Joel and Secondo."

"Signora, really, I'm not…"

"Don't contradict me, Leah. You are; you're just having trouble admitting it to yourself, and the Lieutenant is hamstrung so badly by love that he can barely speak."

She rose, slipped into her coat, bent to give Leah a quick kiss on both cheeks and disappeared out the door.

Leah signaled to Cinzia. A moment later there was a spritzer and a small tray of olives in front of her. What the Signora had told her should have been obvious, and she wondered if one or two of the sad and isolated single women she had run into around town had been duped by Diego or Cecco when they were still young, still capable of falling helplessly and carelessly in love with an older man who flattered them and made promises he had no intention of keeping.

Leah thought over her life. Had there ever been a situation in which she had made herself, unthinkingly, so vulnerable that in the aftermath, she would be angry and feel betrayed enough to kill someone.

There had been such a situation, she remembered. Perhaps she had not wanted to kill, but she had wished the man dead in such a way that he suffered before he died. She had been shocked at the realization, at the admission of this truth about herself. Certain she was pregnant, she had run to him and told him, bright-eyed and happy, excited to see her excitement reflected in his eyes and then their rush to plan a life together. He had avowed all she hoped; that night, the last of her innocence, she kept the secret to herself and slept happily and dreamt happily: her future family, her life.

He disappeared the following day. No note, and he never wrote.

She had escaped an illegitimate birth by the skin of her teeth. The pregnancy had been a false alarm. She went on with her life, told people that after many talks they had decided the relationship wasn't right for either of them, and they had broken up. As she lied, she hated herself for protecting him by not speaking of the betrayal, of his cowardice. She threw herself into her studies, silently working through the shame of her own gullibility and the loss of what had been a dream.

If Leah had been of a different character, perhaps his perfidy would have been enough to incite her to murder.

She finished her spritzer and, laden with this painful memory, walked back to the Lieutenant's office.

Freya was sitting at her desk. "He's gone to lunch with a farmer who lives up by Amiata."

"A farmer who had dealings with Diego and Cecco?"

"Yes, he said it was a long shot, but one he'd try anyway."

"Have you had lunch?"

"No, I didn't feel like going alone, so I'll get a sandwich and eat here. I've got some work to do anyway."

"Let's go together and get a pizza. I could use the company, and I'm hungry."

"Great. How about going to Paradiso?"

"Perfect."

They walked along the edge of the piazza and turned down a side alley to the steps leading to a low courtyard and the door of the restaurant. The smell of warm, fresh-baked pizza crust wafted through the door as they opened it and stepped inside, taking deep breaths.

"I'm having artichoke."

"Me too. And a glass of wine."

"How come you could use company?"

Oh, you know how every once in a while memories come back to give you a gut punch?"

Freya shook her head. "Boy, do I! What was yours?"

"A man I knew when I was much younger. I thought I was pregnant. He disappeared."

"Were you pregnant?" Freya gasped.

"No. And it all happened when I was so young I never told anyone, and I never went to the doctor."

"I'm sorry, Leah."

"It doesn't matter now. I got through it. But it made me think more about Diego and Cecco. It made me think more seriously and wonder if a young woman, finding herself pregnant and deserted by some jerk who didn't have the courage to take responsibility, could be angry enough to kill. I dismissed the idea earlier, but thinking about it again, I wonder."

"I can imagine it. Wow. It seems like we're coming up with more reasons for the murders, except Giacomo's. The more we talk about it, the more it seems his death is a separate thing, a normal death. I talked to a woman earlier that I think could as easily have killed me as look at me."

"Who..."

"What are you two up to?" The Lieutenant stood just a few paces from the table.

"We're eating. What else at lunch time in a restaurant?" Leah piped up, "What are you doing here?"

"Even the police get hungry. And Italian police, unlike the American police of television, do not grab a sandwich on the way to a crime scene. If we have to hurry, we forego eating until we can eat decently. It's better to be hungry than to eat in a slovenly way."

"Thank you for the lecture, Lieutenant. The next time I'm back in the States, I'll be sure to tell all the Montana detectives and police that they need to straighten up and eat right."

The Lieutenant laughed. "Yes, tell them, Leah. I'd like to think my comrades-in-arms get a good meal once in a while, although they may think a good meal is at your MacDonald's."

Freya gestured at the empty chair next to them. "Sit with us, and stop arguing."

The Lieutenant sat down and signaled the waitress, pointing at the pizza and the carafe of red wine. After he'd been served, he looked at Leah and Freya in turn. "I wanted to talk to you both anyway, and we may as well talk here since the place is almost empty.

Freya started. "Okay. I went this morning to talk to a woman who runs a little farm by herself just south of the implement store, the one across the river on the hill. The woman's husband died about twenty years ago, and since then, she's been running the farm by herself with some help from hired hands once in a while or from her neighbors. I knew about her because I'd asked one of my friends from the COOP if she knew of anyone who had had business dealings with Diego or Cecco. She told me about this woman.

"I found her in her barn dealing with a cow that was having a hard time calving. I had to wait because she was pulling the calf. What grizzly business! But she was able to do it, and she saved the calf. Amazing to me that she was strong enough.

After she got cleaned up and the calf wiped down and next to the mother, we chatted for a while. She was personable and seemed happy to have a visitor. When I was able to bring the subject around to Diego and Cecco, she said that about a year ago she needed money for some equipment. She went to Diego and Cecco for a loan instead of to the bank, because she needed the funds fast, and she had done a little business with them earlier that went okay.

"She asked why I'd asked and if I were planning to do some business with them. Before I could answer, she laughed and said that with my looks, I'd better be careful.

"I told her I hadn't had any business with Cecco and Diego, that I worked in the police station and had been asked to talk to her. I told her somebody had told the police she had business with the two men, and I was hoping she might have some useful information.

"Suddenly, she was furious and ordered me to leave. It scared the begeebers out of me. She followed me out, yelling and jabbing the air with her finger about how it wasn't my business how she ran her farm, and it was unprofessional of me to come instead of a uniformed policeman.

"I ran to the car and locked the doors. She was still yelling at me as I drove away, and I think that unless she murdered those two, she was right to be angry. I *was* being sneaky and underhanded."

Freya faced the Lieutenant, who had just taken another bite of pizza, "And I'm not going there or doing any more work to get information for you. I'm not the devious type. It's your job, not mine. I don't know why I agreed in the first place. The woman was huge compared to me, with big, strong hands. You two can go talk to her if you want, but not me. I like my office job, and calm evenings with my sweet boyfriend."

The Lieutenant laughed aloud. "Calm down, Freya. I apologize. I didn't mean to put you on the spot or make you be devious. I won't ask again, I promise. I really thought you might just gather some names for me. I didn't mean for you to do the legwork that Montaro and I should be doing."

He grinned and winked at Leah. "But, who is this boyfriend, Freya?"

Leah and the Lieutenant leaned toward her and spoke at the same time. "Tell us."

Freya blushed. "It's not that I didn't want to help. I just don't want to do it again. He owns a restaurant in Grossetto. His name is Maurizio."

"Long distance romance."

"It's not that far, and the restaurant is local, very few tourists, so he closes on Sundays, and we spend the day together. If things are slow around here," she nodded at the Lieutenant, "and you give me a day off, I go down and help at the restaurant."

"Is he good to you?"

"Leah! What a question! Why would you ask that?"

"Sorry. I've got Diego and Cecco on my mind and Baccia, Lodoletta, and Pagolo. It's just rotten. All of it. And after talking to the Signora, I was thinking there must be at least one or two young women here who have paid dearly because of those two."

Freya took a sip of her wine and another bite of pizza. She swallowed and shook her head. "I don't think I've ever met anyone like you, Leah. You're not police material, and yet you are. You never think things through; you're all instinct, from what I can tell. You blunder along like a cottonwood fluff on the breeze, but then you take root for a little while, and you always find something, usually after almost getting yourself killed. You're a little like Don Quixote, just bumbling along. I can't tell what you're going to do or say next. I don't think anyone can. How did Nick ever live with you?"

Realizing what she'd said, she put her hand over her mouth and glanced at Leah.

"I'm sorry. I didn't mean…"

Leah laughed and answered without looking at the Lieutenant. "Don't worry, Freya. I've been the way I am for most of my life, probably all of it, if I could remember that far back. I gave my parents, and Nick, no end of trouble. The Don Quixote thing is too much, but with a stretch, I guess it fits in some way. I'm not offended at all. For now, I can only tell you I'm not applying to the police academy, and I've never held down a real job for long, but I do have some thoughts." She glanced at the Lieutenant, who sighed.

Leah continued. "When I talked to the Signora, she wouldn't give any names, but from what she indicated and from her look, if I read it right, there are at least one or two young women who may have been taken in by Diego or Cecco and were either strong enough or cunning enough to go after one or both of them. The trouble is, no names. The Signora said for sure there were young women terribly wronged by those two men. She didn't go so far as to say these women might have killed them, but she did set me thinking that a trusting young woman who had given herself to someone like Cecco or Diego, someone who could fool them into thinking they appeared to care and did support her during their affair could believe he would marry her and take care of her. And if he didn't, if he cut off the relationship once she was pregnant, then, well, she might want to kill him. Or maybe she got involved with a married man who promised he was going to divorce his wife for her. Then she gets pregnant, and the married guy cuts off the relationship. Add those hopes to the guy being one of the richest men in town. If a young woman has family troubles or an abusive situation at home and few prospects of work, might she trust too much on an affair or on the power of a pregnancy?"

"True. Unfortunately, it sounds like you're talking about Lodoletta, right?" The Lieutenant asked.

"My god!" Leah blurted.

"It's not the same, but it's close enough to make me think of it." The Lieutenant muttered and put his hand to his forehead.

"Don't think of it, Lieutenant. I don't think that's the case. When I went to see Maria Teresa, she told me about Arrammundu fighting over Lodoletta with another young man named Gerardo. And from what I gather, Lodoletta is back with Arrammundu now, and whatever happened with Gerardo is over. So, it's your turn."

"My trip to Amiata was a complete bust. The man I went to see was in Eastern Europe at some agricultural convention. He's been gone for over two months touring and talking to farmers there. This means we're back where we started, unless some young woman actually did commit the murders, and it also means that Giacomo's death was just a simple heart attack like we thought." He glanced toward Leah.

"No worries, Lieutenant. I'm befuddled and bewildered, and any other synonym you want to give it. The only thing we can do now, it seems, is look for a young woman and follow up on the farm woman Freya saw."

"What was her name, Freya?" The Lieutenant asked.

"Signora Adoranda Giusti."

"Okay. I'll go see her again. She might be more amenable when she sees a uniform. Leah, you can come along if you want. We'll emphasize the cowgirl aspect of your upbringing. Maybe if she knows that, she'll soften her response." He grinned.

"I'm hardly a cowgirl, but I'm familiar with farm and ranch life, and I'd like to come along."

"Because you're curious to see her reaction, aren't you?" Freya laughed.

Leah hunched her shoulders and grinned.

Chapter Forty

They rode in companionable silence to the farm. It had rained in the night, and the countryside was vivid with winter wheat and the yellow and orange of the fall grapevines trailing the undulating hills of southern Tuscany. These moments of calm comfort in the company of the Lieutenant surprised Leah, but she had been unable to understand her feelings well enough to know if she loved him enough to spend a life, however long that meant, with him. Even if she did love him well enough for a lifetime, could she let go of her freedom, her erratic drive to wander? Would she end up damaging his life by her impetuous behavior, which she seemed still unable to control?

She ached for Italy, for Tuscany, for her friends, for the countryside, the morning to evening walks along the vie cave, for tozzetti and spritzers, pasta with truffles, Tuscan bread, and forests, for the beautiful sight of *ciclamino* growing along the roadsides and in the forests, for the market on Thursdays. She wanted to know the Italian lace makers and the Italian cooks and the unexplored areas of the land; she wanted to know the children, and the history, and the housewives.

At the same time Leah longed for her daughter and son-in-law. She wanted to experience the daily life of the ranch, the warm hide of cattle, and horseback rides into the mountains, heavy snow, beef stew and homemade bread, the warm smell of her horse in the barn in winter, the cold air of -30-degree winter, the scratchy feel of the hay when she fed the horses.

And she longed for the Lieutenant's gentle, sensual touch, his kisses.

There was so much in the world; she wanted to live it all. At times, the choices nearly broke her, and she knew her choices sometimes hurt those around her, because she could not erase the need to keep going, keep experiencing, keep loving. For her, there were not only four directions in the world; there was north, there was south, east, and west, there was up and there down, there was kitty corner and circuitous, straight and angled, hundreds of directions in which to move, hundreds of trails to explore.

Today, sitting silently next to the Lieutenant, she was convinced that in a permanent relationship with her, the Lieutenant would not be able to accept her way for long.

Only Nick. Only Nick.

A sadness settled on her shoulders.

They found Signora Adoranda Giusti in the barn, checking on the new calf, which was standing sturdily on all fours and enthusiastically sucking and butting at its mother's teats.

"Signora Giusti," the Lieutenant called from the barn door.

She swirled around and strode toward them, her index finger at her lips.

"Please don't yell, Lieutenant; the calf's nursing." She looked Leah and the Lieutenant over. "My goodness! Yesterday a strange, skimpy, nosy little woman, and today a uniform with another skimpy little woman. Cecco and Diego, right?"

"Can we talk? I'd like to explain about yesterday."

She shrugged. "Come ahead. I'll always talk to a uniform." She glanced at Leah. "But don't move quickly or loudly." She poked a thumb over her shoulder. "She's a new mother and skittish with strangers around her calf."

The Lieutenant entered on tiptoes.

Leah walked beside him, chuckling.

"No need to tiptoe, Lieutenant," Signora Giusti snorted. "It's not *that* serious; just be gentle; she's protective of her new calf. And you," she turned to Leah, "you were giggling at our very careful Lieutenant, too. Do you know about cows and calves?"

"A little."

Signora Giusti smiled and reached her hand toward Leah. "Call me

Adoranda. Adoranda Giusti. I'm glad to meet you, but maybe not so glad about your company."

The Lieutenant extended his hand, "Lieutenant Cavour."

"And I figure you're here on business, Lieutenant, unless you've decided on a switch of careers and want to go into farming." She winked at Leah. "But I have to warn you. Nobody in their right mind goes into farming at your age. It's better to be born into it, to get acclimated to the hardships and uncertainties."

"Thanks for the warning, Signora, but I'm not interested in taking up farming. I've come on official business."

"The murders. My dealings with those scum Diego and Cecco?"

"Exactly."

"You know, I would have told the young woman from your office if you'd been along. I don't mind talking about it—well, maybe a little—but I thought her coming was unprofessional."

Leah and the Lieutenant laughed aloud. The Lieutenant explained. "It might help to understand that there are so many questions to this case that I've elicited the help of some civilians. And Freya, from yesterday, won't be back. You terrified her."

Adoranda laughed. "Well, maybe she needed it. If she comes back, I'll be nicer. She sure locked those doors fast when she jumped in her car!" Adoranda laughed again, wide shoulders shaking, dark eyes sparkling.

It crossed Leah's mind that this woman, who could pull a calf, give it tender and protective care, and laugh enough to put troubles in their rightful place, could not possibly be a murderer.

"So, you two want to know about my dealings with Diego and Cecco, yes?"

Leah and the Lieutenant nodded.

"Well, come up to the house. We'll have coffee, or a little vin santo if you prefer, and talk. And I might even scrape up a piece or two of *castagnaccio*."

Lieutenant and Leah looked at each other, wide-eyed, and smiled. Both of them loved the chestnut flour, walnut, and pine nut cake.

In the entryway, Leah and the Lieutenant, following the Signora's lead, pushed off their shoes and slipped into the simple, soft "ciabatta" slippers the Signora had provided for visitors to use.

The large, high-ceilinged kitchen was immaculate and redolent with the smell of stew cooking on the stove. The Signora gestured toward the big round table in the center of the room; it was a beautiful piece made of Holm Oak, finely polished by the Signora's hands.

"Coffee or vin santo?" The Signora asked from a workspace near the stove.

"I don't like to turn away vin santo," the Lieutenant answered, "but I'd better stick to coffee. The cake will be a pure delight."

"I'll take coffee too, please," Leah added.

Within minutes, the Signora had spread a cloth and set three glass demitasses on the table and three small plates with a piece of castagnaccio on each.

When they had finished with the cake and coffee, the Lieutenant asked, "I understand you've been in farming for a long time."

"Yes, my husband, may he rest in peace," she crossed herself, "and I. And our parents too. They were mezzadri and my grandfather, mezzadri here and in America."

"Mezzadri in America?" Leah was startled to hear it.

"They didn't call them that, of course. It was in your state of Mississippi. They called them 'sharecroppers,' I think. But it was nearly the same. My grandfather was one of the first to go to the Sunnyside Plantation in what you call, if I remember, the Arkansas Delta. There were Italians who had gone to America and become Americans, and they made a big business of convincing Italians like my family to go to America. They made it sound like heaven. But the truth is the people who owned those 'plantations,' as they called them, made you pay them back for your fare over and for the food you ate. So, my grandfather started in debt, and he stayed in debt. For him and others like him, it was like being slaves or serfs. In fact, my grandfather and the other Italians worked alongside the Blacks. Both the Italians and Blacks were at the bottom of the scale. The Ku Klux Klan hated Italians and Blacks.

"But Italians and Blacks got along." The Signora suddenly brightened.

"Someday, I'll play you my CD of *Spaghetti Juke Joint.* Do you like Blues? My grandfather was in just the right place to get that, at least. He said there was a kind of bar near the plantation where the Blacks and the Italians used to go and listen to Blues on Saturday nights. My grandfather loved Blues ever after, and he passed that love along to us."

"It never occurred to me you'd like the Blues."

"C'mon, you know about farmers; you should know we don't live the stereotypes people have in their ignorant heads. My grandfather knew Blues, Classical, opera, and every other kind of music you can think of. And my mother, too."

"What happened to your grandfather? From what you say, he made it home."

"Yes. Some did. It took many years, but he made it home by saving pennies at a time. And the treatment of Italians on that place you call the Delta was mixed. Some people, especially like a woman writer he told me about named Emily Reed, understood and appreciated us, and since then, well, you know your great playwright, Tennessee Williams, he wrote about us. He thought the Italians were full of vitality!"

Adoranda laughed, "But the way he got home was this: He found some work he could do on Sundays in a local grocer's store, which happened to be owned by a Siciliano. My grandfather said they did better than the Italians from central Italy, because they stayed close-knit in town and had little stores.

"Anyway, this Siciliano hired him for Sundays, and he saved all that he made there for getting home.

"So why am I telling you all this? I don't know. I just got started on the story. Or maybe I'm just old and like remembering the old stories.

"Anyway. You want to hear about Diego and Cecco. The thing is, around here, our word has always been a contract. I mean with the other farmers and neighbors and tradesmen in town. And I thought it would be the same with Diego and Cecco. I'd had the cost of some new equipment and needed money fast in order to pay the hired workers during the *vendemia*. Someone told me those two would help for a fairly good interest rate, so I went to them and made a deal by handshake, but when it came time to pay them back, they robbed me with some rigmarole about interest rates at the bank going up.

"I yelled at them and pleaded with them, but it didn't do any good. I had to pay, and after, it was rough, all because of them."

"Did you threaten them?" The Lieutenant stared at her to see if she might lie.

"Of course I did! I told them they wouldn't get away with it. I even threatened to kill them."

The Lieutenant waited.

The Signora laughed. "Did you think if I were going to kill them, I would have waited this long? That I'd work my hands raw to pay them back and then kill them? Do I seem that stupid to you, Lieutenant?"

"No, Signora, you don't seem stupid to me in the least, but if you know anything about my work, you know that I've seen revenge simmer for a long time before a murder."

"I understand. I didn't mean to be snippy. I have an explosive temper, it's true, but I don't hold anger for long, and I'm not much for revenge. I like my farm, and I like my work; the neighbors understand and accept my character, and I guess I'm just basically too happy to murder anyone. Have another piece of cake."

Both Leah and the Lieutenant laughed, and the Lieutenant responded, "I guess you are Signora. You're still on our list because of that threat, but you don't seem like a murderess. Did I ask you where you were when they were killed?"

"No. You forgot that one. What day was it?"

The Lieutenant told her.

"Well, I don't keep a calendar of the days I murder people, so I can't tell you exactly, but I imagine I was here, feeding the cows or mucking out a stall."

Chapter Forty-One

Freya, Montaro, Leah, and the Lieutenant were gathered in the Lieutenant's office. The Lieutenant started. "Okay, let's go over it all again."

He counted things off on his fingers: "Pagolo appears to have an airtight alibi; Baccia is in jail, but we know she was neither capable nor inclined to murder even if she has confessed; Lodoletta may have had the opportunity, but it's unlikely she would have been capable of overwhelming the men, she is too small and not strong enough especially since the attacks were frontal. Arrammundu had motive, but doesn't know he had motive; Signora Giusti seems very unlikely to be a murderess, although we'll keep her on the list." He paused while the others considered what he'd said.

"Anything else?"

"We haven't considered the young women?" Leah said.

"Right. Montaro has something to say about that." The Lieutenant opened his palm toward Montaro.

"I have two names, but I haven't talked to the women. As I told the Lieutenant, I think it would be better if either you, Leah," he nodded at her, "or you Freya, or both of you, go to talk with them. They'd be more comfortable talking to women I think."

He pointed with both forefingers toward his chest. "A big hairy guy like me is not usually the kind women want to spill their intimate details to. I don't blame them. I can be intimidating, I guess." His voice had an edge of sadness.

The others laughed. Montaro was one of the gentlest, most modest men in town, but in looks, he was a gangster off the streets. He was perpetually unshaven, his uniform was soiled and stained with splotches of food, and he had missing buttons. He rarely combed his hair, which twisted wildly in the wind, and he spoke in a deep, rough dialect.

The Lieutenant let all of Montaro's sartorial shortcomings pass. He dealt with the issue by ordering an extra uniform and shaving kit with a comb and brush for Montaro. These the Lieutenant kept in his own locker to give to Montaro so the junior official could run to the showers and make himself presentable in the event of an unpredictable visit from regional officials. When those officials came, the Lieutenant excused Montaro, telling the officials Montaro had been up all night on a difficult surveillance. Then he sent Montaro off to the showers to clean up. This ruse had worked for years; the Lieutenant wanted to keep him, whatever the minor problems. Montaro was a fine officer. He had strength when it was needed, was brave in action, and knew when to push and when to go easy on suspects.

"Those women just don't know you, Montaro. But you may be right. It might be best for Freya and Leah to go." He turned to the two women with open palms, "Okay?"

They looked at each other and nodded, "Okay," Freya answered for them. "I said I wouldn't anymore, but if Leah is going, I'll go with her. We'll need the names and addresses, and some sort of official written document that we have the right to talk to them. I mean, this is highly unusual, no?"

The Lieutenant laughed. "Almost everything we're doing is highly unusual. Having you two involved at all, for starters. Montaro and I would be out of a job if the head office found out. I think the best thing is for me to go with you, at the beginning to make it official," he turned to Leah, "like we did with Signora Giusti. That seemed to work well. Sorry, Freya, I really put you on the spot with her by not going along with you."

"I know you did! And like I said, I won't go alone like that again."

"I'll go with you this time. Once I've explained the situation to the two women, I'll wait outside while you talk with them unless they indicate that I should stay. Does that sound okay with you two?"

"Do you think they'll mind having a foreigner there?" Leah pursed her lips.

"You're hardly a foreigner anymore, Leah. People here know you, even if they haven't spoken to you. Your Italian is good, and you're not threatening," he paused, smiling, "well, not most of the time."

They all laughed.

"Okay, okay. I think you're wrong about the way I'm perceived. I am seen as a foreigner, but thankfully, not one of the bad foreigners, and people do accept me. And you do have a point about the two women being more comfortable talking to women." Her look and voice had turned serious, "I know how tender this subject can be."

"I trust you, Leah." The Lieutenant let his eyes rest on her for a long moment.

"The names?" Freya asked.

Montaro held out a sheet of paper. "One is Germana Boscolo and the other, Luigina Trevisan. These are the phones and addresses."

"Venetian surnames?" Leah asked.

"Yes, some grandfather or great-grandfather maybe. Who knows? Think of the Signora. Venetian to the core, yet here she is."

"She's never said why she's here," Leah responded, "and she won't tell me the story of how or exactly when she came."

"She won't tell anyone, Leah." The Lieutenant added, "And we love her too much to push it by asking.

With Leah and Freya by his side, the Lieutenant knocked on the door. It was opened immediately by a young woman with short cropped black hair, large dark eyes carefully made up with shadow and eye-liner, high cheekbones, and full lips accentuated by a subtle apricot-colored lipstick that heightened her smile and made her teeth seem even whiter.

In that first, expectant look, she was lovely, but when she recognized the Lieutenant and saw Freya and Leah, her smile faded and a cloud covered her eyes.

"Lieutenant? Can I help you?"

"I see you know me, but I don't think we've met. Are you Germana

Boscolo?"

A voice from inside the apartment called out. "No, she's not. I'm Germana Boscolo."

They heard steps, and Germana appeared beside the other young woman. Unlike the woman who had opened the door, Germana had chin-length dark blonde hair and wide-set brown eyes, but like her friend, her cheekbones were high and prominent, and her lips full, sensual. She wore no makeup; her natural beauty would only have been marred by any addition, and she seemed to know it. The Lieutenant could see why Diego and Cecco may have been attracted to either one.

Germana took the other woman's arm. "This is my friend, Luigina Trevisan, Lieutenant. I'm visiting. As you probably already know all about it, Luigina and I have some things in common: our dealing with those scumbags Diego and Cecco. And I bet that's why you're here, no?"

Germana looked at Luigina. "It's okay, Luigina. They just want our side of the story. Can they come in?"

"Okay. But why the women? I know Freya; she's okay. And I've seen the other one, but..."

Leah stepped forward and held out her hand. "I'm Leah Contarini. We've seen each other around town, but we've never met."

Both women shook hands with Leah. Leah noticed that Germana's handshake was much firmer than Luigina's. Both of them looked her in the eye.

"Well, come in then," Luigina gestured toward the worn, stuffed couch and chairs that sat around a battered coffee table. "Would you like coffee?"

"We just had, thanks," the Lieutenant lied. "It is about Diego and Cecco we wanted to talk to you. I brought Freya and Leah along because I thought you might be more comfortable talking to women about your relationship with those two."

"You mean you deputized them!" Luigina and Germana exclaimed in unison.

The Lieutenant laughed. "No, I didn't deputize them, but I trust them to listen carefully and ask the right questions. Anyway, it seems like you two are willing to talk to all three of us. Am I right?"

Luigina and Germana looked at each other. Germana leaned to whisper something in Luigina's ear. Luigina whispered back; then they both nodded at the Lieutenant.

Germana spoke, "Yes, we'll talk to all three of you. It will be official, Lieutenant, with you here as well. And we want it to be official."

"I appreciate that. We want to track down the killer or killers as soon as we can."

Luigina spoke, "You know you could save yourself a lot of trouble if you just let it go. Those guys were pigs; whoever killed them did the town a favor, maybe especially some of the women in town, but for sure other people too…"

"Could you tell us about your relationships with the men?" Leah looked at each in turn. "Germana?"

"What can I say? It was a couple of years ago. I was still fairly innocent, not completely innocent, but enough to believe that an old guy, like Diego, rich and surprisingly virile would maybe want to marry someone like me."

She laughed, but the laugh was bitter. "Just ask the psychiatrists and read the magazines. It's the same old story: my dad left my mom when I was twelve, and I've been looking for a dad or a granddad ever since. And besides, I thought if I let a few things go, like Diego's gut and his not—so—handsome face, he wasn't bad. He acted like it was puppy love at the beginning. Everything: flowers, trips to Rome and the seashore, expensive dinners. I'd never been treated so well in my life. He treated me like a princess, and I was convinced he adored me. And he loved my body. He was like a teenager that couldn't get enough."

Leah glanced at Freya.

"What?" Germana asked, "Am I embarrassing you? Or are you just thinking, what a dummy this one is?"

Leah answered. "No, you're not embarrassing us, and we're not thinking what a dummy you are. We're women, Germana, and you're not the only one who's been taken in before by putting your trust in a man. Men get taken in by women, too. It's a reality; some people are mean and untrustworthy.

The only choice we have, man or woman, when that happens is whether or not it makes us bitter. I think each of us chose not to be bitter. Didn't you, Freya?" She looked at Freya.

Freya nodded. "It took me a while, but, yes, I made the conscious choice not to be bitter."

"Well, bully for you, aren't you two goody-goodies," Germana spat the words. "Did either of you have a child by the guy?"

Leah and Freya shook their heads.

"Well, there you are with your choice! There's a big difference when there's a child. A broken heart and the shame of being a fool is one thing, but a broken heart, the shame of being a fool, *and* being pregnant, being sent away alone, and returning without the child, without a love, *with* the stigma *and* broke, *and* with no recourse, is another. I was bitter as hell. And I still am. Sometimes, I wish I could dig him up and kill him all over again."

The others jerked.

"Oh, calm down. I didn't mean it like that. I didn't kill him, for god's sake. I just meant I get mad when I think about it too much. I thought my life was set and secure, and now my baby is living with some stranger, and he'll never know who I am. Why shouldn't a woman be able to get revenge? Why shouldn't she!"

Her voice broke, but, determined not to cry, she cleared her throat and rubbed her eyes with the back of her hand, wiping away all trace of tears. Her face had gone hard.

"You guys haven't even asked me where I was when Diego was killed. Aren't you supposed to do that?"

"Yes," the Lieutenant answered, "we are supposed to ask."

"Well, the jokes on you—or more likely on us. We were here, together. We're each other's alibis!" She threw her head back and laughed uproariously.

The Lieutenant put his hand to his forehead. "Oh my god. For how long?"

Luigina nodded her head. "Germana's water's off, so she's been staying with me for…How many days, Germana?"

Germana hunched her shoulders. "Geez, almost two weeks."

"And we've hardly left the apartment. Only to go to COOP. And we went together. We've had coffee here, and cooked and chatted and watched movies. Sorry, Lieutenant." She smirked.

"It's not funny. Both of you have a strong motive for killing each of the men." He studied their faces. "I'll let it go for now, but we're not done. Tell us your story, Luigina."

"It's a different story, Lieutenant. Although it comes down to the same thing. Cecco, as you know, was married, but he was unhappy, and he convinced me that, with me, he was happy. You see? Same story in some ways as Germana. I had the broken family too, but mine was coupled with abuse, not serious but real neglect, so I was ready to be important to someone, to be loved, and I fell for Cecco's sassy, confident character. He was full of charming bravado. Actually, he was a dirty coward, but I interpreted it the way I wanted it to be. He wasn't all flowers and trips, and I was working anyway, but he was great in ways that mattered—if you know what I mean. He made me feel like some sort of goddess. The feeling you get from good sex can make you think everything is perfect and you forget real life in a way; you forget other people's feelings, and you even forget your own troubles. There was some little voice in me that knew it was a dead-end street with Cecco, but I kept wallowing in the pleasure of it, the good sex, yes, but also the dinners, the presents. We all do it, for god's sake, we love people who stroke our egos and if you're a little uncertain or hurt, you soak it up and let the pleasure take over. It makes you feel above the cesspool you've been stuck in for most of your life."

She grinned, but her eyes had filled with tears. "When I got pregnant, he gave me the money to go to Rome, to that horrible place for unwed mothers. I went willingly. I thought I'd have the baby, come back, and he'd be there waiting, ready to take care of me and the baby, even if we didn't marry. I didn't care much about the marrying part.

"But once I was gone, it was as if I didn't exist. I never heard from him again. The baby died." She took a deep breath and clenched her jaw. "The doctor had the choice of me or the baby, and he chose to save me. I wish to God he hadn't."

She started to cry and spoke in broken words, sucking at the air. "I wish he'd saved the baby. Maybe as a boy, the baby would have had a better life."

To help Luigina, Leah spoke, "And when you came back?"

"When I came back, the pig wouldn't even look at me, or take my phone calls. He didn't even goddamn care what had happened to the baby. He never asked, not one question, and I guess he's never known. I can see why someone bashed his skull in, just like I can see why someone stabbed Diego. They deserved it, goddamn liars."

Her face had turned red with anger.

Germana laughed. "So there you are Lieutenant and sidekicks. You've got two angry women that had good reason to kill those scumbuckets, and you'll have to figure out whether we did or not. We've only got each other for alibis, and maybe someone at the COOP. God knows both of us had motives, and both of us, as you see, are strong women. So, what do you think?"

They grinned like Cheshire cat twins.

Leah, the Lieutenant, and Freya walked away from their meeting with Germana and Luigina frustrated.

"Lieutenant, I'm sorry, but I have a doctor's appointment. Do you mind if I cut off here," Freya indicated a street leading away from the office, "I'm already a little late."

"Of course. Go ahead, Freya."

When she hurried away in the opposite direction, the Lieutenant faced Leah. How about you? Can you come back to the office to talk for a while?

"You sound frustrated, Lieutenant. Don't let it get to you. The Persians say: 'It will become known'."

"How in the devil would you know a Persian saying?"

"It's a long story, Lieutenant, and sometime I'll tell you about that too, but right now I want to think about Germana and Luigina—and for that matter, about Adoranda Giusti, and Baccia, Pagolo, Lodoletta. How did we get so many suspects?"

"We don't have that many, not really, although it seems like it. I think we're letting things confuse us. Stop and think. We know Baccia didn't do it. Granted, she's right-handed, but it's beyond credibility that she's strong enough to give a single blow that would have disabled Cecco enough to allow her to go on beating him. And the same for Diego. She's just not strong enough to have driven that knife so far into his body."

The Lieutenant stopped walking and stared up into the air. "I read something about volleyball: if a woman hits the ball over the net as hard as she can it's traveling on average about 80 kilometers an hour. That sort of thing happens all the time in women's volleyball, and the one that's hit shakes her head a little, and that's that. She goes on playing. But if a man were to hit the ball his hardest, it would be going about 242 kilometers an hour, and the woman who was hit definitely wouldn't shake her head and keep going. She'd be out cold, at the least. Granted, the weapon in our case was probably much harder for Cecco and sharper for Diego, but you get my point. And Baccia is not a young woman; she doesn't have the same force as a young woman, let alone the force of a man."

"I see I'm not the only one who knows strange things, Lieutenant. Those are impressive statistics. They work for Lodoletta too, just as we've been saying: she's too small and not strong enough to have killed either Cecco or Diego. We've known this from the beginning, but Baccia won't budge on the confession until she's certain Lodoletta and Pagolo are in the clear. So, where do we go from here?"

The Lieutenant counted on his fingers. "Okay, Baccia, Lodoletta, Pagolo, and, I think, Adoranda Giusti are off the suspect list."

"Adoranda doesn't have an alibi."

"You're right, but did she seem to you, in any way, like a suspect? I couldn't detect a trace of guilt or fear or deception in her manner with us, or of what she says of her behavior with Cecco and Diego. And why would she have waited so long?"

"Okay," Leah laughed, "I'll give you Adoranda too. So, how many do we have left?"

"We've only Germana and Luigina, or some unknown person that we have yet to meet."

"I need to write each name down, with a little information at the side, and think about each one. It's getting confusing, and I want to straighten it out in my mind."

They had arrived at the door of the station.

"I plan to do the same thing, but first, come into the office for a minute; I want to talk to you in private."

Leah's eyebrows raised, "What about?"

"Inside." He opened the door and motioned for Leah to come inside.

Chapter Forty-Two

They sat on the chairs in front of his desk. As he was adjusting his chair to face her; Leah saw his face was flushed. He cleared his throat several times.

"Leah, I want to talk about us. I want to know what's happening. When I kiss you, I know you have feelings for me, but it seems like we're either at each other's throats, or we're sharing a passionate kiss, always at the most awkward, inopportune times, and then one or the other of us hurries away. It's driving me crazy. I need to know how you feel, beyond those kisses."

"Those kisses are pretty difficult to go beyond!" Leah smiled at him.

"Don't tease me. You know what I mean. They *are* delicious," he exhaled heavily, "but I want to know if there's love behind the kisses and not just passion. I want to know what you're thinking and feeling. What you want."

"Lieutenant, I think the kisses you and I have had are, as Ingrid Bergman said, 'tricks of nature to stop speech when words are superfluous.' I never thought I would feel like that again after Nick died, and I never did feel like that since Nick, not until you kissed me."

"Then…"

"Wait." Leah took his hand. "I don't know what it means. I know how strongly I'm attracted to you. I know I respect you. I know that even when we fight, and we do! So often! I still want to be near you. But is it just wanting more of the kisses, wanting more of you? Is it just lust and ego on my part? I am egotistical, you know that. I can talk wise sometimes, but the truth is, I like doing what I want to do when I want to do it. I like having my freedom, and part of what you're asking me is if I care enough about you to give up some, or maybe more than some, of that freedom."

"That's not true. I'm not asking you to give up your freedom. I'm asking you to know your feelings about me and to let me know what those feelings are. I know I love you. It's been like the slow ride up a ski lift, and then suddenly, you're off the lift on the way down, fast, and you know what it is to ski. I've known you in every mood I can think of. I've had time to see your joy with Nick; your irresponsible courage; your grief; your sincerity and straightforwardness; your vivid self-respect; your anger; your tenderness with people and with animals. And I've experienced in less ways than I would like," he cast a sideways smile, "your passion and your desire. And I want it all. I want every part of your character, even the most frustrating parts…"

In an abrupt motion, Leah stood, "Lieutenant…"

He rose and looked down at her.

She put both hands to his face and drew him to her. He took her in his arms, kissing her with a blend of passion and affection that made her feel the stars climbing up the night sky.

When they drew away from each other, Leah spoke. "I can't answer you, Lieutenant. I can't answer. I want you, and I want you in my life. But forgetting is so long."

She rushed away and was gone.

Chapter Forty-Three

From across the piazza, the Signora watched Leah rush out of the police station to the back side of the fountain, where she always hid when she wanted to think. The Signora headed for the fountain.

"Leah," she said in a calm voice as she approached, "why have you run away from the police station and hidden yourself?"

"I'm not hiding myself; I just wanted to sit and think for a minute, alone."

The Signora stood directly in front of her. "Well, I'm not going to leave you alone. You looked like you were running the 100-meter dash, and I can see that your face is blotchy; you look terrible. Has there been another crisis? Another murder, God forbid?"

Leah laughed despite herself. "No, Signora, not another murder. We have enough to do trying to figure out the ones that have already happened. I'm sorry I was blunt; I didn't mean to offend you. Come sit." Leah patted a spot next to her on the stone bench.

"Bad news from home?"

"No, Signora, nothing like that. It's the Lieutenant. The Lieutenant and me."

The Signora emitted a long, loud sigh. "Then all's right with the world. You don't have to say anything else. I'm quite aware of the contortions and struggles of people in love…"

"But I didn't say I was in love with him!" Leah exclaimed louder than she wanted.

The Signora patted her hand. "Of course, you didn't. You probably don't even know if you are or not, or anyway, you're not yet aware if you are or you aren't. The nature of love is uncertainty. And you two argue so much that it boggles the mind. You fight, and then you fix whatever you were fighting about, and then you kiss each other passionately—like you must have just now." She eyed Leah. "I suppose all the ups and downs indicate love. I couldn't take it myself. But you two probably have less ego than I do."

"How…"

"How did I know you were just kissing passionately? Your lips look as if someone's been pounding them with a hammer, Leah. I can only imagine it was some kiss!"

Leah burst into peals of laughter and hugged the older woman. "What would I do without you?"

"That's a very good question to ask yourself. Now, let's change the subject. Your relationship with the Lieutenant will work out, and if it doesn't it will work out anyway. So, tell me about the case and how it's going."

"We went from having no suspects to having three new ones, all women. And I still think that Martelli's death is somehow tied into it all, but I've stopped talking about it because the Lieutenant doesn't agree, and we only fight if I push the issue."

"Who are the new suspects?"

"Adoranda Giusti, Germana Boscolo, and Luigina Trevisan."

"The two Venetian girls. Well, they aren't really Venetian, but their fathers. And Adoranda…" The Signora grunted. "Ridiculous to even imagine her. If she wanted to kill someone, which she never would, she would have done it on the spot as soon as she realized they'd tricked her and taken her money. She has a temper, but she isn't capable, in any sense, of long-planned revenge."

"That's what the Lieutenant and I thought. Still, she doesn't have an alibi, so we have to take the possibility seriously."

"She'll prove to be telling the truth. But why are you still thinking about Giacomo's death?"

"I don't know. I just have this instinct. I guess it's because Signora Martelli feels so strongly about it. A woman knows her husband."

"Not all of them do, my dear, but I agree with you; she's a woman who does. I went to visit her the other day, by the way. She asked about you, and I hope you'll go see her."

"How is she?"

"She's doing well. Lonely, frustrated with the police, I think. By the way, I saw Lodoletta there in Chieto, just across the street from the Martelli's building, where the bus stops."

"She must know someone there."

"I suppose. I waved to her." The Signora gave a little wave. "With her usual sweet manner, she raised her middle finger at me. I'm beginning to believe it's her usual greeting and parting gesture, and I should be honored to receive it." She made a face and shook her head in little jerks. "I actually think somewhere inside Lodoletta's rough exterior, there's a beautiful young woman, but she's succeeded in building a fence around herself and won't allow herself to come out. I feel for Baccia."

"Baccia understands too well. And Lodoletta has reason. Baccia, Pagolo, and Lodoletta all have reason to, as you put it, build a fence around themselves. They've been abused and beaten so badly for so long, it's a wonder they're anywhere near normal. And there are cracks in Lodoletta's armor. She actually came to me to apologize for being nasty one day in the piazza."

"That's a start. Maybe love is doing her some good."

"You mean with Arrammundu?"

"Of course, with Arrammundu! Who else? They've been together a long time. Angelica was happy about it, and that's one of the reasons I continue to care for Lodoletta. If Angelica loved her, then there is certainly a fine young woman behind that middle finger."

Leah laughed. "I guess so, but I think there was some trouble. I thought Lodoletta was seeing a guy named Gerardo down by Valentano."

"That was a long time ago, and he's since engaged to a girl from his own neighborhood."

Leah put her arm around the Signora and squeezed her in a gentle hug. "Signora, you're amazing. I don't know where you get so much information; it astounds me. You should write books."

"What? Exposés on all the people in town? Wouldn't they just love me for that! Wouldn't you just love me, exposing all your kissing with the Lieutenant?"

They both laughed.

"Leah, I need to get along. Don't worry about you and the Lieutenant. When you know, one way or the other, you'll know. It's inevitable." She paused. "Although with you…well, we'll just have to wait and see. With you, it's hard to tell anything for certain."

Leah watched her walk away, back straight, shoulders squared. Her fur coat looked as beautiful and new as ever, her head held high as ever. What a mystery she was! A Venetian lady of means in a small Tuscan village. What was she doing here?

Calmed after her talk with the Signora, Leah walked back to her apartment, hung up her jacket, and made a cup of tea. With the ginger and honey tea steaming in front of her, she took a few deep breaths, pushed the sweet kiss of the Lieutenant from her mind, trembling as she did, and sat at the kitchen table with pen and paper to begin jotting notes.

She began with Baccia, but after writing and crossing out several lines of useless thoughts, she wrote "not a true suspect," and went on to Lodoletta. As soon as she had spelled out the name, she remembered what the Signora had said. The older woman had seen Lodoletta in Chieto, across from the Martelli's apartment. What was Lodoletta doing in Chieto? Friends? Leah made a note to ask her.

Pagolo's alibi, as Leah thought about it, seemed too secure. The neighbor had sworn, but it didn't make sense. Pagolo had to have eaten, had to have used the facilities, had to have taken a break. And how late at night had he worked?

The neighbor himself must have had other things to do besides the job of cleaning the cantina. He had to have had daily chores, a coffee or wine at the bar, a visit to the bank or the pharmacy. It was impossible to believe that they both could have stayed in the cantina working every minute. What was the Lieutenant thinking? Perhaps he knew them too well. Trusted them too much?

And how precise could the coroner really have been? The bodies had decomposed less than they would have in summer, but still, they were decomposed. How exact were the signs? What was the temperature in the cave and at the mill? All these questions must have been answered by the forensic reports, which were stuck in a pile of things to do on some forensic expert's desk in Florence. She made a note to remind the Lieutenant to call again. Having the answers would make things so much clearer.

Leah made another note to talk to Pagolo's neighbor again.

Germana and Liugina. She would need to talk to the Lieutenant about these two women. Their "alibi" was as full of holes as was Pagolo's. It was impossible to believe that if they were so much together, over the span of time that the murders must have taken place, someone besides a few people at the COOP would have seen them or heard them. They said they'd gone for food; they had to have made cooking sounds, or had to have laughed, or moved furniture in the apartment, sounds which the neighbors would have heard. And they had to have gone out, at least for an evening's walk; everyone did. And they must have gone to the bar at some point. How could they be young single women and not go for a coffee or a glass of wine unless, it suddenly occurred to Leah, they were afraid of something?

Something else bothered her. If Gerardo had dated Lodoletta long before Lodoletta got involved with Arrammundu, why had the two men had such a fight at the farm as Maria Teresa said they had? Who could have been the other woman? Was Arrammundu double-timing Lodoletta with Gerardo's girlfriend/fiancé?

It didn't concern the case, but Leah was perplexed. She decided to let the murders of Cecco, Diego, and possibly Giacomo, sit for a while and see what she could find out about the fight. Maybe it would tell her at least some truth about Arrammundu and Lodoletta.

She put away her notes and looked up Maria Teresa's phone number.

"Hello?"

"Maria Teresa, this is Leah Contarini."

"Who?" Maria Teresa shouted into the line, "It's a bad connection. You'll have to speak louder!"

Leah shouted, "This is Leah Contarini."

"Oh, Leah. I'm happy to hear from you. How are you?"

"Fine, just fine. I need to talk to Gerardo. Can you give me his number?"

"Of course! Hold the line a minute."

Leah thought she could hear a shuffling, moving away and then back.

"Are you there?" Maria Teresa shouted.

"Yes!"

"Do you have a pencil?"

Leah laughed and shouted back, "Yes! I have a pencil."

"The number is 800 711 6921. Leah, is something wrong?"

"No Signora, nothing. I will come see you soon and explain."

"Alright. I'll be happy to see you."

"Goodbye, Signora."

Leah hung up the phone and dialed Gerardo.

"Hello."

"Gerardo, my name is Leah Contarini. I'm a friend of Maria Teresa and Antonio. Would it be possible to meet with you sometime?"

"I know about you from them. They said you were friends with Angelica and Arrammundu and that they'd told you about the fight."

"That's what I wanted to talk with you about, but I'd rather not over the phone. May I come see you?"

"Are you in Scansansiano?"

"Yes."

"I'm coming up there tomorrow. I have a meeting at 9 a.m., but I could meet you in the bar on the piazza at 10 a.m."

"I appreciate your willingness. I didn't expect it."

"If Maria Teresa trusts you, so do I. I've got nothing to hide, Signora, and I regret what happened. I wanted to commiserate, not to make Arrammundu angry. Look, I have to go now, but I'll see you tomorrow."

"Okay, yes." Leah hung up the phone, wondering what he meant by wanting to commiserate.

Chapter Forty-Four

The following morning, after a long trek from her apartment in heavy rain, Leah entered the bar at 9:45 a.m. She poked her umbrella back out the doorway, shook it, and set it in the umbrella stand that stood to the side of the door.

Within minutes the barmaid, Cinzia, brought Leah her usual: cappuccino and a brioche. While she drank the cappuccino and took a few bites of the brioche, Leah stared out the window. The market was not for two days, it was raining hard, so the streets were almost empty, and the bar had few customers.

"A fortuitous convergence of circumstances," Leah thought. Usually, the bar was noisy, making it possible to talk about anything without people at the next table hearing your conversation. And today, it was nearly empty, which also created the space to talk without being overheard. Leah did not want other people to hear her conversation with Gerardo.

A handsome young man stepped into the bar, shook his umbrella out the door and put it in the umbrella stand. Then, at first missing Leah in the corner by the window, he stood looking around the room.

"Gerardo?" She said in a raised voice.

"Oh, there you are. Yes, I'm Gerardo." He held out his hand. Leah took it and was pleased by the firm grip.

He stood straight and tall, with shoulders back in what seemed an almost military stance. His crow-black hair, dark skin, and sincere dark eyes gave Leah an immediate sense of ease and trust.

"Please." Leah gestured to the empty chair across from her.

Gerardo shed his jacket, laid it to the side of Leah's poncho, and sat down. "Can I order something for you?"

"How about what you're having? I haven't eaten anything yet today."

Leah turned to Cinzia, who was already watching with great curiosity and interest. A man this handsome was always a curiosity. She fixed the cappuccino and cornetto carefully on a plate and brought it to the table.

"I haven't seen you in here before," Cinzia smiled at Gerardo.

"I'm not from here, Signorina. I'm from Valentano."

Leah gave Cinzia a look.

"Lucky Valentano," Cinzia quipped and turned back toward the bar.

Gerardo laughed. "These Scansansianese girls!! Now," he turned to Leah, "You want to know my story with Arrammundu, right?"

"That's right. But even more, I want to know why you fought over Lodoletta."

"Lodoletta?"

Gerardo was obviously surprised. "We didn't fight over Lodoletta!"

"But Maria Teresa said the fight was over a woman. And when I learned you had dated, or were dating, Lodoletta, I assumed…"

"You've got it all mixed up." He was calm, straightforward.

"We weren't fighting over Lodoletta. My relationship with her is ancient history, and Arrammundu knew all about it, or knew anyway that it was some guy from around Valentano."

"But from what Maria Teresa said, you said her name during the fight."

"I did, but it wasn't about her. I was trying to tell him that from what Lodoletta had said, I thought he knew what I'd just told him."

"And what had you just told him?"

"We were working in the barn, and I told him I was glad to meet him, and I was sorry about the loss of his mother and particularly sorry about how she had suffered in her life because of what had happened when she was young. He asked me what had happened. When I realized he didn't know about the rape, or the way everyone thought the death of her husband had been arranged, I tried to get out of it and back off, but he grabbed me and asked what the hell I was talking about. He pinned me down in the hay and forced me to tell him the story I'd heard about it. I was afraid he was going to kill me, so I told him. But that wasn't enough for him. He started punching me. I tried to fight him off; we rolled out into the lane, and he kept beating on me. He's not as big as I am, but I'm not really a fighter, and he beat the stuffing out of me. That was when Maria Teresa and Antonio came out."

Leah leaned her elbow on the table and put her forehead in the palm of her hand.

"I'm sorry to upset you, Signora; I know he's your friend, but he was as violent as I said he was. I wanted to console him, not make him mad. And I'm amazed you, a foreigner, knew the story and he didn't."

Leah raised her head. "His mother and friends were trying to protect him. And no one blames you, Gerardo. You were an unknowing messenger, and you didn't do anything wrong, so please don't take it on yourself. Arrammundu knew nothing about his mother's history on the farm. The knowledge of it came unexpectedly; it was a shock, and I think he wasn't fighting you, he was fighting the reality of what had happened."

"I wouldn't have said anything; I thought it was public knowledge."

"I think it became that over the years, in whispers. I don't think it was ever spoken about openly around Arrammundu, and I know his mother did everything to shield him from it. So sad. If it had been talked about openly and dealt with, maybe, just maybe, none of this would have happened."

"You mean the murders? You don't think Arrammundu…"

"I can't believe he would, but I need to talk with him."

"You?"

"I mean the Lieutenant and I; I work a little bit with him."

"Oh."

Gerardo looked confused, but did not ask, and Leah did not try to explain.

"I would appreciate it, Gerardo, if you would keep our conversation between you and me and the wall. I don't want to cause any trouble by gossip."

"And I don't either. I learned my lesson from that beating."

Chapter Forty-Five

Leah walked from the bar to Arrammundu's apartment. She knocked on the door and waited. She knocked again. When there was no answer, she put her ear to the door. Sensing the emptiness on the other side, she held hope that Arrammundu would appear. She knocked again.

"You're wasting your time, Signora."

Leah twirled around, startled by the voice, and saw a short, very thick little woman, with wild gray hair, face as wrinkled as a withered apple, with a soft fuzz along her upper lip, and sparkling dark eyes.

"I'm Gelsomina, Angelica and Arrammundu's neighbor." She made a sad face. "I guess just Arrammundu's now."

Her voice was deep, like a man's, and she seemed to exude such a good nature that Leah smiled. "Hello, Gelsomina. I'm glad to meet you. I'm Leah Contarini, a friend of Angelica and Arrammundu. I'm looking for Arrammundu, and it's urgent."

"Urgent. Well, he's just left, and he seemed to be in a hurry as well."

"Do you know where he's gone?"

"I can't say for sure, but he wasn't carrying a pack, and he didn't take his car, so I imagine he was going to the via cava across the bridge below. That's where he goes when he has his PTSD spells, and it looked like he was in the middle of one."

"What are his PTSD spells like, Signora?"

"From what I've seen, when he's in the middle of one, he fluctuates between anger and gloom. I hightail it back to my apartment if he's in an angry one.

It's not something you want to see, and it can last two or three days. I'm glad he gets out of here when he's in a rage. I think it worried Angelica, but she was never scared like I was. She said she understood."

"Thank you, Signora. I'll come back later."

"I'd give it a day or two if I were you."

Leah nodded and slowly walked away, thinking. She needed to talk with Arrammundu before she told the Lieutenant what she had heard from Gerardo.

Outside, it had begun to rain hard.

By the time Leah stepped off the lip of the piazza onto the descending trail, her clothes had soaked to the bone and made slapping sounds with each step. Only her boots were waterproof and warm. She moved quickly, bounding from short step to step downward, brushing against the tall culms of bamboo that added a shower of drops to the steadily falling rain.

On the flat, twisting with the trail as it meandered along the river, she thought of how she would approach Arrammundu. If he were having an episode in reaction to PTSD, he may be angry, but maybe not dangerously so. If he had killed Cecco and Diego, and he thought she had discovered the truth, he could be dangerous, contrite, or suicidal.

At the bridge, she struggled up the berm, crossed the road, and dropped down the other side, slipping, falling, and getting up again as she approached the field below. The grasses in the little field had grown, and water ran off in sheets from her poncho down her thighs and legs.

It was a relief to enter the via cava. The sheer walls on either side and the overhanging holm oak above sheltered her from the heavy rain. She watched each step; the tufa trail under her feet was slick and running with water along the narrow canals cut into the rock at the sides and down the shallow trough cut along the middle of the trail. Leah panted with the exertion of the upward climb and with the weight of her wet clothing.

By the time she came to the cave where Cecco had been murdered, she was exhausted. She stepped inside just enough to be out of the rain and stood waiting for her eyes to adjust. A minute or two passed.

"What are you doing here!" The voice was ragged, broken.

A jolt of adrenaline coursed through Leah's body; she twirled around. He was sitting on the bench at the back of the cave, wet as she was, hunched over with his hands gripping at the edge of the stone bench. His hair hung in strands against his face, and he had a wild look, like a hunted animal brought to bay.

"I said, what the hell are you doing here!"

She took a deep breath. "It's me, Arrammundu. I came to find you. I know that you know about what happened to your mother, and I wanted to talk to you before you talk to the Lieutenant."

"I know all about you talking to Gerardo. I saw the two of you in the bar. Like always, you were meddling, digging into other peoples' lives, uncovering their secrets, pretending to solve problems and bring justice. You make me sick. Why couldn't you stick to lacework, to making my beautiful mother's memory last in one of your articles? Why didn't you leave the spaces between those threads alone and just deal in beauty. You don't have any idea what justice is. You and your Lieutenant."

He bolted to his feet and began striding back and forth across the floor of the wide cave. His voice raised to a shout.

"You play at being in love with him, and you play at being a detective, and you play at being a friend. You weren't my mother's real friend. You just wanted to use her for your article, just like you're doing to Baccia, just like you've done with everyone you've ever written about. You take their information, their lives' work and turn it into glory for yourself. It's *your* name in the big print under the title.

You don't know what friendship is. You don't know what brutality is, or justice. My mother didn't tell you her story because she didn't want to tell you. And she didn't tell me because she wanted to protect me. She loved me and wanted to protect me. They killed him, you know. Theirs might not have been the hands, but it was the same thing. They killed him. And she lived a lifetime of silent suffering so I wouldn't have to bear her pain as well as my own. Where was my mother's justice? Where is the justice for all the women whose lives have been ruined by shitheads like Cecco and

Diego? Dirty fascists, kissing the asses of the Germans, raping any woman they want. Where's the justice? Cecco got what he deserved. The stupid fool thought I was his son. Idiot! My mother was pregnant when he raped her. He raped a pregnant woman! He deserved to die."

"And Diego and Giacomo?"

"I didn't kill Diego; I wish I had. He and Giacomo were part of the whole ring of bastards who took what they wanted when they wanted it. The sort of men that our lovely townspeople fawn over because they're rich or they're toadies to the rich, nothing more than servants, like Giacomo. I'd like to kill them all."

"You didn't kill Diego?"

He stopped pacing and stared at Leah. "It was Cecco that raped my mother. Diego encouraged him, I'm sure of it, but he didn't rape her." Arrammundu started to pace again.

"Who did kill him? And Giacomo?"

"Why ask me, you crazy bitch? And what do you mean about Giacomo? Why don't you go away, run to your Lieutenant, and tell him where I am? Go on. Tell him. But I promise you, you won't find me when you get back. You'll never find me."

Leah stepped toward him and reached for his arm. "Arrammundu…"

In one motion, Arrammundu took a boxing stance, as if his training had suddenly come back to him, shifted his weight a little to the front leg, dipped slightly, dropped his front arm about a foot, twisted clockwise, and executed a powerful uppercut. Leah crumpled to the floor, unconsciousness, her head bouncing slightly against the stone.

"Stupid bitch," Arrammundu muttered over her body before rushing into the rain and up the trail.

Chapter Forty-Six

Leah woke shivering. An intense pain shot up her jaw, and her head felt like someone had driven an axe through it. She tried to sit upright, but a wave of nausea overwhelmed her, and she fell back, vomiting on the floor beside her.

"Arrammundu?"

There was no answer. Moving inch by inch, she pushed her body sideways to see the back of the cave. He was gone. It was dusk.

She lay still.

When she woke, it was dark outside. She tried again to rise and fell back. Nauseated, her head pounding, she felt the darkness close in on her.

Sometime later, she woke again, her body trembling uncontrollably with the cold. Slowly, she put her palms on the floor of the cave and gingerly pushed herself upward. She reached a tilted sitting position, mostly on the side of her thigh, and balanced herself with both palms to the side.

She waited a few minutes, pushed herself onto her knees, waited, and then slowly rose onto her feet, trembling from the cold, unsteadied by the blow. She shuffled to the mouth of the cave and leaned against the wall. Her eyes had adjusted to the dark. It had stopped raining, and the moon was out, making the trail visible enough for her to follow, if she watched her steps.

Steadying herself against the walls of the via cava, she shuffled, rested, and shuffled forward again at a snail's pace. It was nearly first light by the time she could detect the highway across the meadow. When a car passed, she cried out, but her voice was weak, and the driver didn't hear. The grass, wet from the night's rain, tangled at her feet making her forward motion even more difficult. She pushed on until she reached the berm, where she lowered herself to her knees to crawl up and over.

The exertion was too much. At the edge of the highway, she blacked out.

"I found her on the edge of the highway, Lieutenant, and brought her here to the hospital. She was unconscious, and she's damn lucky I didn't run over her. There was an oncoming car, and you know how narrow that bridge is. It's a wonder there wasn't a wreck. Isn't she the American woman, Conti, or something like that?"

"Contarini. Leah Contarini. You did well to bring her to the hospital and to call me, Giorgio. Thank you."

"You're certainly welcome. It gave me a start, I can tell you. A body at the side of the road. I thought she was dead. But of course, I stopped; it's what anybody would do. Nobody would leave a person out there in the cold. But what in the devil do you suppose she was doing out like that at night and in the rain? And on the via cava? She'd obviously been out a long time. She was soaking wet. Do you think she'll make it?"

"She'll make it. I don't know what she was doing out there; she'll tell us when she's awake." The Lieutenant wished Giorgio would go away.

Giorgio looked straight at the Lieutenant, wondering at the hard tone of his voice. The Lieutenant's words sounded like he was giving the woman an order to get well, even though she was asleep. "That's good then, Lieutenant. I'm glad to hear it. We've got good doctors here, and they'll bring her through. Is it okay if I go now? They asked me to stay until you got here, but I'm up early, and I've missed a good part of my morning's work. There'll be hell to pay if I don't get to it, body by the road or not."

The Lieutenant sighed with relief. "Of course. Thank you. You've certainly saved her life. I think lying there much longer would have drained her of what little strength she must have had left."

"Well, with that bruise on her face, something, or someone, hit her mighty hard."

"Yes." His word carried all the force of his anger. "And listen, if they give you trouble at work, have them call me, and I'll straighten it out."

Giorgio nodded, "I appreciate that," and left, mumbling to himself. "Boy! Not a job I'd want."

As soon as Giorgio was gone, the Lieutenant sat in the chair next to Leah's bed and took her hand. "You idiot," he said softly. "What were you doing? Why didn't you come to me? I'm so angry at you, I could punch you myself."

Leah started. "No!"

The Lieutenant jolted out of his seat and gently stroked her forehead. "Shhhhhh. Shhhhh. It's okay. It's me. No one's going to hit you. Rest, just rest."

The tension eased out of her body, and Leah fell again into a deep sleep, dreaming of crawling over rough tufa stone, trying to get there in time. Where? Looking down at her knees—rubbed raw and bleeding.

When Leah awoke the next morning, the Lieutenant was asleep in the chair beside her bed. She watched him sleep, his handsome face tilted to one side. He would be furious with her; still, here he was keeping watch, as he must have been through the whole night.

Leah tried to recall exactly what had happened, but the question of Arrammundu persisted. Where had he gone? He'd admitted to killing Cecco, but not Diego and not Giacomo. He'd seemed surprised that Leah thought Giacomo was murdered. The worse thought was, what would he do next?

The Lieutenant awoke with a start, "Leah?"

"I'm here, Lieutenant, and more awake than you are." She cast a wan smile.

"Leah, for God's sake what happened? Why were you out in the rain, in the night and how'd you get hit. I know you were doing something crazy, I…"

"Calm down, Lieutenant. I'll tell you everything, but you'll have to be patient. I'm not in shape to move—or to think—quickly."

Her lips bumped against each other as she mouthed the words, and for an instant, the Lieutenant forgot his anger and worry and smiled at her.

"What's so funny?"

"You. I'm not laughing. It's just that your lips can barely move."

"Well, laugh away, Lieutenant. You'd be in the same predicament if you'd taken a direct uppercut."

His face went serious. "Who was it, Leah?"

"Arrammundu."

"Arrammundu! But why? And where?"

"Yesterday, or whenever it was; what day is today?"

The Lieutenant pointed at the big calendar on the wall."

"Okay, day before yesterday, I called Gerardo, the one who had the fight with Arrammundu over a woman. He said he was coming to Scansansiano, so I wanted to meet with him because something the Signora said made me think the fight might not have been over Lodoletta."

"You sound totally confused and tangle-brained."

"What kind of a word is tangle-brained, Lieutenant? Just be quiet and try to follow me, okay? This is not easy. Okay, or not? You're looking at me, but not responding."

"Yes. Okay. I'm listening."

"Okay. Gerardo told me that the woman they'd been fighting over was Arrammundu's mother, not Lodoletta. Gerardo knew the whole story about Cecco raping Angelica, and in thinking to express condolences to Arrammundu, he mentioned the rape and that he was sorry for it. Do you see? This was the first time Arrammundu knew about the rape."

"My god! " The Lieutenant shook his head sadly. "A motive."

"Yes. That's why they fought. Gerardo said Arrammundu was livid, but he kept it to himself; I imagine he didn't want to let anyone know he had a motive, and who would think to ask Gerardo?"

"You." He rolled his eyes.

"Unfortunately, Arrammundu saw me talking to Gerardo and guessed what we were talking about. I didn't know he saw us, and I went to see him, before I talked to you…"

"Leah, damn it…"

"Just listen, before you start chastising me, would you? Let me get the story out. I'm tired, and I want to finish."

The Lieutenant nodded and wiped his hand over his mouth, as if to silence himself.

"I wanted to make sure I understood, and I wanted Arrammundu's side of the story. But when I got to his apartment, he was gone. The neighbor told me that when he has a PTSD "event," she called it, he often goes to the via cava, down by the bridge. So, I went after him."

"Naturally. Afternoon, raining hard, a possible killer, and you wanted to talk with him alone on an isolated trail in the forest. Perfect sense."

Leah ignored his sarcasm.

"I found him in the cave where Cecco was killed. He was in a fury like I've never seen him. At first, we talked, but he was so angry and yelling about justice, how foolish you and I were, and how I'd never seen the spaces between the threads of his mother's lacework. He swore he didn't kill Diego, only Cecco, and he didn't know anything about Giacomo. He thought Giacomo just had a heart attack..."

"And so do I!"

Leah tried to purse her lips but could only groan. "I wanted him to come back with me to see you. I reached for his arm, thinking to tell him so, but he took a boxer's stance and slugged me in the jaw. I think I must have hit the stone floor with my head. If I'm remembering, he only hit me in the jaw."

"The doctor agrees with you. Do you have any idea where he went?"

"No, I was out cold. I wasn't even aware he'd left until I finally woke up. And I had to concentrate on getting back to the road. It took a long time."

"And you're lucky you didn't get run over. You collapsed on the top of the berm. Giorgio Biano found you." The Lieutenant heard a noise at the door and looked up. Freya was standing there, her face ashen. She nodded at Leah.

When the Lieutenant turned, he saw that Leah had once again slipped into sleep. He rose and stepped into the hallway.

"Freya, I want you to go back to the office. Tell Montaro to get 5 or 6 men from the office in Chieto. Tell him they should bring boots and rain gear, some dry clothing, and to prepare for a long day's work, so they might want a few sandwiches. And Freya, you call me here at the hospital when they get here and are ready. In the meantime, pack me some food, and get the dry clothes out of my locker, and put it all in my pack."

"What's it all for, Lieutenant?"
"We need to start a search for Arrammundu, if he's still nearby…"
"Arrammundu?"
"He's the one who attacked Leah. He killed Cecco."
"My god!"
She turned and rushed off down the long hallway.

Chapter Forty-Seven

The Lieutenant, Montaro, and the men, plus a police dog, gathered at the cave where Cecco had been murdered.

"From here, we'll move upward in a group until we reach the point where the trail divides. At that point, Bernardini, Corridori, and Pellegrini will turn north and follow the trail up to the road; Montaro, Vichi, and I will go straight ahead past the old water fountain until we come to the road aways further west. Whenever the trail breaks into open area, I want you to fan out and search for any signs that someone has passed by or for any place where someone might hide. He will have sought shelter. He has no food, no dry clothing, and it's likely he's exhausted and emotionally distressed.

Don't approach alone if you find him. He's got PTSD from his service in the Middle East, and he's having some sort of emotional breakdown. That could mean crying and or it could mean wild aggression, and you may not be able to tell which reaction he'll have by looking at him. He's got specialist training from the military; he's just killed one person and attacked another, so he's not hesitant to use his training. But remember: we're not in America. I don't want any knee-jerk reactions on your part, any precipitate or impulsive use of your guns because you feel threatened. Arrammundu is sick and confused and probably feeling caged by his own mind and by us.

"Do you all understand what I'm saying? I don't want any mess-ups! We're here to capture him, not to kill him—and not be killed by him."

The Lieutenant yelled in frustration. "Respond, damn it! Do you understand what I'm saying? You're policemen; this is your job, and part of it is to put your lives on the line when it's demanded."

"Yes, sir," they yelled back in unison.

The Lieutenant bent to hold a shirt he had taken from Arrammundu's apartment next to the dog's nose. The dog bayed and pulled against the leash.

"But Sir," Corridori spoke up. "The rain. Omero won't be able to smell anything."

The Lieutenant glared at him. "Are you on the K9 squad, Corridori?"

"No, sir."

"Well, it's a damn good thing you're not. Vichi, he's your dog; straighten Corridori out."

"Yes, sir."

Vichi turned to Corridori and spoke in a friendly voice, trying to ameliorate the Lieutenant's gruff manner. "You're thinking what most people think, Corridori, but it's false. Rainy weather, like today's, especially when it's not too hard, is actually good for a K9 hunt. Dogs have an increased sense of smell in the rain, and the moisture in the air carries the scent better than dry air. Omero will find him, if he's in the area, and will give us a warning before we see him."

Vichi gave a companionable nod to Corridori and turned back to the Lieutenant.

When the men crested the trail into an open field that spread out from a steep decline above the river, Omero suddenly loped forward to the edge of the precipitous slope, baying and yelping. The Lieutenant ran to Omero and looked down. He saw only the stand of downy oak and the shadow cast by the oaks' winter-brown leaves. He squinted. A long lump, which at first appeared to be a log, lay beneath a tree a few feet into the grove.

With a little hop, the Lieutenant jumped down, heels first, digging into the wet soil of the slope and bouncing his way down the steep decline, waving his arms to keep upright. His men followed, careening downward, waving their arms wildly through the air for balance.

They found Arrammundu among the oaks, shivering and feverish, mumbling incoherent sounds to himself.

"Montaro, you stay with me. Vichi, take Omero and the others back up to the road. Go upriver aways to find a place where you can climb without falling. It'll be faster. Once you're back on the trail, get to the road and the others and down to the car as quickly as you can. I want you to bring Doctor Pelligrini, a stretcher, warm clothes for Arrammundu, and blankets.

And don't talk to anyone but the doctor! That's an order. I don't want the gossip mill to start churning until it's unavoidable."

The men rushed away through the oak to the trail and turned upriver, scanning the hillside for a way to ascend through the thick forest.

The Lieutenant removed his coat, knelt beside Arrammundu, and laid the heavy wool garment gently over him, speaking in soothing tones to calm the broken man.

Montaro, who had brought his little flask of whiskey with him for warmth, pulled it from his pocket and gently lifted Arrammundu's head. He tilted the flask so that a full shot of whiskey filled Arrammundu's mouth. Arrammundu emitted a weak cough as the whiskey gorged his throat. With another cough, he opened his eyes, staring at the two men as if he were looking through them, into another world.

"Arrammundu, it's us, the Lieutenant and Montaro. Help is on the way. You'll be alright."

"C-c-old. I killed Cecco and Leah."

"Not Leah. You punched her hard, but you didn't kill her. She's recovering in the hospital; when she fell, she hit her head on the floor."

Tears came to Arrammundu's eyes. His body shook, trembling with cold, with relief, with grief. His moans fell like knives against the ears of the Lieutenant and Montaro. It was as if each sob, each tear from his eyes, was slashing the flesh, creating a body of scars.

For Arrammundu, this moment of being saved created a flood of memory and pain that joined with his physical pain. All the laments of his life: the horrors of the explosion in the Middle East, the children's body parts flying through the air, the useless loss of life, the anger and hatred of which people were capable, and perhaps most of all, the knowledge of his own mother's lifelong anguish caused so casually, so arrogantly, by cruel, selfish men.

Before he killed him, Arrammundu had asked himself a hundred times why Cecco should live, and a hundred times, the answer came that Cecco should not live. The sight of his mother lying on the floor, dead from cancer, gray and shrunken, and sad from years of carrying the burden of her secret, years without her husband, who had been put in harm's way by these empty men. What good were they in the world? How did they deserve the world?

He could at least get rid of one of them.

Montaro turned his head aside, but the Lieutenant watched silently. He knew Arrammundu's tears were the language of pure anguish, of remorse, and profound grief. He knew there was no grief like the grief kept silent.

Under this gentle mist, the Lieutenant was witnessing a soul in which, for a moment, ego and evil had won out over the drive to the good. This was the pure torment of every good person who, damaged or confused or momentarily distracted from his own spirit, had given way to anger or evil and then realized what he had done.

There were those who never experienced the knowledge of their own wrongs, but this was not Arrammundu; the Lieutenant knew for certain. Arrammundu was a guilty man, but also a boy who desperately wanted to protect his mother, even if whatever he did was too late.

The Lieutenant lifted Arrammundu gently to a sitting position and held him close in the embrace of one who understands no person on earth lives without suffering. No person escapes their own or others' malevolence.

There would be enough time for the law.

Chapter Forty-Eight

"Where is he now?" Leah asked the Lieutenant.

"He's just down the hall, heavily sedated, so don't even think about going to see him. And you're not allowed anyway; he's under guard; nobody can go in except me or Montaro."

"I won't press charges."

The Lieutenant sighed and shook his head. "Of course you won't. Concussion, a close call with a broken jaw, and you won't press charges! I fail to understand how you can be so tenderhearted when the guy almost killed you."

He didn't almost kill me!" She lowered her voice, "He did almost break my jaw, I admit, but that's an 'almost,' so it doesn't count, and besides, you can't stand here and act tough with me. Montaro's already told me how you cradled Arrammundu on your lap until the doctor got there. So don't play tough cop. Neither one of us want him to make it worse than we know he's already had and is going to suffer in the coming months and maybe years. He'll either have to go to jail or to a psychiatric lock-up. And that will be enough; I'm going to encourage psychiatric lock-up to whoever will listen."

"Don't get on your high horse. I agree with you. I think he needs psychiatric help, and it'll be my suggestion in the official report, which I think will carry weight. But, *mia cara*, our worries aren't over; we've still got Diego's killer to figure out."

"And Giacomo's," Leah added.

The Lieutenant rolled his eyes and changed the subject. "The important thing now is for you to get well and get out of here."

"I'm well, and I'm getting out tomorrow. I passed all the tests, and the doctor says I'm ready to go."

"The doctor is wrong, and you're stubborn."

With a last shake of his head, the Lieutenant turned on his heel and walked out the door.

Leah was released the following morning. After she had signed the papers and said goodbye to the nurses and doctor, she walked slowly down the long, sterile hallway to the steps that would take her to the street. Her head felt a little woozy still, but not enough to impede her walking.

Outside, she looked at her watch and realized it would be another ten minutes before the Lieutenant was coming to take her home. She sat on the wooden bench by the outside steps, tilted her head upward, and closed her eyes, enjoying the warmth of the autumn sunshine.

"Signora?"

Leah opened her eyes and looked over her shoulder.

"Lodoletta! Hello. I'm happy to see you. Are you visiting Arrammundu?"

"I'm going to try, but I heard that he has a guard on his room, and they won't let anyone in."

"That's what the Lieutenant told me."

"Are you going to press charges?"

"No. I think the murder charge is enough, and I think he needs help, not jail. But how are you doing, Lodoletta?"

Lodoletta sneered and released a flood of sarcasm. "Oh, fine. Just trundling along my merry way. Now that my dad and my grandfather have been murdered, I can concentrate on fighting this goddamn depression and anxiety, living with persistent toxic shock: the memories of years of abuse, the memories of my sexual promiscuity probably caused by that lifetime of abuse or maybe just the result of me being part of the dregs of humanity, or maybe because I didn't give a damn, and, plus these things, wondering if the only man who's ever really loved me is going to die. So things are just aces!"

"I didn't mean to offend you, Lodoletta. I know you've suffered, and I know the effects are lasting. I just meant, how are you today."

"Geez! I'm sorry. I just hate the world right now. There's no life in all this violence. I feel like every day, I'm closer to death. And I'm young. I'm not ready. I want to climb out of this damn hole, this morass of sick humanity, and have a normal life. I want them to find Diego's killer and maybe Giacomo's too."

"So you think Giacomo was killed?"

"Maybe not intentionally. But for sure, he was like my dad and my grandpa. They were three of a kind, although Giacomo was a wimp. He did whatever they told him to do."

"Who do you think might have killed him?"

Lodoletta's eyes darted to the door of the hospital. "Ahhh, I don't know anything about it. See ya." She bounded away up the steps into the hospital.

"You're looking pensive this morning. Are you feeling okay?" The Lieutenant had appeared around the corner from the parking lot just as Lodoletta disappeared through the hospital doorway.

"I'm okay. I just had a disconcerting conversation with Lodoletta."

"About?"

"About herself and her difficult life, which she's got good reason to talk about. She's worried about Arrammundu—and she wants to find out who killed Diego, and she thinks Giacomo was probably killed too."

"That bad-penny idea turns up again. I thought we were done with that. He died of a heart attack."

"I never really questioned that. The question was whether someone shocked him, or scared him enough to cause a heart attack. I trust his wife, and so does the Signora, and so does Lodoletta, although I can't figure out why she has an opinion or even cares."

The Lieutenant spoke gently. "It seems he was involved in some of the abuse, maybe not directly, but indirectly. He was into drugs for a while, and he was thick with Cecco and Diego earlier on, from what I hear. He worked with them on the farm."

"You mean they gave the kids...?" Leah was startled.

"Let it go, Leah. What they did should be only for understanding their kids now. And all of them are gone, and I hope if there is such a place, they're in

Hell with the knowledge of what they did eating away at them every second of eternity. They were the scum of the earth, all three of them.

And even if someone caused Giacomo's death, if they did it without touching him, I don't see what I could do about it. The coroner says he wasn't touched, or poisoned, or stabbed, or anything else. He simply had a heart attack strong enough to kill him."

"Maybe not so simple."

"Oh, come on." He held out his hand to help her up, "You're going to addle that brain of yours even more than it already is addled. I'm taking you home."

"Are you releasing Baccia?"

"I can't yet. There's still Diego; remember, she's confessed to that one, too. She's sticking to her story."

The Lieutenant dropped Leah off on the road just below her apartment. Leah took the back steps that lead up and into the old city and to her door. She entered gratified for the lingering smell of lavender and pleased to be back where she could completely relax. A vestige of headache still pecked at her temples, and her neck was sore from the moment it snapped backward from the contact with Arrammundu's fist.

The stay in the hospital not only allowed her to heal; it allowed her to think, and her thoughts had persistently strayed to Pagolo's neighbor. If he provided an alibi for Pagolo, the reverse was also true: Pagolo was an alibi for him. Someone had mentioned that the neighbor, Signor Monaci, was another one who had been duped by Cecco and Diego. Who had told her that? Leah searched her memory. It must have been Freya. Leah set her things down and called Freya.

"Hello."

"It's Leah, but don't say my name. Can you meet me in an hour at the little pizzeria behind the church?"

"Are you buying?"

Leah laughed. "Of course. Don't even hint to the Lieutenant that you're seeing me. He'll have a fit if he knows I'm out of the apartment."

"I won't say anything."

It wasn't yet noon when they met, and the pizzeria was empty except for one teenage boy, who ate his slice of artichoke pizza in three bites and was gone, off to work or to hang out with friends in the piazza of the new city above.

Leah and Freya both ordered the elegant, simple potato pizza with thin slices of crisp-edged potato covering the dough and drizzled with olive oil. The cook smiled at the order. Potato pizza was the one he most liked to make. After years of making delicious pizzas of all types: pizza con carciofi, pizza al formaggio, pizza di Pasqua, pizza dolce, pizza rustica, pizza alio olio, pizza Margherita, pizza quatro Stagioni, ai funghi, and even Nutella pizza for the kids, after all this, he prized most of all potato pizza, and the women in front of him seemed even more beautiful than they were because they ordered it.

The cook gave Leah a particularly wide smile when he handed the plates of the steaming slices to them. They turned away, flushed with delight at his look.

"What's he smiling about?" Freya whispered.

Leah laughed, "Who knows?"

They carried their plates to an isolated table in the far corner of the L-shaped room where they could speak freely.

"So what's the big secret?" Freya asked, taking up her fork and knife.

"Are you the one who told me that Signor Monaci lost money to the Cecco and Diego?"

Freya snorted. "Maybe. I don't remember if I did or not. But practically anyone in town could have told you the same thing; it's common knowledge."

"Monaci never told me, or the Lieutenant."

"The Lieutenant's known about it all along."

"Then why wasn't Monaci a suspect? He should have been brought in, no?"

"It was a few years ago, and the Lieutenant's known Monaci since he, I mean the Lieutenant, first came to Scansansiano. Monaci's not a murderer."

"I'm going to talk to him anyway. I can't believe those two didn't take a break of some sort during the time Diego was killed, and if they're vouching for each other, saying they didn't, somebody's lying."

"So why not Germana and Luigina too? And maybe Arrammundu's lying. Or maybe Lodoletta's lying?"

"Okay. Okay. I know there's still lots of work to do." Leah leaned forward with her elbow on the table and her head in her hand.

"Eat your pizza before it gets cold. You're a glutton for punishment, you know that? Talk to the Lieutenant and let him do his job. You need rest, you idiot. You've just had a trauma to your head."

"I'm not traumatized, and I feel fine. A bump on the head. The Lieutenant doesn't think much of my hunches right now. He wants me to sit around and vegetate."

"I wish you would! Or at least that the two of you would just get married. You're both such a bother; it's like living around an old married couple that fights all the time with intermittent moments of lovey-dovey. *Mio dio.*"

"Well, that was a non sequitur. You want me to vegetate or get married? We're not like an old married couple! I don't even know if I want to continue the relationship and…"

"You haven't even started a relationship! Once in a while he grabs you and kisses you, you kiss him back, and then you get angry at each other again, and then you get in some dangerous fix and he's all upset for days worrying about it, and I have to work with him and put up with his wrinkled forehead and sad sighs."

"Okay. Okay. It takes me a while to make decisions."

"*A while?* Years is *a while?*" She gave a loud laugh.

Monaci had been whistling to himself as he swept out the corners of the cantina and was just reaching to wipe away a cobweb that had formed on the ceiling above. At the sound of Leah's voice, he whirled around so fast the broom went sailing out of his hands and flew across the room.

Leah ducked just in time, and the broom hit the doorframe and dropped with a clamor to the floor.

"Signora," Monaci came running, "I'm so sorry. You startled me."

"There's no harm done, Signor. Don't worry about it. I'm fine. But I never knew a broom could make such a fine weapon!"

Her remark relieved Monaci's tension, and they both laughed.

"I'm sure you haven't come to talk about brooms. How can I help you?"

Leah noticed a tightness in his voice now that the laughter was over.

"Signor Monaci, I can't get it out of my mind that neither Pagolo—nor you—simply couldn't have worked all day the day of Diego's murder without a break. It just doesn't make sense. You would have to have eaten, have to have used the facilities, or made a phone call, or run an errand. Perhaps to bring something for the cantina, or to settle something at the bank. Do you see what I mean? You've vouched for him being here every minute of that day, but it doesn't jibe with the reality of life. People don't work every minute all day without some sort of break."

"Well, Signora, you're right." He was wringing his hands. "We did take breaks, but in my house, which is just up the street, two minutes away. I couldn't account for every minute, but since there were so few, certainly too few to get down to the mill and back without me noticing."

"Is it true that you yourself had a run-in with Cecco and Diego some while ago?"

Monaci's forehead was sweating and his face flushed in anger. "Yes, but that's none of your business. Many people know about it, and they have the decency not to mention it. It almost ruined me, and friends here in town know that and are polite enough not to bring it up. Including the Lieutenant, I'll add; so it makes me think you must be here snooping around on your own, without his permission, and I'd like you to leave."

"Signor Monaci. The Lieutenant asked me to help out as I could. I'm not just snooping. A man has been killed…"

"Yes, a disgusting devil of a man who deserved death and eternal suffering. So why not let it rest; why keep prodding and upsetting people's lives? Why not let sleeping dogs lie."

Leah was angry; her words poured out. "Because Baccia is still in jail, and she may have to stay there, only in a jail somewhere far away from her children. She's confessed to a crime she didn't commit because she wants to make sure her children aren't blamed. Should she be the one to take the punishment if she's not guilty, while some coward—like yourself, I'm beginning to think—hides behind a false alibi and dares to whistle along cleaning out his cantina, like everything is good and all's right with the world—as long as nobody knows he's guilty?

Is that what you want? Baccia to take the fall for you, while you drink your homemade wine, stuff yourself with your wife's pasta al pesto, and take a nap every afternoon? You're not telling the truth, and I know you're not."

"Go away, Signora! Go away! I don't want to talk to you. I want the Lieutenant. You're not police. Go away!"

He was near tears; Leah could feel his anguish, but knew she could not stop. He was on the verge of breaking.

"No, I won't go away. Not until you tell the truth. Stop being a coward and tell the truth, for god's sake."

He broke, his voice in shreds. "I didn't do it. I swear I didn't do it. I was here working the whole day, except at lunchtime; I went home to eat. I swear it. You can ask my wife. I just went home for lunch."

"And a little siesta, maybe?"

He shouted, "Yes, for God's sake, yes. A little siesta. Leave me alone. Go away."

It was the desperate plea of a man who had lied, a man who felt guilty. Watching the anguish on his face, Leah remembered a sentence from the ancient Roman dramatist Plautus, "Nothing is more wretched than the mind of a man conscious of guilt." Contrary to the harsh way she had forced the truth from him, she felt a strange compassion. How many times in her life had she been guilty of lies, lies smaller than murder perhaps, but still lies, still guilty?

She turned and left Monaci to work on his cantina.

Leah opened the door to the station, and hearing the sound, Freya glanced up from her work. "Well?"

"I went to see Monaci."

"And?"

"And like I thought, he was lying. He went home at lunch and he had a siesta."

"*Mio dio*! That means Pagolo…"

"Exactly. Is the Lieutenant in?"

"He is, and you're going to have to suffer his wrath, which means I'm going to suffer it too. Will you ever be normal?"

"I hope not." Leah winked and knocked on the Lieutenant's door.

"Come."

Leah put on her most flashing smile and walked into the Lieutenant's office.

"Why are you smiling like that? Something's wrong, isn't it? When you distort your mouth like that, I know something is wrong. Tell me. With no preface. I don't want explanations or excuses. Just tell me."

"Okay, Lieutenant. Signor Monaci was lying. He wasn't there all day with Pagolo. He went home for lunch, and took a siesta, and he doesn't remember how long of a siesta. That means Pagolo could have left work, dashed down to the mill, and gotten back before Monaci came back to the cantina after his siesta."

He hesitated before answering.

Leah was surprised he wasn't angry at her for having gone alone to see Monaci. Was it a signal of more trust?

"Arrammundu saw Pagolo," the Lieutenant muttered, as if to himself.

"For at most a few minutes, and we don't even know if it was at lunchtime. And we don't know for sure if Arrammundu was telling the truth about seeing him. That part of it is unclear, no? So what are we going to do?"

The Lieutenant sighed. "Damn it. I've known Monaci for a long time; I never would have expected him to lie to me. It's a murder case, for god's sake. I'll have to go see him now."

He rose and stepped around the desk to stand in front of Leah. "You stay here. I want to talk to him alone, and then you and I will find Pagolo and see what he has to say. I hope we catch him before he gets wind of your conversation with Monaci, but I imagine Monaci has already called him."

"*Oh dio!* How stupid of me; I didn't think about it. Of course, he would call Pagolo."

"It's too late to worry about it now. How are you feeling?" He put his hands on her shoulders and studied her face.

"I'm fine. Slight pecking of a headache at my temples, but otherwise fit as a butcher's dog. And energetic."

"I'm glad of it." He bent and kissed her on the forehead and walked to the door. His hand on the door handle, he turned. "Please, please stay here, Leah. I'll be back in a half hour. Visit Baccia why don't you."

Leah did as the Lieutenant suggested. Freya took her to the back cells. The opening to Baccia's cell clanged open, and Leah entered to sit next to her. Baccia's face had grown thin and pale, and although she flashed a wan smile at Leah, she dropped her head and fiddled with a handkerchief she had rolled in her hands.

"Baccia, you don't look well. Aren't they feeding you appropriate meals? You've grown very thin."

"No, Leah, don't think badly of the Lieutenant or Freya. They've been ordering the best meals for me, but I'm not hungry. Being a prisoner is a boring and depressing life. I know I chose it, and I know I must do it, but it drains the appetite. Do you think the Lieutenant might allow me to have my lacework here in the cell? Could you ask him for me? I know it's unorthodox, but I think he would trust me not to use it for anything other than the lacework."

"I know he trusts you. I'll ask him about it. But Baccia, we know you're not guilty; won't you please recant your confession? It's not doing any good. Arrammundu has already confessed to Cecco's murder, and all of us know you didn't kill Diego. Please. Pagolo and Lodoletta need you."

"I haven't seen them for a couple of days. And just before you came, I got such a strange phone call. It was from Mrs. Martelli. She said Pagolo and Lodoletta had been there to visit, to tell her how sorry they were about Giacomo's death, and that they hoped she was doing okay. I didn't know they even knew her."

"They didn't tell you about going there?"

"No. I don't know her, though, so they must have met her sometime when I wasn't there, or through someone else. It's an enigma to me. When they come again, I'll ask them. And I hope it's soon. Two days is an eternity in here, and it's on top of several eternities already."

Leah stood. "I have to go; I'm sorry. I'll be back."

"But, Leah, so soon? You only just got here. I would love to sit and talk for a little while. Life is so monotonous here."

Leah leaned down and kissed her on the forehead. "I'll be back. I promise."

Leah rushed out to the office. "Freya, can you come with me? We need to get over to Chieto to see Giacomo's wife."

"Why? And shouldn't we wait for the Lieutenant? He said he'd be back in a half hour."

"We can't wait. Are you coming? I can explain it on the way."

"Okay. Okay. But I've got to leave a note."

"Write!"

When the Lieutenant learned from Monaci that he had called Pagolo as soon as Leah left, the Lieutenant rushed back to the office to find it empty. He read the note, called Montaro, who was out at the bar, and told him to meet at the car.

They arrived at the Martelli's apartment just a few minutes behind Freya and Leah and caught up with them on the steps of the building.

"What are you doing here?" Leah asked the Lieutenant.

"No, the question is, what are you doing here? And Freya, if you're going to make a habit of rushing out of the office and leaving the door open, I'm going to fire you." The Lieutenant was truly angry; Freya turned red.

"Don't be angry, Lieutenant. It was my fault. I needed her to come along because I wasn't sure what we'd find."

"Perfect. You thought there might be danger, so you invite all ninety-five pounds of Freya to come. Great thinking."

"But..."

"Don't bother explaining, Leah. I can put two and two together. Monaci told me he called Pagolo after he talked to you, and Freya's note said Pagolo and Lodoletta had come here."

Leah interrupted. "Baccia said she hasn't seen them for two days."

"I can't quite figure out why they came here, or when, exactly, but we'll ask Signora Martelli. They're on the run, for sure."

Signora Martelli answered the door on the third knock. "Such a group of you! I'm getting more visitors than I've had in years. Come in. I'll make coffee."

"Thank you, Signora." The Lieutenant's voice was cordial, and he spoke slowly. We don't have the time now, but we will take a rain check if that's alright with you."

"Of course, Lieutenant. Then how can I help you?"

"We understand that Pagolo and Lodoletta Bini came by to see you. We're anxious to get in touch with them, but their phones seem not to be working. I'm wondering if you have any idea where they are?"

"I don't. They didn't stay long; it was a condolence call, really. They just wanted me to know they were sorry for my loss, and they hoped I was doing well. That was it. And then they left. It was odd—I don't know them really—and the visit was strange enough that I peeked through the curtains to watch them as they left the building. They didn't have suitcases when they visited me, but when I saw them from the window, they were walking away with those rolling suitcases, so I suppose they were going on a trip somewhere. They didn't mention anything about it to me, but I imagine they were going to the train. The bus is only once a day now, and the bus people have cut several routes so it's difficult to get out of here." She laughed.

"Yes, I imagine they were going to the train."

"Thank you, Signora. The next time, we'll be more social and stay a little longer to take your offer of coffee."

"Well, I'll be glad to see you all. It gets lonely…"

The Lieutenant, as if he were not in a hurry, took her hand and raised it to within an inch of his lips. "Goodbye, Signora."

On the street, the Lieutenant yelled. "We'll go in one car and come back later for the other one. Hurry."

The train station thrummed with travelers, most of them Italian with suitcases, but a few foreign backpackers hovered in a corner of the waiting room. The backpackers had laid their maps on the floor of the station and were pouring intently over their routes. A few men and women stood on the *binario*. Smoke twisted upward from their cigarettes, and some leaned against the railing of the wheelchair ramp. Most of the people waiting sat in the plastic chairs of the waiting room, their luggage gathered at their feet like chicks around a mother hen.

Leah, the Lieutenant, and the others scanned the faces of the travelers. In the far corner of the L-shaped room, a man and a woman stood in earnest conversation with their backs to the main part of the room. Their suitcases sat beside them.

"Freya, you and Leah stay here. Montaro and I will talk to them."

"But…"

"There's no arguing, Leah. I'm not being bothered with taking you to the hospital again. Stay here!"

"Pagolo, Lodoletta, you're traveling today?" The Lieutenant spoke as if meeting a friend by chance.

The two of them swung around, a flash of fear across their faces. They looked at each other, at the Lieutenant, and then at the door.

In one quick move, Pagolo shoved the Lieutenant in the chest, and Lodoletta pushed Montaro. Leah saw the Lieutenant jerk backward and Pagolo break away in a run toward the street door. She swung from Freya and took chase. Just as he was passing through the doorway, she made a flying leap toward his back, caught him by the shoulders, and both of them crashed to the ground, Leah on Pagolo's back, still grasping his shoulders.

At the moment Leah took chase after Pagolo, Lodoletta broke from Montaro, but he was too sure on his feet, and thrust out his leg to trip her before she'd taken her second stride. A crowd gathered around them, and another around Leah and Pagolo. The Lieutenant had run to Leah. Seeing his uniform, the people parted in front of him and let him through, where he found Leah astride Pagolo's back, holding his hand behind him.

"Handcuffs?" She asked.

Someone in the crowd laughed. "Looks like she should be the one in uniform, Lieutenant!"

The Lieutenant turned toward him. "I'm in complete agreement."

Chapter Forty-Nine

"But why, Pagolo? Why now? You could have come to the police. If a complaint had been made, I could have done something. I've asked your mother many times over the years to make a complaint; you know that. So why now?"

Leah saw the Lieutenant was near breaking. He had done what he needed to do; he had carried out the law, but it felt not enough, wrong and right at the same time; and he hated himself even as he asked the questions for which he already knew the answers.

"I know exactly why I did it. I did it because I stopped being a coward, and that was thanks to Arrammundu."

The Lieutenant's mouth dropped open in surprise. "What's Arrammundu got to do with it?"

"Don't be surprised you didn't know; even Arrammundu doesn't know. I followed him up the trail that day—the day he killed Cecco. When he went into the cave, I wedged myself into a depression in the rock and listened. I heard their conversation, and I heard the murder; I was there, you guys..."

Pagolo raised his chest, "...and I was proud of him and he gave me courage. I was glad—overjoyed!—that my father was dead, and I realized I could take Arrammundu's strength and rid the world of Diego as well. Do you have even an inkling of what my mother, Lodoletta, and I went through as children, and even until now? I think you can't know. I wonder sometimes if people in your line of work know what true malevolence is. There is evil in the world. You two should know that."

He stared both the Lieutenant and Leah in the eye. "You may have brushed against the edges of it, but you don't *know* it, not in the way we do. My father and grandfather had to be stopped, and Arrammundu gave me the courage I should have had long ago. For years, I've been backward parenting, keeping quiet, trying to defend my father even though he was the devil himself. It happens with abused kids like me; I've read about it until I'm sick.

But that moment, listening to my father—who would have shunned my mother and Lodoletta and I in a second if he could have proved Arrammundu was his son—listening to him whine and plea, gave me strength to do what needed to be done to finish the job."

"Pagolo," Leah's voice was a plea. "You know the law has to take over. I won't speak for the Lieutenant, but I want you to know that I can speak in court about your family, the closeness of you, your mother, and Lodoletta. And I can speak for Arrammundu. Don't give up hope. There may be justice beyond the justice of the law."

"I don't care what they do to me. Just take care of my mother and Lodoletta."

There was nothing more to ask. Leah and the Lieutenant both stood. The Lieutenant, no matter what he felt or wanted to say, knew he needed to be silent now. They both shook hands with Pagolo; the Lieutenant called for the guard, and they left the cell.

Back in the Lieutenant's office, Leah asked, "But why was Lodoletta running? Was it simply because she wanted to be with Pagolo? It doesn't make sense. She had to have felt guilty. Did Pagolo hide part of the story?"

"Questions we have to answer, Leah. She's in the back. I haven't charged her yet, and Pagolo swears she didn't know anything about it. But something happened."

There was a knock at the door. The Lieutenant pulled his chair around to the front of his desk so they could all sit together. When they were seated, the Lieutenant began.

"Lodoletta, we're only beginning to get the picture; we need you to help us."

"Why should I? You haven't helped us before; you haven't helped any of us, not Angelica, not Arrammundu, not my mom, or Pagolo, or me."

The Lieutenant's face reddened in defensive anger. "You were all silent! Silence, hiding problems, especially such heinous problems, doesn't do anyone any good. I know it's complicated, but so is the law; we depend on it, but things have to be known for it to work."

"Do you know anything about shame, Lieutenant? Do you know what it means to a six-year-old or a nine-year-old who wants so badly to be loved by her father and grandfather that even if they beat her and do unspeakable acts to her, to her brother, to her mother, they defend them to the last punch in the face? Do you know that children like that are ready to fight to protect the very men who've abused them? That they'll go crazy if someone criticizes them. Pagolo and I and my mother were just beginning to get the courage to act; we were just beginning, and Arrammundu, poor bastard, was the one who led us into the final step of courage."

"But why not come to the police then?"

"And what, rat on Arrammundu because he rid the world of a dangerous and sick pervert? Because he honored his mother by redressing an evil that had ruined her spirit? All of us loved our parents, and we wanted them to love us. But Angelica was the only one that did. We kids, maybe we were weak, but at base, we were good; we were children who wanted to be good and adults who wanted a decent life, but we were joined and twisted by pure evil. There's not an easy answer. We did things wrong, and I'm sorry for that. I know we have to pay, but I also know that you and many people stand behind us, even though we did wrong. We'll pay; we'll pay and do it with heads held high."

Leah leaned forward, "But you've done nothing, Lodoletta. You're here only because you were with Pagolo."

"There's so much you can't understand and so much you don't know. I'm the one who caused Giacomo's heart attack."

Leah and the Lieutenant swiveled toward each other, wide-eyed in surprise, Leah because she wouldn't have guessed Lodoletta but was proved right about Giacomo, which she had begun to doubt, and the Lieutenant because what he had refused to guess was true, although it seemed impossible.

Leah turned back to Lodoletta. "Did you watch for the right laundry day?"

"How did you know that?"

"It was the only thing that made sense. The only time the door would be left open for the few minutes you needed to get in and up the stairs. You were lucky. Someone could have been in the hallway, or on the steps."

"Once I got in, I could have pulled it off even if there had been someone in the hallways. Visitors go there all the time."

"But not to the Martellis," Leah added.

"No. I did have to be careful there."

"How did you give Martelli the heart attack?" Frustrated, the Lieutenant broke in.

"I actually didn't mean to kill him. All I meant to do was to confront him with what he'd done and to tell him I was going to tell his wife. As easy as that. I didn't even know at the time that it killed him. I only found out later—and I was glad it killed him," she said defiantly.

"What did I tell him? I told him I knew about his role in Lorenzo's death—an accomplice to murder. I told him about Cecco and Diego's treatment of Germana and Luigina, and other girls in town, about Adoranda; I told him how they had cheated farmers out of their money and taken advantage of restauranteurs struggling to stay open. I told him everything I knew—and I know plenty about them—and finally, I told him in slow and complete detail what Cecco and Diego did to my brother and me and my mother. The kind of people he'd chosen for friends.

By the time I got through with him, he was sobbing, begging me to stop. I stopped, and I left, and what happened, happened. I didn't touch the guy; I just told him the truth, and the truth killed him."

Crazed by her own memory, Lodoletta began to laugh. Within seconds, she was laughing uncontrollably.

The Lieutenant stood and gently helped her to her feet. "Lodoletta, I'm going to ask the doctor to come and give you something to calm you." He gestured with his head toward the door, hoping Leah understood she should ask Freya to call for the doctor. "You're in the cell next to Pagolo's, so you can rest."

Lodoletta moved meekly along beside the Lieutenant, out the door toward the cells.

Chapter Fifty

The following morning, early, Leah and the Lieutenant met in the small bar at the side of the piazza. It was the bar known as the 'old men's' bar' because only a few older men gathered there, traditionally in the late morning, when they drank spritzers and ate snacks while their wives were home cooking lunch.

Leah and the Lieutenant found a table in the corner, relieved to be the only customers.

They sat across from each other, silent, saddened by the outcome, particularly for Baccia and Arrammundu, but also for Pagolo, Lodoletta, Signora Martelli, and for Angelica and Lorenzo, those who were purely innocent and those who, in their crimes, were also innocent in some sense of justice.

"What now?" The Lieutenant asked, and Leah understood that he was asking about more than the murders and their young friends.

"Now we go on; we continue."

"And do we—you and I—continue, Leah?"

She took his hands in her own. "We continue, Lieutenant. I'm not sure in what way; I'm not sure of the outcome, but we continue."

Epilogue

The courts found the circumstances surrounding the murders of Cecco and Diego to be ameliorating factors in the final verdict. Both Arrammundu and Pagolo were given greatly reduced sentences and, within two years, were released under the supervision of the Lieutenant and Signor Monaci, who employed them in his shop. Lodoletta was found not guilty of any wrongdoing, but was strongly advised to seek psychiatric help, which she did, along with her mother, Baccia. Arrammundu, who shared a small apartment with Pagolo, became family with the Binis and eventually married Lodoletta. Their son, Guglielmo, gave great joy to his grandmother, Baccia, and the rest of the family. He showed a great interest in science and professed on his 6th birthday that he intended to become a doctor.

Leah and the Lieutenant continued to continue.

Acknowledgements

It takes the work of many people for a book to see the light of day. I cannot list everyone who helped me write this book, but I would like to name a few.

First of all, I thank Steve Siporin, who brought me to Italy, to the ancient Etruscan trails, and to the small-town rural life of lower Tuscany that I love so much. He listened to me on countless countryside rambles, drove me along rugged back roads through thick forests so I could search for a hidden cave, and shared his own deep knowledge of the area. In addition, with grace and patience, he has always been my first editor, improving various versions of the text, graciously allowing me to interrupt his own work so many times I should be embarrassed to admit it.

If it was Steve who brought me to Tuscany, it was the people here in Tuscany who welcomed me, fed me, took me on walks to sites I would never have seen on my own, lent books, shared their knowledge of the area's history, and were willing to tell me their own stories: The Nizzi family, Signora Elena Servi, Enzo Giuliani and Maria Rosa Pucci, Elisabetta Peri, Carlo Fe, Luigi Cerroni. After the book was completed, readers, foremost among them author Greg Stout, friends Mary and Steve Sharp, and my editors at Level Best Books, Harriette Sackler and Verena Rose, read the manuscript and made suggestions to improve my work. Level Best editor Shawn Reilly Simmons caught typos and misspellings and made me look like a professional. I am fortunate to know all of these people, and I thank them all for their generosity and friendship.

Any errors in this book are entirely my own.

A Note from the Author

This novel is entirely a work of fiction. The story, names, characters, and incidents portrayed in this book are the work of the author's imagination. No identification with actual persons (living or deceased) is intended or should be inferred.

Libi Siporin asserts the moral right to be identified as the author of this work.

About the Author

Ona "Libi" Siporin has lived and worked between the U.S. and Italy for many years. Siporin delights in short get-aways to Italy's great cities, but is content to spend most of her time walking the Tuscan countryside and trails and figuring out what her protagonist, Leah Contarini, will do next.

SOCIAL MEDIA HANDLES:
Instagram: libisiporin
FB: Ona Siporin

AUTHOR WEBSITE:
www.onasiporin-writer.com

Also by Libi Siporin

Leah Contarini Mysteries:
Bitter Maremma
If Two of Them Are Dead

9 781685 126391